K. C. Williams was born in Church Village in 1983 and has remained in the Rhondda Valleys his whole life. He attended college and became a bricklayer at 18 before joining his father and brother in the construction industry. He married his partner of 11 years in 2013 and they currently live in Llwynypia.

K. C. Williams

MY EUPHORIA

AUSTIN MACAULEY PUBLISHERS
LONDON • CAMBRIDGE • NEW YORK • SHARJAH

Copyright © K. C. Williams 2024

The right of K. C. Williams to be identified as author of this work has been asserted by the author in accordance with sections 77 and 78 of the Copyright, Designs and Patents Act 1988.

All rights reserved. No part of this publication may be reproduced, stored in a retrieval system, or transmitted in any form or by any means, electronic, mechanical, photocopying, recording, or otherwise, without the prior permission of the publishers.

Any person who commits any unauthorised act in relation to this publication may be liable to criminal prosecution and civil claims for damages.

This is a work of fiction. Names, characters, businesses, places, events, locales, and incidents are either the products of the author's imagination or used in a fictitious manner. Any resemblance to actual persons, living or dead, or actual events is purely coincidental.

A CIP catalogue record for this title is available from the British Library.

ISBN 9781398434363 (Paperback)
ISBN 9781398434370 (ePub e-book)

www.austinmacauley.com

First Published 2024
Austin Macauley Publishers Ltd®
1 Canada Square
Canary Wharf
London
E14 5AA

Table of Contents

Prologue	7
Chapter 1: Home	10
Chapter 2: Academy	13
Chapter 3: Unearthed	22
Chapter 4: Posting	29
Chapter 5: Cover	40
Chapter 6: Luna	47
Chapter 7: Sample	55
Chapter 8: Uncover	62
Chapter 9: Spreading	72
Chapter 10: Grease Monkeys	79
Chapter 11: Bonding	84
Chapter 12: Mare Imbruim	88
Chapter 13: Funeral	95
Chapter 14: Party	101
Chapter 15: Stirring	106
Chapter 16: Moon	110
Chapter 17: Orbit	119
Chapter 18: Reposting	125
Chapter 19: Meeting	128

Chapter 20: Confusion	133
Chapter 21: Chaos	141
Chapter 22: Calm	148
Chapter 23: Deck Four	153
Chapter 24: Below	161
Chapter 25: The Spire	168
Chapter 26: Above and Below	176
Chapter 27: Distraction	184
Chapter 28: Tension	187
Chapter 29: Fresh Sample	189
Chapter 30: Saving Grace	191
Chapter 31: Break Point	196
Chapter 32: Reunion	200
Chapter 33: Test	205
Chapter 34: Orders	211
Chapter 35: Evac	214
Chapter 36: Together	220
Chapter 37: Departures	224
Chapter 38: Bridge	226
Chapter 39: Waiting	229
Chapter 40: Choices	232
Chapter 41: Last Chance	234
Chapter 42: Captain	239

Prologue

She opened her eyes, yet everything was still dark. She tried to move, her arms still at her sides. Her chest felt constricted, it was difficult to breathe. There was mass. Weight on top of her. She lurched her shoulders left and right. Cold dampness on her back. She tried again grunting sharply and her right hand felt free. With the weight still pressing down on her, she leaned to her left threading her arm up towards her face. She squealed as her forearm snapped past her elbow stopping against her chest. From there, she guided her hand upward. Finding a groove in the mass she pushed. Surprisingly, she got through it easily as if there was a parting. Everything around her felt cold, wet. Sticky almost. *No, it was definitely sticky.*

With her hand past the weight holding her down, she was able to move her fingers freely. Just air the other side. Air she now realised she desperately needed. Pushing her hand up again. Illumination made her pupils shrink in her sapphire eyes. It was not bright, but it was better than nothing. She tried to take in a good breath of air but the mass covering her would not allow her lungs to expand. Adrenalin began to soak through her skin. Her lip began to quiver, and her eyes started to glaze…

No stop it! You didn't come all this way for nothing! You didn't go through all…THIS for nothing!

"Get the fuck up!" She yelled aloud and began rocking her body from side to side again. More of the mass shifted and there was a thud. Then another thud and the laser point of light opened in front of her. Now able to move both arm she reached up, steadied her hands on both sides and pulled. The intake of air was intoxicating as she sat up. Her hands were wet with a Scarlett liquid. Her long blond hair was stiff. Her peach body-hugging vest clung strongly with the maroon glue. She instinctively put her hands over her mouth, painting the cold liquid on to her face. She was buried in a pile of people. Dead people. Torn up people. Shredded people.

Five of the men and women around her wore white flight suits with blue lapels. Three wore red, although the technician colours were barely visible in the collage of carnage. The last one was different. Still as mangled with deep cuts and gouges as the rest but this one had a thick vest with several pockets. He had badges on his shoulders and a breathing mask that made his face look mirrored. This man was one of the security personnel. She scanned the faintly lit room. The gun metal grey walls were high around her with a red framed catwalk spanning the entire room at around ten feet. Only a hand full of the oval shaped lights were working, and two of them flickered constantly. Pushing bodies aside slowly she clawed herself free.

She jerked forward and stumbled; her right foot still imbedded in the pile. With a slippery pop she was out, sprawling across the orange tinted floor. Laying on her back again she took several deep breaths. She moved her slick hair off her face and noticed it was thick with gloppy blood. Her nosed wrinkled as her adrenaline lowered and the Metallic smell of blood and the vomit inducing smell of shit danced around her nasal passage. The catwalk began to vibrate with the sound of heavy booted footsteps. She slowly rolled onto her side and onto her knees, her cream trousers sticking to the bloody surface below.

She tilted her head peeking up at the catwalk where a tall stocky figure stood. In the badly lit room, she managed to make out the bright orange lapels on the grey padded jacket and orange discs over the knees of padded trousers. She remained completely still staring in silence at the figure. The figure took hold of the railing and leaned forward. They began shifting from side to side, paused and lean further over the rail.

"Kara?" The figure whispered in a rough new Zealander accent. she squinted for a second and turned her head fully to focus on the man.

"Luca? Is that you?" Karabina whispered back in her gentle Ukrainian accent.

"Yes, it's me Kara. Are you hurt?" Luca asked searching the platform for a ladder.

Kara did not answer. Her shoulders began to tremble. Her eyes pooled into tears.

Luca found a vertical ladder taped in yellow and black.

"I'm here. I'm coming down to you," Luca reassured. Luca reached the bottom, his legs danced beneath him on the blood slick floor. He tightened his grip on the ladder and looked back at Kara's distort form. With the entire floor slick like oil, he crouched. With a strong push he slid on to his knees across the room and threw his arms around Kara hunched body. She buried her oval face into his chest and threw her dripping arms around him.

"Are you hurt?" Luca asked again. Kara shook her head sharply.

"Thirsty," was the only word she could muster.

Chapter 1: Home

Karabina opened her eyes and quickly threw her forearm across her face, blocking the sun light that streamed through her bedroom window. She rolled in her bed, putting her back to the bright light. Beside Karabina's bed her digital clock stared back at her. The green L.E.D. lit numbers seem to glow in its white oval case. After a moment she shoved it away, the clock gently sliding across her bed-side table before dropping to the floor. Karabina tucked her knees in and closed her eyes again. The sound of footsteps started upon the staircase below. She quickly pulled the blue duvet over her head before the bedroom door opened.

A man of average height stood in the doorway. He was broad and slightly balding. He folded his muscular arms stretching his grey shirt.

"I do know you're awake," the man finally said. Karabina through the blanket off her face with a grunt. She looked down the bed toward the man who was now leaning on the doorframe.

"Morning sweetie," the man said gently.

"Morning Father," Karabina replied, sitting up in the bed. She adjusted the blanket around her to cover the cream vest she wore.

"Your mother has already started breakfast. Come on," her father said before turning and heading back down. Karabina threw the rest of the duvet off her thin legs before getting up. She grabbed her bra back off the bedroom floor before going to her steel chest of draws. Placing her thumb on a small red panel, it turned green and gently slid open. Taking a fresh grey vest and short shorts from the draw, she tapped the unit, and the draw began to slide shut. It stopped. Karabina rolled her eyes. *Bloody thing*. She pushed it with her knee, and it finally closed.

Karabina lived in the Frankivskyi district of Lviv City. Which was situated in the western side of Ukraine. Being an only child, she never wanted for anything growing up. She always thought that a brother or a sister would have improved her childhood. *A sister*. But she knew she had everything needed for a strong future. An excellent education in a top school and academically minded friends like herself. So many of those friends had left the area to pursue bigger and better things now but she was still at home with her parent's. After a quick shower, she headed downstairs and into the kitchen. Her father was already enjoying a plate of potato pancakes while reading from a Cyber Station. The un-shaded light emphasised the lines in the lose skin on his head. His Cyber Station like so many similar designs were an almost paper-thin digital screen with instant access to the net. Karabina sat to his left at the table. Her mother turned from the kitchen unit and smiled at Karabina.

"Borscht?" Her mother asked.

"Yes, please Mother," she said reaching for a hot glass of Uzvar that had been placed for her. Her mother was not tall, but she made up for it with her firm and perky form. She had always been in decent shape in Kara's memory with regular sessions of in-house exercise classes. Her golden hair was pinned into a ball at the back of her head. But the skin pulled tight by the style did not hide her creasing face. After a moment, her mother brought a bowl of Borscht with a small plate of Pampushki. Placing the food in front of her she gently stroked Karabina's long blonde hair. Although Karabina was now 18 years old, her mother still looked upon her as her baby girl. Her father looked up from his Cyber Station. He glanced at his daughter then up at his wife.

"Sofia? Don't," he ordered staring at her. Sofia scowled and marched back to the kitchen unit and started loading the Utensil Steamer. Karabina looked at her father and then at her mother, her father still staring in Sofia's direction. Karabina had just broken a Pampushki to dip in her Borscht when her mother started blubbering over the kitchen unit.

"Mother?" Karabina asked rising from her chair.

"Don't," her father said softly taking Karabina's right hand.

"What's going on Father? What's happened?" Karabina demanded.

"Everything is fine. Sit down," Karabina sat again. Her mother turned sharply.

"This isn't fair Prokip," Sofia said, her cheeks wet with tears. Prokip closed his eyes and took a deep breath.

"Alright let's see shall we," Prokip said tapping at his Cyber Station. As Sofia approached the table and sat opposite her husband, Prokip slid the Station toward Karabina. She looked down at the screen.

"What am I looking at?" she asked not yet processing the words.

Prokip locked his hands together with his elbows now on the table.

"It's from the USC…Euro section." He smiled. Karabina scrolled the screen with her index.

"The United Space Council?" Karabina said surprised. Prokip covered her hand and gave it a gentle squeeze.

"You want to travel? You want to be somebody?" he asked.

"Yes of course Father."

"Well, your father put in an application for you." Sofia snapped, folding her arms, and leaning back in her chair. Karabina smiled.

"I've been excepted," she said standing.

"I've been excepted!" She shouted jumping into the air. Sofia's face dropped from smugness to sadness as Prokip stood. Father and daughter held hands, and both jumped up and down in delight.

"Isn't it fantastic," Prokip said, grabbing Karabina by the shoulders.

"It is Father. It is," Karabina hugged her father tightly.

"You want to go?" Sofia interrupted. Karabina released her father and hugged her mother from behind.

"Yes Mother," Karabina moved round her mother to look her in her teary eyes.

"I want this Mother. I really want this."

Sofia smiled softly and touched her daughter's smooth face. Taking a deep breath, she said, "If it's what you want…I won't stop you."

Returning to his chair Prokip slid the Station back to himself and scrolled through the text.

"You need to decide what roll you want to take."

Still with her arms around her mother, she thought.

"I'm going to be a flight officer Father," she announced smiling again. Prokip nodded in approval. Sofia squeezed her daughter around her thin waist.

"Yes, you will my dear and you'll make the whole family proud," Sophia praised.

"Yes, but you have a long road ahead before you get out there." Prokip confessed. Karabina release her grip on her mother and returned to her place at the table. She picked up her broken piece of pampushki and dipped it into her bowl. After taking a bite, she smiled again.

"I'll give you my recipe before you go," her mother said smiling at her girl. Karabina nodding as she took a spoon full of Borscht into her mouth.

Chapter 2: Academy

It did not take Karabina too long to adapt to life at the U.S.C.A. in Germanys capital of Berlin. She shared a room with two young ladies around the same age and living quarters were surprisingly spacious. Each room was fully-decked with ultramodern technological equipment. They each had a personal Cyber Station which was link to the main server of the Academy. They had a cleaning bot which would glide along their floor collecting any dirt or dust. Karabina had noticed quite quickly that the bot spent a lot of time in Charu's area. But according to Charu that was not the case, then again, she had also insisted her name meant attractive.

Which was clearly a lie. She was incredibly sweet though and Karabina appreciated that. Charu had the look of an owl about her with her jet-black hair, hooked nose, round face and a sari head wrap that could have been replaced with feathers. Charu came from a wealthy Indian family who lived in the Banjara Hills of Hyderabad. And although Karabina's family was nowhere near as wealthy, their circumstances were similar. Both coming from a life where joining the service was not necessary. *Why do you want to go into space when your family already has money?*

People would ask but it quickly became boring. Aubrey, the third girl in the room share was attractive, stunning even in Karabina's eyes. Aubrey was tall and slender with the smoothest face and cutest nose, her bright lime eyes marrying perfectly with her red hair. Aubrey was well experienced in keeping her area clean since she had obviously had to clean up after herself unlike Charu.

Kara caught sight of Aubrey bending over in underwear that enhanced her peachy bottom. And she kept looking. She did not notice Aubrey speak at first.

"What's the matter Kara?" Aubrey asked looking back from a bending position. Kara quickly slapped herself mentally.

"Nothing…You missed a bit," Kara said quickly, suddenly realising she did find Aubrey attractive for real. *Well shit.* Aubrey turned to face Kara after scooping her clothes up off the floor.

"I'm not cleaning the floor sugar," Aubrey stated before dumping her clothes into the wash machine, which instantly closed its lid with a whirlpool motion before sliding itself into the wall. Aubrey had come from France, the Corsica in the south which meant her being at the academy made a lot more sense. But where they had come from was not important in anyway. They were all working together to get out there to the great beyond.

"How many classes for you today?" Aubrey asked taking her hair straightener off her desk.

"Four today," Kara replied watching Aubrey straighten and brush her hair in one motion with the Hair Tech Brush.

"Damn you have it rough. How about you Charu?" Aubrey asked flicking her hair toward the floor.

"Only two," Charu muttered, while fixed to her Cyber Station. Aubrey pointed the Hair Tech at Kara and she stood. Turning to the side she allowed Aubrey to apply the straightener to her hair. After three strokes around Kara's head Aubrey said.

"Your hair is stunning sweetie."

Kara smirked with embarrassment.

"Aww thanks'…How many classes do you have?"

Aubrey rested her elbow on the arm she put around her waist, pointing the straightener up at the ceiling.

"None for me today…Which means I'm going out…With Josh." Charu turned in her desk to judge Aubrey.

"What?" Aubrey asked spreading her hands.

"He's handsome, funny," she continued.

"And going to be an engineer," Kara interrupted smiling. Aubrey turned to another desk that had red and white deco and slid the straightener into a casing that protruded from the desktop. The straightener locked in place and slid itself into the desk disappearing.

"That doesn't mean anything. I like the guy. And he is treating me to a romantic day out," Aubrey said putting her hands together in front of her and gently swinging side to side in a mocking I am so in love sort of way.

"He'll get you suspended," Charu said in the same mocking tone.

"Yeah, from the ceiling sugar," Aubrey replied with a big playful wink. They all laughed.

By around 9.30 am, all the girls had dressed for the day. They all wore the same style of flight suits although in varying colour. Charu's suit was a light green indicating she would be joining the medical division. Already having some training before deciding on the academy, it was the obvious choice. Aubrey was in a light grey since she was going to become a kick-ass security officer. Her suit was clearly hiding an outfit underneath for her skiving day.

Kara's was a light blue, a baby blue even with a chrome bar on each shoulder that proved she would, eventually become main flight crew. Kara was well on her way to becoming a flight officer, a coordinator that would help map route's through deep space. The three left their room into a busy hallway. Young men and woman in similar coloured suits passed them in either direction. *Just like my days at school.* The girls gave their traditional morning hug's and parted way's. Kara began her walk slowly watching Aubrey head toward a young man with thick brown hair and a faded orange flight suit.

She watched the pair embrace with a deep enthusiastic kiss before turning away and heading down the hallway to her first class of the day.

Kara made her way into the room which was teared upward to the rear. Each desk had a computer terminal a little larger than a Cyber Station screen with a chair connected on its right side, but they were turned outward, awaiting an occupant. At the front was a large glass table, like a pool table that was a pearl white all around the frame. Beside the table was a bulky built man with a painted face. The marking were tribal tattoos of his Samoan heritage. He stood patiently with a solid posture that help to emphasise the militaristic style of his uniform. The student's filed into the room and began taking their seats. Kara sat at her desk, halfway up the class and thumbed the terminal.

The screen illuminated with the words. 'ONLINE, GOODMORING KARABINA FARION.' Before loading in the necessary document and displays for the days lesson. The man at the front turned to the large table and thumbed a small black panel on its side. The table lit and a galaxy hologram projected from the table.

"Ok, Guys and Gals. Today we will be going over obstacle collisions…in space," the man said as he held out his hand at the galaxy and rotated his fingers, causing the image to zoom in fast to the Sol System. He turned back to the class.

"which of you is awake this morning, who can tell me why the Sol system or any system is dangerous to navigate?"

An Asian man to Kara's left raised his hand. The man pointed at him.

"Niran, go," he ordered.

"Professor, it's the gravitational pull of the planets," Niran answered.

"Yes, but that gravitational effect will help to eliminate any debris in a ship's flight path," the professor added bringing the system much tighter and displaying the asteroid belt between Mars and Jupiter.

"The asteroids of our system gather here." The professor explained.

"From this Hologram, the belt itself looks impassable, but that simply isn't the case," he continued. The Professor turned back to his class.

"And the answer for this is?" he asked the class, with seven students raising a hand. After a moment, he single out a girl with short blonde hair that had been shaved off on one side.

"Jamie?"

"Professor, the asteroids are spread out so much we can easily navigate the belt," Jamie explained. The Professor clicked his fingers at Jamie with a point.

"Yes, do you know the density of the belt?" The professor added. Jamie nibbled on the side of her index finger as she thought.

"We've covered this Jamie, 4% of Luna's mass," the professor added. Jamie tilted her head to the side. Then the answer struck her mind. Straightening up again she said.

"Three, point two by ten, twenty-one…professor." The Professor clicked another pointed yes at Jamie before scanning the class again.

"Kara? How many Earth's can we fit in the belt?" The professor quickly asked her. Kara stroked her hair behind her ear's.

"Fourteen…" She paused; the Professor peaked his head.

"Sextillion," she finished. Another click of approval, and she smiled. The professor scanned again.

"Friedrich? How many suns in that space?"

"Eleven-quadrillion," Friedrich immediately answered. Another clicked from the Professor. For the next forty minutes, the professor guided the class through a course in SNA, Space Navigation Assistance which was a reference for guiding a ships computer through its many star system's and charts to plan the most efficient route through space. These where the best times for Kara, working her brain was the most exhilarating part of her training at the academy. What she hated was coming up next…Zero gravity exercises.

After the morning's lesson, Kara made her way down the main corridor. Its high white wall's looked like ice, but Kara felt warm. She made a right turn into a tighter corridor, which was quite literally a tunnel. Her footsteps became louder as the floor underfoot became a metal grated catwalk. There was light beneath that seemed a long way down. She stopped at a grated staircase with red and white railings at either side. She took a long deep breath then descended. The light got dimmer as she made her way down. The staircase felt way too long to not any landing platform's in between. When Kara reached the bottom, she rubbed her shoulder's feeling the chilly air glide over her. *The ventilation fans don't help.* The fan peppered the upper side of the arching tunnel she was in. Although great in number, they did not turn extremely fast. More like a breeze than a blow. Every few paces the darker tunnel splayed off at both sides, showing glimpses of pipe and duct work. On the sixth splay, she stopped. She stood completely still listening for any strange sounds. She began to step back very slowly.

Two hands came lunging out from the right. Then the arm's and the rest of the body.

"AAAAAAAAH!" A man with thick blonde hair and a strong stubbled jaw leapt into the middle of the tunnel. He stood there in a wide stance, for a moment then straightened. He looked behind, then back in front. He turned again and began down the tunnel. Suddenly she was on his back, arms and legs around him as he dropped to his knees.

"Oh Shit!" he yelled.

"I got you, Nathan," Kara laughed as she stood over the man on his knees. She released her grip on his throat. Nathan looked up as his attacker smiling.

"Yeah, yeah, you got me," Nathan said rising to his feet. Nathan threw his arm around Kara's head giving a squeeze. Kara swung her hand down, tapping Nathan's groin.

"Ooh." Nathan grunted releasing Kara from the head lock.

"We're going to be late, let's go," Kara said slipping away. Nathan stood straight, holding himself. Taking a breath, he followed Kara down the tunnel. They stood together at the end of the tunnel at a thick steel door. Nathan reached out pushing the control panel, several jets of air leapt into the tunnel from the door seals.

"Do you think you'll be sick again?" Nathan asked placing a hand on her shoulder. Kara looked up at him as the door opened at the centre and slid into the wall's in four sections.

"You ever been kicked in zero G?" Kara asked with wide eyes.

Kara and Nathans introduction were probably the oddest experience of her life. During the first Zero Gravity lesson, the men had gathered, the same as the women and it was clear each group was sizing up the other. Either group made comments about the other in whispered tones, but Nathan stood in silence. Kara glanced back from the circle to see him looking straight at her group. *Or Her*. His muddy hazel eyes were soft looking, kind even but his staring glaze was cringe worthy. She continued to talk with the girls until a brown-and-white striped rubber football appeared in the centre of the group.

All the woman looked over at the men and Nathan was still looking at them arms parted at his waist. She did not know why but Kara directed the ball with her foot before kicking it back toward him. Nathan stopped the ball under his foot and smiled.

"Weird," One of the girl's said before chatting again. Kara just looked at him puzzled.

Was that a pickup technique?

Shortly after inductions from the two teachers, a man and woman. The antigravity panels that covered all surfaces fired up and all students were gently gliding back and forth across the large space. There was laughing and joking of plenty with the odd yell or scream from a messed-up transition. On Kara's third transition from the floor to the ceiling, she saw Nathan again. Spinning toward her at high speed.

"I can't stop myself," Nathan said as he got closer. Kara stretched out her hands, grabbing his shoulders as the momentum took them both. Nathan got his arms over hers and pulled them into a turn. A second later they slammed into the wall. Nathans back hit first taking his breath away as Kara slammed into him. Being shorter than him, Kara's head hit his chest.

"Are you hurt?" Nathan asked looking down at her.

"I think I'm okay," Kara whispered, head still against his chest. *His chest is firm*. She slowly looked up at him.

"Am I okay?" Kara asked him.

"Your far more than okay…What's your name?" Nathan asked.

"Karabina." She blushed.

"Karabina Farion."

"And where is that name from?" Nathan questioned.

"Europe, Ukraine." They moved their arms at the same time, making a small space between them.

"I'm Nathan Ellis. England," Nathan said moving to Kara's side. Taking her hand, he gently pushed off the wall, sending them back out.

Despite there being a definite attraction between the two, they decided to stay friends at the academy. The idea of falling behind or even failing due to their feelings was too much of a risk. They quickly became symbiotic, Kara being rough at times like a buddy would and Nathan being caring and sensitive like a girl, friend would.

The duo headed into the large Zero Gravity chamber where several classmates had gathered. Nathan greeted several of his male colleagues with fancy handshakes and one asked.

"Is Kara still single?" Nathan looked at him like he had asked to fuck his mother.

"What? You're not dating her," he continued.

"She won't be dating anyone while she's here, so leave it." The discussion was halted as the Teachers entered the chamber. The lady of the pair raised her hand.

"Good day to you all. Today we will be doing something a little different." She began.

"You will be learning the most important lesson of all," the Man continued.

"What happens to fire in zero gravity." The class spread out into a line and stood at ease. The lady instructor carried a long cylinder across the room and fed it into a hole in the wall while the other turned to an operating console and began pushing buttons. The floor in the centre of the room began to shift and slide open. Storage crates, tables and chairs rose from the opening. The crates where long carbon fibre blocks with steel reinforcements along its edges with clasps made of titanium. The Tables where smooth with arching legs and oval tops of white and silver. The chairs although similar in design had wide arching back rests with seat restraints made of titanium and Kevlar weave.

"Arrange yourself into mixed groups please."

The class began moving into pairs and Nathans colleague glided toward Kara before Nathan grab the collar of his flight suit.

"Not going to happen Ray," Nathan said pulling him back and moving past him. Kara saw this and clapped her hands together and brought them up to her face.

"My hero." She mocked swaying from side to side.

"I'll call him over if you like," Nathan said. Kara quickly dropped her hands.

"Oh no don't do that," she said looking over at Ray.

Kara and several other students were directed into the chairs. Each one restrained themselves in place with the harness straps. The remainders lined up at the walls.

"The cylinder is filled with liquid H20 to simulate the fire. There is no smoke or an actual flame. You would see fire as dim blue balls rather than lashing flames." The female teacher explained. The other teacher stepped forward.

"When Mrs Colins releases the liquid, it will spread fast though the chamber. Fire would move much slower through the space unless, like this instant it comes from a leek…A pressurise fuel tank."

Mrs Colins began turning a red valve on the tank set in the wall and nodded to her colleague. He stepped back toward the Control Terminal.

"You must reach your partner before the liquid does…Good luck." With that, he pulled a lever on the Control Terminal and everything in the room lifted off the floor. The teaches held on to the panel's they occupied as the gravity left the room. All the students were several metres off the floor now. The designated rescuers were sliding up the wall's as they watched the crates, tables and student's restrained in chairs float upward and begin twirling.

"Fire!" Mrs Colins warned pushing a red button on the wall. Clear balls of liquid water began drifting from the cylinder across the room.

The rescue students pushed off the walls toward their targets. After a few moments, the twirl that Kara was stuck in, started to make her feel dizzy. She tried to figure out which rescuer was Nathan every time they appeared in her vision. She saw one Girl collide with a table and flip away toward the ceiling. Another student hit a crate sending it across the path of two others, throwing them backward. *Where's Nathan?*

One reached out, grabbing the chair of his partner. With his momentum, he took the girl and her chair into the oncoming liquid. Nathan rocketed past all the chairs near the ceiling on the far side above the expanding cloud of water.

Stopping against the wall he turned quickly to single out Kara. Another girl reached her partner and began swirling round with the chair trying to undo the restraints. The dispersal cloud of water balls was getting wider and closer to the restrained students. Kara caught sight of the pair in a twirl get drenched by the water bubbles as she drifted backward. *What the…?*

Kara got progressively further away from the spreading orbs when she heard Nathans voice.

"Don't be sick…" Nathan warned. *It was already coming.* Kara came to a stop at the far wall as Nathan moved round to her front.

"Seriously. Don't be sick." Nathan continued fumbling at the round clasp at her waist. Kara covered her mouth and coughed. The clasp clicked open, and they both began pulling Kara's shoulders free of the harness.

"Where's the water?" Nathan asked pulling the harness down from her crotch. Kara looked across the chamber.

"Ten…Nine…Eight," Kara counted.

"Okay, okay." Nathan snapped as he tucked his legs in before kicking the chair downward. The pair floated upward until they stopped at the ceiling.

"Ok class, this means only five of you would have survived if that was real…Come on back down," Ms Colins called out to the scattered class. Kara focused on Nathan again.

"You've got a habit of saving me," Kara told him.

"I didn't want to fail the exercise," he confessed. They both smiled.

"I meant saving me from vomiting too."

"If you were sick…it would have been in My face," Nathan confessed again and they both burst into laughter as the Gravity effect began to rise, gently pulling them back down to the chamber floor.

Chapter 3: Unearthed

MISSION DATE: D:15 M:8 Y:2264
EUPHORIA LOCATION: KUIPER BELT: PLUTO MOON: CHARON ORBIT
MISSION LOCATION: CHARON: NORTH POLE REGION
MISSION OBJECTIVE: MINIRAL ANALYSIS
MISSION CREW NO.: 5 (2: SHUTTLE. 1: LANDER: 2: SPACE WALK).

There was a gentle dim thud inside the helmet of Astronaut Grey as the bolt from his harpoon hit the surface. The Compact bolt gun he used was attached to his suit at the waist, anchoring to the ground by titanium cable. He pressed retract on his belt and was gently pulled down to the Moon surface. With the cable tight at his side, his feet were on the surface.

"Okay, I'm hooked in. Furukawa come on over," Grey ordered through his helmet radio, turning slightly in his bulky space suit. He could see the Lander in the corner of his large dome helmet. It had an Icosahedron ball sat on a cylinder base with its landing legs spread like a spider. The tips of the legs plunged into the ground with eight anchor cables around it. He saw Furukawa's legs appear from the base. She pushed her way down to the ground the best she could before using thrusters on her back to turn over. She held the underside of the lander and gave Grey a thumb. Grey thumbed back and Furukawa pushed off. Drifting forward she used the thrusters again to turn over and added an additional boost to glide downward toward greys out-stretched arm. She grabbed on with both hands and pulled her legs in to the ground. Grey held on to her by the belt as she used her bolt gun.

After Furukawa was anchored, she attached a second line to Grey's belt, linking the pair.

"Are you okay, Furu? You sound a little panicked," Grey asked hearing her quick breathing. He watched her as she began to slowly crouch.

"I'm fine Boss, let's get it done," she said taking a metal container from her belt.

"Her heart rate is elevated but she's good." A third voice announced over the comms. Furukawa rolled her eyes. "I just said I'm fine Cole."

"Yes, and I just confirmed that," Cole said watching their bio-monitors inside the lander.

"Okay, I'm moving on. Five metres…If you're okay, Furu?" Grey asked again.

"Just go will you," Furu snapped into her headset. Grey detached from his ground anchor and used his own thruster to propel forward. Using short bursts to keep him from rising off the surface he reached the five-metre mark and fired a second bolt into the ground. Furukawa glanced up at him as the reeling from her tether stopped. She was already swinging a small pickaxe, similar to a rock hammer into the ground. Although the surface looked soft, the Moons brown surface dust was as hard as stone.

"How we doing Furu?" Grey asked beginning his excavation, listening to Furu's grunts.

"I'm good. This stuff is harder than I thought," she confessed.

"Get what you can of the surface then go to the drill."

"Copy that." She used the axe to drag what she had broken into the metal container. Furukawa returned her axe to its pocket and brought out a small two-handed drill from the bottom of her thruster pack. She pressed it to the ground and fired it up.

Grey's grunts were drowned out of her headset as the vibration from the drill resonated through her suit. The inch-wide drill bit ploughed through the rustic dust into the ground beneath. The tip slowed but stayed constant. She lifted the pressure off the tip regularly pulling dust out of the hole. When the drill had reached four inches, she took the drill out and set it back. She placed a needleless syringe into the hole and pulled its plunger up collecting a full sample of refined dust.

"Drill and surface sample done," Furukawa announced stowing the syringe.

"Good work. Cole how's are time?"

"Eight minutes before your suit's start to freeze."

"Copy that," Grey said pushing his drill to the ground. Grey's drill had a cylinder attachment on the end that he used to core drill a rock sample out.

Furukawa moved on to a second sample site 5 metres in the opposite direction and after anchoring again began the strenuous grunting again.

"Oh, come on," Grey mumbled over the radio while the core drill spluttered whenever it got stuck.

"Do you think we will bring back better samples than the last crew?" Cole asked over the comms.

"I hope so. I called in a lot of favours to get the most northern spot," Grey admitted.

"So, any decent find will be down to you. Thanks boss," Cole replied.

"Yeah, just remember that when we become famous."

"Oh, don't worry you get all…"

"Aww shit!" Grey interrupted.

"What's wrong?" Furukawa asked drilling her second sample.

"The drill's stopped working, it must have over heated."

"Is that even possible at this temperature?" Furukawa asked turning on her knee to look in Grey's direction.

"Well, the thing's not turning, and I've got nothing on the trigger," Grey pulled at the drill. It didn't move. He repositioned and tried again. Nothing.

"What's happening Boss? Heart rate climbing."

"I'm trying to pull this thing out…It's stuck," Grey stated having a third crack at it. Furukawa listened to Grey's maddening grunt's as she gathered her sample with a second syringe.

"I'm coming over," Furukawa told him. Grey turned to face her.

"No, you stay…damn it," Furukawa was already coasting toward him. Grey stood and turned, Furukawa getting close. He reached out with both arms before Furukawa made contact. The pair locked together, and Furukawa quickly placed her feet and reeled the cable between them into a two-foot line. Lifting gently off the ground she fired a fresh bolt into the ground and winched herself down.

"God damn ice ball!" Grey ranted, kicking at the core drill.

"It probably refroze in place when it stopped," Furukawa assumed.

"How we doing for time Cole?" Grey asked, taking a moment.

"Four minutes."

"Alright Furu get that side," Grey said moving to the top side of the drill. Furukawa held the bottom half.

"Pull…Pull…Again," Grey said between strenuous grunts from himself and Furukawa.

"…It's no good. It won't budge," Furukawa confessed, hands on knees.

"Any ideas?" Grey asked settling back straight.

"We could reverse our thrusters to pull but we still need to crack the ice seal," Furukawa suggested.

"If you do free the thing, you could get stuck in your trajectory and launch off into space," Cole admitted over the comm.

"We need solutions, not more problems," Grey said. Furukawa opened a pouch on the front of her suit and took out a second drill bit.

"Yes, I knew I brought a spare. We drill both sides," Grey bent down and began unscrewing the drill from the core attachment.

"Then what?" Grey asked her.

"That's all I got."

"It's a start, get drilling," Grey said excepting the drill bit. Furukawa set her drill tight against the core drill and began drilling. Sparks began to jet of the drill bit every few seconds and quickly cooled in the frozen atmosphere.

Grey began drilling on the opposite side.

"I've got something. But it's risky," Cole eventually said.

"Let's hear it."

"We blow it out with combustion…Or at least loosen it enough to pull free," Cole explained.

"I'm with you so far," Grey said as they both drilled.

"The only way we can do that is with your air tank."

"Are you insane we need air to breathe," Furukawa interrupted. "Yes, I know but you'll only need a burst in the hole you're drilling."

"Then get a spark off the drill," Grey finished.

"Your nut's," Furukawa said.

"You got a better plan…Keep drilling," Furukawa was shaking her head but continued drilling. Cole unstrapped himself inside the lander and floated to the suit locker where his suit hung. He unhooked his astronaut helmet off the wall. He opened the inner airlock below.

"Boss…You have to be sure to break the seal on the helmet side…I'm dropping a spare into the airlock ready," Cole told him releasing the helmet into the air lock and resealing behind.

"Hole drilled," Furukawa said sliding it out of the hole.

"Furu, you need to remember the number's on Grey's suit to reset after changing the mixture for the burn, also don't forget the pressure when the seal is broken," Cole explained.

"This is a real stupid idea you know that," Furukawa told Grey.

"I'm not leaving without what's in that core," Grey insisted.

"Two minutes guys."

"Come on Furu, I'll spark it," Grey said getting himself ready.

"Fucking hell alright," Furukawa said moving behind grey and taking note of the tank read outs. "Alright. How much oxygen?" Furukawa asked.

"As small as you can. Helium off. Nitrogen as is. Oxygen two percent should be enough," Cole said.

"Ready Grey?" Furukawa asked hand on the control panel just above the tank. With her free hand, she held her small pickup ready.

"Do it."

Grey took a deep breath and Furukawa quickly tapped at the panel changing the mixture in the tank. Using her pick, she severed the hose near Grey's helmet. The pressure burst out pushing her back. She quickly pushed the hose down to the drill hole and held it there for several seconds. Grey fired up the drill, the bit spinning. Furukawa pulled the hose away and she was resetting his mixer when Grey grinded the drill bit down the side of the core attachment into the hole.

The drill and core launched into the air ahead of a jet of flame that instantly disappeared. The blast threw Grey backward. He spun upside down from the blast. The anchor point on Furukawa kept him from disappearing for good. Furukawa was jerk off the ground, throwing Grey into a whip back toward the ground. The core was going higher and higher.

"No, no, no, no!" Furukawa yelled. She disconnected her anchor, flipped her thrust vector and launched after it with her thrusters.

"Furu No!" Cole screamed into the radio as he watched the scanning screen with their signals separating.

Furukawa thrusted up toward the core with it slowly tumbling away. She stretched and reached and grabbed it. She stopped her thruster and pulled the core tight to her chest. She did not stop going. She curled the best she could and tried to turn. She could not adjust. She reached to her side again re-reversing her thrust. The burn of air thrust stopped her forty metres above the surface. With a small spluttering puff, the thrusters were empty.

"Fuck." All she could hear was her breathing while suspended in nothing.

"Grey?...Grey?...Talk to me." There was no response. Her breathing became much faster and heavier. It was even colder here than forty metres below her.

"Cole?...Cole?...Come in god damn it!" Her voice began to tremble. She attempted a swim to adjust herself but there was nothing to push against.

"Cole!...Cole!..."

The comm crackled and she took a deep breath in relief.

"Furu! I'm here...What the hell happened?" Cole finally replied.

"The blast threw us around...I don't know if Grey is alive...And I'm stuck," she said, panic in her voice.

"Fuck! I've got nothing on Grey's bio-monitor...I think he's gone," Cole said back, his voice just as panicked as hers.

"Oh god no. I can't turn to look for him," Furukawa said, now trying to twist.

"What about the core?...Did we lose that too?"

"Fuck the core! Grey is dead!" She screeched back.

"And he died for nothing if it's gone Furu!" Cole shouted back.

"I've got the core."

"Oh, thank god...Alright can you secure it on your suit," Cole asked clambering out of his seat back to the suit locker.

"Yea I think so...why?"

"I need to get you down...You going to feel a jolt when I reach you and we can't lose that sample," Cole said climbing into his suit. He checked his mixture on the pack and slung it on.

"Okay, okay, okay," Furukawa said, breathing fast. She pulled on her hip cable and spooled it around the shaft of the core.

"What is that?" She said quietly spotting what seemed to be black grease on the surface side of the core that had crystallised in the freezing temperature.

"Say again Furu I didn't get that."

"Just get me out of here...I'm starting to feel cold in here." Her thruster and air tank pack had already started freezing, she looked at her gloves, ice was crystallising on her suit too. She finished spooling and hooked her cable on the drill end of the core. Her breath was frosty.

"Cole! Hurry! My suit is shutting down...Cole!" There was no response. Silence.

"You better be on your way Cole...Cole!"

The air in her lungs was punched out of her. Blood leapt from her mouth when she coughed. She squeezed her eyes tightly feeling pain. Shaking profusely, she tried to look at her right side. Something had punctured her suit. And her lung. She coughed again with much more blood.

"Co…Cole," she mumbled hoping he was on his way. Her eyes began to feel heavy as the pain intensified. Something pulled her. From the inside. She began convulsing violently as her lung began tearing inside her smashed rib cage. The pain and pull continued and she felt her boot's touch the floor. She attempted to turn, only her head moved. She saw Cole tight at her side. There was tugging at her belt. More blood coughing, sticking to the visor as it froze.

"I'm so sorry." She heard Cole say through her radio. Then something pushed her. She began to spiral seeing the surface then space then surface again. On Her sixth rotation, she saw Grey face up on the ground. His visor was smashed, his skin shining blue and white. There was a crackle, and her radio went silent.

Vibration sounded through her helmet; she shook inside her suit. Then darkness. Silence…

Chapter 4: Posting

Kara sat patiently outside the Academy office. She sat alone on the spoon shaped chair mounted to the wall, although there were five other chairs. The soft cushion was black on the white carbon frame and the hallway was a faded grey. She lifted her Cyber Station from the chair beside her and thumbed the screen. With a ping, it illuminated. After a quick search, she scrolled through images of A class star ships. All were enormous and refined. Some were long and cylinder like and others were more compact in a rectangular prism shape. She marvelled at their incomprehensible size and technical achievement. After her four years at the Academy, she had a newfound appreciation of the Research and development and engineering divisions of the Space Programme. She would never be able to fly without them. The tinted glass door of the office opened and a lady in a white body cone dress stepped out. Her hair was blonde and lightly curled to one side of her head. She approached Kara and smiled.

"The Professor will see you now…If you'd care to follow me." The lady said before turning on her white heels and heading back toward the glass door. Kara quickly shut down her Cyber Station and gave chase. The lady opened the door and held it open with her posterior. She invited Kara with her hand and Kara walked inside. The room was four metres square with a large white desk in the centre. The lady followed her inside and took her seat at the desk. Adjusting the skirt of the dress she glanced up at Kara.

"You've never had to come here before, have you." She inquired.

"No, never," Kara confessed.

"Oh, I am sorry the door on your left." The lady pointed and Kara moved toward the door. It was a solid wooden door. She had not seen one since she was a child. She took a deep breath a knocked.

"Come in," replied a deep, male voice. Kara turned the old cast iron knob and pushed her way inside.

With a grunt of effort Kara was in the room, almost stumbling in. The Academy Director studied her entrance while rubbing his hands gently. When Kara had regained her composure, she approached the Director who was sat at a huge solid oak desk in a throne like chair. Although the rooms deco was incredibly old fashioned, the Director's clothes were extremely modern. His crisp white suit almost sparkled in the glow of sun light, streaming through the window behind. His short-greased hair and clean skin made him look much younger than he should have been. The Director leaned forward, resting his thick padded elbows on his desk.

"Yes? Can I help you?" The Director asked. Being taken aback Kara took a step closer.

"Uh…Yes…Director…Uh…Karabina…Karabina Farion, Sir." The words fumbling from her lips.

"Sir?" He questioned. Eyes wide.

"This isn't the Military Karabina. My name is Martin Parker. You can address me as Director." Before Kara could respond, he stood up smiling.

"Or you could plant yourself in this chair in front of me and call me Martin like everyone else, what do you think." The Director chuckled, offering the much smaller wooden chair with his hand. Kara moved sheepishly but did sit in the chair.

"Well, Director? Or Martin?" he asked taking note of her deer in the headlights look.

"Martin is better," Kara finally said. Martin slowly stepped back and lowered into his chair.

"Why?" he asked.

"Why? Because it is less formal. Creates a more relaxing environment," Kara explained.

"Is that what you what from life…A relaxing environment?" Martin probed.

"I don't understand?"

"I'm simply trying to ascertain why you came to the Academy, why you what to fly and why you're the best damn Navigator we have here," Martin's voice became progressively louder until his punch line.

Martin leaned back to a relaxed position in his throne.

"Is it because you want…a relaxing environment," Martin said mockingly making his statement again.

"No. You're twisting my words…Martin," Kara bit back. Martin leaned to his left and opened a heavy draw in the desk, reaching in he pulled a green binder of papers out and placed it on the desk.

"There's the fire I've heard about," Martin said opening the binder.

"Why are you still here? Why haven't you been deployed?" Kara glared down at her feet.

"I don't know," she said quickly. Martin glanced through the first few pages.

"Shall I tell you why?" Kara lifted her head.

"Please."

"Your record states that you have never left this site. No vacation time, no tours, not one single expedition off this planet," Martin told her.

"I…I wanted to concentrate on my studies."

"Yes, study is good. Experience is better," Martin finished, closing the binder, and sliding it across the desk toward her.

"You need off world experience. But I cannot deploy you on a ship to get it. I can't have an un-experienced Cadet replacing any seasoned Navigational officer," Kara regarded the binder for a moment.

"Paper has only used for off world transport," Kara realised.

"Yes, keep going."

"Information can be broadcast to a Ship before leaving Earth dock," Kara continued.

"They said you were smart…Anymore?" Martin said smiling widely.

"The only reason you would give me these paper's is for shuttle flight…Which means your…" Kara paused.

"You are sending me to the damn Moon!" Kara burst out, leaping from her chair. Martin's faced dropped realising her disappointment. He slowly stood from his chair.

"This is your one and only chance to apologise and except this posting…" Martin began, Kara attempted a interject.

"Your one and only chance to get any off-world experience," Martin continued. Kara stood to attention.

"I apologise for my outburst Director and gladly except my new posting on Luna," Kara spoke robotically before turning on her heel and marching out of the office.

That afternoon kara had dressed in tight black leggings and a loosely fitting white shirt, finishing the look with a short black jacket that stopped below her chest. She began to pack all her things ready for her posting. Her clothes, her equipment her keep sakes. The Hair Tech that Aubrey had gifted her when she left for her deployment on the USC Comado. The black under short's that Nathan had given her as a joke gift, claiming one day they would get to see what goes in each other's draws. And a gold bracelet with links of sun's and star's that Nathan finally gave her when she had agreed to give him a pair of her underwear too. *I hope your both safe and happy.* She gathered everything into a silver-coloured carbon fibre case with a thumb print lock that she pushed. She pulled the case toward the door and scooped up her Cyber Station.

Moving into the busy hallway she took a deep breath and made off down the corridor. When she approached the front entrance to the Academy, she approached the front desk where two men in white suit jacket's over black shirts stood.

"Karabina Farion," she said handing her Cyber Station to one of the desk attendants. He smiled and placed the device in a chrome block that the Station fit perfectly in, then placed it within Kara's reach on the desk.

"I.D. and Clear code please?" he asked. Kara thumbed the Cyber Station screen with her free hand.

"Clear Code…Ellis," Kara stated before removing her print. Taking the block back the attendant removed the Station from the block and slid it into a stack unit, which blinked green when the Station was delivered.

"Your transport has already arrived Miss Farion." The attendant added gesturing toward the large sliding doors of the building. Kara thanked the attendant with a nod and walked to the large door's dragging her case behind her.

When the door's opened, she saw her transport was a black civilian shuttle. It was low arched and the thick treaded tires were barely visible. As Kara approached the driver stepped out from the far side and moved quickly to help with her solitary case.

"Shall I put this into the back?" The woman asked reaching for the case. Kara allowed the transfer and the driver, who Kara believed may have been Latino waved a hand at the vehicles rear. The back compartment opened, and a slow ramp of weaved metal uncoiled. The Case had been laid upon it and was pulled into the compartment in the same coiling motion. By this time, Kara had slid open the front passenger door. The driver paused for a moment before following up to close the door for her.

"Thank you," Kara nodded before her escort had scurried back to the driver's seat. The driver who was maybe in her mid-forties started the silent electric engine with a thumb scan.

"The Space Port, isn't it?" The driver asked pulling her a brown leathery harness over her thin body.

"Yes…Thank you," Kara said, mentally waving goodbye to the place she had called home.

After five miles of silence, the driver turned to Kara who was still gazing out of the window.

"You're the first fair I've had up front in…maybe a month," she announced.

"Really" Kara said turning to face her.

"Oh yes, most like to sit behind and get lost in their Cyber Station's," the driver continued.

"I've just handed mine in. Beside that's just rude," Kara explained.

"Ha, you don't have to tell me it's rude." After a moment, the driver spoke again.

"I'm sorry…You handed yours in?"

"Yes, I'll be issued a new one when I reach my posting. I'm going to Luna Base," Kara continued to explain.

"Have you been there before?"

"No, have you?" Kara asked her.

"Yes, Once. With my husband." The Driver confessed. Kara turned her body in her seat with interest.

"What's it like?"

The Driver sat quiet for a moment.

"Like a winter wonderland…At night. We Stayed in the Armstrong Dome Hotel." The Driver explained.

Kara began to imagine how that could look, although she quickly realised, her time on Luna was no Vacation. It did not stop her imagination whirling. She could see herself running through the grey dust, so well-lit it looked like snow. She saw herself kicking through the snow in her ankle wrapped shoes. Inside one of Luna's domes. Like a figure in a snow globe. She began to twirl around and round, arms stretched out wide. She fell, the snow erupting like a cloud around her. She began to laugh. Another voice is laughing with her…A girl's laugh. Aubrey appears on top of her also laughing from the fall. Aubrey rises to a kneeling position over her. The pair smile and stair into each other's eye's. Kara can hear a voice calling. She looks in aww at Aubrey's beauty as the snow falls upon her hair. The voice call's again and Aubrey slowly looks to her right. Kara follows her gaze.

The two girls smile deeply as Nathan comes into view. He runs toward them. He starts to wave with his right hand. Kara looks up at Aubrey and then back to Nathan. Nathan is waving both arms? Wildly? Kara feel's Aubrey's grip tighten on her shoulder's. She looks up at her again. Aubrey's eyes are wide. Too wide. Those magnificent green eyes begin to redden. Blood seeps from her eyes. The blood does not touch Kara's face but spreads outward. The globs of suspended blood continue to ooze from Aubrey's eyes as she screeches. Blood leaking from her mouth. Her grip like knifes in Kara's shoulder's. Kara reaches out for Nathan, both girl's screaming now. Nathan has not closed the distance; he is still he was. Kara grabs at Aubrey's face trying to stop the skin tearing grip. Aubrey's floating blood begins to crystallise. Her mucky blood pooled eyes begin to freeze. With a crack of air, Aubrey is shredded off Kara. She rockets to the ceiling of the dome. Her body erupts into a cloud of blood, flesh, and bone as her mass crushes into the glass of the dome.

Kara lay there in horror as her friend's body continues to impact and erupt into mere particles of mist. Kara's teary eyes begin to harden on her cheeks. She looks to Nathan for help. Nathan hurtles toward her through the air now. She reaches for him as he gets close. The dome explodes apart. Huge pieces of glass ten inches thick come thundering down. Nathan overshoots her reach. His head explodes against the side of the dome as the rest of his body plunges through the impact. Kara hears the whoosh and looks up as a massive section of glass hit's her.

Kara leaps in her seat banging her head against the passenger window.

"Fuck!" She yelled as the driver recoiled from her.

"Are you all right. You were having a nightmare," the driver told her.

"I reached out to wake you and you jumped out of your skin," she continued. Kara rubbed her head and check her palm for blood but there was none.

"Yeah. I'm okay," she said rubbing her head some more.

"I didn't mean to startle you."

"It's okay, honestly you did me a favour," Kara admitted. The driver touched her on the shoulder and nodded toward her window.

"We've arrived unless you need a moment."

Without speaking Kara reached for the door lever. The door slid forward, and she got out still holding her head. The driver quickly made her way to the rear and collected her case. She approached her slowly and handed the case over.

"Are you sure you're, okay?" she asked again.

"I'm really fine honestly. How much for the ride?" Kara asked.

"I was paid before I arrived." The Driver confessed as she closed the rear compartment and heading back to the driver's door.

"Good luck on your posting," the driver said climbing into her seat. Kara bent to the window and raised a hand and the Transport shuttle pulled always from the departure bay. Kara turned on her heel and paused. She studied the building exterior. The front had huge, mirrored doors with golden pillars at each side. Above the glass doors was a large disc, the emblem of the U.S.C. with what looked like an old space shuttle. That was bending unnaturally around a red planet. Kara rubbed her head one last time before making her way inside.

Kara scanned the large accessible area of the Space port entrance. The blue marble pillars were wide and plentiful. To the left of the Security booths, she spotted the departure stands. Kara approached the security booths easily with nobody really queuing there. The booths were being guarded by armed personal, Identity scanners, cameras and Alsatian dogs. She heaved her case onto the conveyor to the right. Two women in navy blue uniforms surrounded in black body armour stepped forward with their left hands raised. Kara froze in place.

The first security office held the grip of her small compact weapon. A white box like thing that made Kara think of the sticky draw in her bedroom. The second had a camera and monitor unit that was attached to her armour with straps and supports. Holding the sides like a steering wheel She slowly raised it as the device began to hum. Several green laser beams dance over Kara.

"Raise your arms please ma'am," the armed officer asked as a male, dog hander stepped forward. Without order the large dark coloured dog began to sniff around her body, starting at her feet.

After a few moments, the dog returned to its masters left heel, still silent. The offices parted and waved Kara through.

"Thank you, ma'am," the armed woman said. Kara stepped through an arching frame of white with hundreds of tiny black camera lens running around its inner casing. Her case had been scanned and inspected by a second male officer with thick brown gloves of rubber. He lifted the case off the conveyor and loaded it into a black metal case that was a little larger than hers. Kara watched as he connected a hose to an inch-wide hole on its side. Turning a valve at the far end the hose began to pulse with a hissing sound. He glazed back at Kara.

"Ma'am. Your case will be loaded for you for stability in the shuttle."

"Oh...okay, thank you," Kara said surprised and started to make her way to the departure stalls.

Blue marble covered the front panelling of each stall with a black camera mounted on top. The cameras moved independently, following Kara's every move. Behind each of the three desks sat a woman in bright red blazers and matching berets. All three of them smiled together as Kara reached the first. They almost look identical, Kara thought fumbling at her jacket. She worked her identification card free and handed it to the operator.

"Thank you very much Ma'am," the lady said softly loading the card into her computer that was slightly hidden by the stall. A small box panel rolled up, out of the stall. As it rolled completely over it reveal a thumb scanner. Kara thumbed it quickly.

"Keep your thumb there please." The operator asked glancing back at her computer screen. Ejecting Kara's card and handing it back with a smile.

"All done Miss Farion. Head down the long tunnel to bay seven and have a wonderful day." The operator explained.

"I hope so too. Thank you very much," Kara replied and made off to her directed path.

After the aquatic style tunnel, Kara pushed into the revolving door of bay seven. Inside was a lounging area, carpeted in silver and black. A man in a dark green flight suit sat in one of the eight thick padded chairs studying a Cyber station closely. To Kara's right was a cooper tinted bar littered with cups and glasses. She approached it and saw small vending units which dispensed hot and cold drinks. Working out where everything was set out along the bar, she began preparing a coffee.

"Aww come on! Pass it!" The man shouted, slamming his fist down on the arm of the chair with a quiet thud. Kara glanced back at him then continued to pour her drink. She added two sugar cubes and stirred them in. She turned to face the room and stood quietly, sipping the coffee.

"Aww man, your useless! Get off the wall! Do something!" The man shouted again grabbing at his own thick black hair.

Kara smiled and turned back to the bar and added a little more milk to her drink. She began strolling round the room behind the distraught man. She approached the back of his chair and leaned in slowly. Making sure her hair did not touch him she studied the Cyber Station screen.

"Damn it! Get that asshole out of there!" The man yelled again. Kara looked at the side of his head.

"Who are you talking too?" Kara asked as the man leapt sideways in the chair away from her.

"Holy shit!" He yelled, his eyes bulging out of his head staring at her. Kara burst into laughter. The man grabbed at his chest, still bewildered.

"You scared the life at of me," he admitted.

"I can see that," Kara ridiculed before sipping at her cup. The man looked round the room still half across the chair beside his.

"What are you doing in here? Who are you?" The man asked.

"Karabina. Are you on the shuttle too?" The man leapt out of his terrified pose to his feet.

"Uh, yes Miss Farion. I am James Becker; people call me Jimmy or Jimbo or just Jim. I'm your shuttle pilot," James rambled, standing to attention. Kara studied him for a moment watching the panic in his eyes. James was definitely older than her by at least ten years but right now she was on top.

"Well Just Jim," she finally said setting her cup on a side table. "When is departure?"

"Whenever you say Miss Farion," he stated. Kara smiled and stepped closer to Jim. He glanced down instinctively studying her athletic form. Kara leaned into his left ear, her chest gently touching his.

"Lead the way Just Jim," Kara ordered.

"Yes Ma'am," James said stepping back and quickly turning. Kara followed his quick pace through another door and down a second tunnel toward the shuttle bay.

The shuttle bay itself was large chamber like an old aircraft hangar that had been refitted to accommodate the maintenance of its shuttles. There were twelve in all each with its own colour of striping, but all had a base colour of white and grey. Each was shaped like an elongated egg with a wide stabilising fin that circled the whole craft. It's four air thrusters looked like melting wax droplets at each corner. A streamlined booster engine at the back. James approached a shuttle, scorch marks though it's melon striping. He held on to the fin at the left side where the orb was widest and pulled, raising its door up high. He held it there as Kara came near.

"Your carriage awaits, Miss Farion," James joked smiling at her.

"Thank you, Just Jim," she said taking a step inside. It was spacious with two rows of thick padded benches and two mechanical boosted seats at the front.

"It's Kara by the way," she said looking back. James followed behind and pulled a hand grip set on the inside to close the door.

"And it's Jim…Not Just Jim," James gliding past Kara toward the pilot seat.

"Whatever you say J.J.," Kara teased taking the co-pilot's seat.

James laughed realising she was simply screwing with him and took his head set from a hook in front of him and setting it comfortably on his head. Kara followed suit stroking her hair back with the headset. James began flicking switches across the console and he spoke into his headset.

"Flight, this is Shuttle sixteen in hangar four, pilot James Becker requesting permission to depart over." He placed his hand on a black knobbed level and waited. The headset crackled.

"Shuttle sixteen, you are go for departure on an immediate assent. Do you copy over." A voice replied.

"An immediate assent, copy that flight," James confirmed gently pulling on the lever.

The shuttles small thrusters hissed as pressurised air rushed to the ground. The shuttle lifted and gently moved forward out of the hangars opening. It began to tilt upward as the front thrusters double their output. When the shuttle was ten meters above the ground, James flicked two switches simultaneously and the rear thruster roared. The thruster cone expanded as ragging fire erupted outward sending the shuttle up into the sky. After four minutes, the roaring sound faded. Kara fix her stare on the side panel of glass and pressed her hand against it.

"Oh wow," Kara whispered as the shuttle emerged into blackness. Kara could see distant stars as clean as torch lights outside, with a blue glow of the earth just behind.

"It's beautiful," Kara whispered again, and James turned to her.

"Is this your first time up here?" He questioned.

"Yes," Kara said turning sharply to face him before gazing at the view again.

"Well, I envy you. I don't remember it being so wonderous," James admitted.

James flicked more switches before slouching back in his seat. Kara slapped her hand at the pain of glass again and James smiled.

"It's a ship!" Kara beamed. James leaned forward and toward her shoulder.

"Yeah, that's the Venture," he explained before leaning back again.

"It's massive." She exclaimed.

"That's what she said," James smirked. Kara glared at him and rolled her eyes.

"And then, He woke up," she replied and they both smiled.

"What's it doing there?" Kara asked looking out again.

"Could be outbound or inbound I don't know. It's a research vessel. Science and exploration," James explained. Kara's expression sank.

"I wish that's where we were heading," she confessed lowering her gaze.

"But then you wouldn't have such a handsome pilot," James said quickly.

"Besides, I'd rather be in a place with some real gravity, the artificial stuff makes me dizzy." As James said that Kara leaned forward in her seat setting her gaze on the moon. The Luna base had been constructed in the eastern side of one huge darker area on the moon's surface.

"Now that is pretty impressive," Kara reacted glancing at James. He smiled widely and nodding.

"Yeah, Welcome to the sea of Shadows."

Chapter 5: Cover

He had been in the Captains office before, and every time had been quite pleasant. There were brilliant white wall panels and white leather seating, not forgetting the oval white desk the captain sat behind. The was a cabinet on the left but he had no idea what was in it. The same went for the desk draws, He had no right to know. But today was not an enjoyable time to be there. Today Cole had to give his statement about the devastating events on Charon. David Arthur Cole was of average height and thin, his face was drawn, and his eyes were small. Without good light you would not be able to see his eyes were brown. Captain Stefan Dietrich had been in the military most of his life reaching the rank of Vice Admiral purely on his achievements alone before leading the crew of the Euphoria. And Astronaut Cole knew this would not be an easy sell. He could hear the sound of boots storming toward the room and he leapt from that nice leather chair and stood to attention. The door slid open with a smooth hum. Captain Dietrich stepped in before halting at the door. Cole did not turn. The Captain was broad but overweight. His hair was grey and short, but it had still been brushed back. His uniform was a matte black but the insignias on his shoulders were stitched with gold. His jaw was wide but free of any facial hair. His eyes blue. A deep blue. He watched Cole for a few moments.

"What the hell happened?" He snapped as he waded past Cole.

"My report is on your desk sir," Cole said pointing at it. The Captain glared at the Cyber Station that lay there.

"I'm not reading that shit. It will be full of formalities and stupidly long words. I don't have time for it…I have to send condolence messages to Grey and Furukawa's family's…Video fucking messages!" He paused. "So why don't you tell me in your own words what happened." The Captain stepped to his right and sat in the thick padded chair. Cole glanced down at the Captain before squaring up again.

"We set out with the lander from the shuttle and…"

"Cole! What happened to my fucking Astronauts?" The Captain yelled making Cole flinch and close his eyes.

"On Grey's core drill exercise, the drill got stuck…Furukawa suggest blasting the core out…"

"And Grey agreed to this?"

"Yes sir. He refused to leave the core sample behind. They used Grey's oxygen tank to fuel the blast." The Captain leaned on the desk, his head in his hands.

"And you didn't try to talk them out of it?" He said shaking his head.

"I did try sir. But like I said Grey refused to leave without the core and it had frozen in place."

"What next?" Captain Dietrich pressed.

"The mixture must have been wrong since the blast was larger than they expected. Grey was thrown into a spin and his helmet broke on the ground."

"Jesus Christ. And Furukawa?"

"Her tether snapped, and she was thrown away completely."

"What about her thrusters Cole?"

"Sir?"

"Surely, they were working yes…? So why didn't she come back down?"

"Her bio-monitor didn't go immediately. She must have been knocked unconscious." The Captain stood slowly.

"Well, I hope she never woke up…Drifting through space knowing there's no hope must be terrifying."

"Yes, I can imagine sir."

"Now explain how you were able to retrieve the sample?"

"I moved as fast as I could…I really did sir. I couldn't see Furu when I got outside. Grey was on the ground face down. The drill was still attached to his belt, so I brought it back after seeing that Grey's body was frozen solid," Cole's eyes began to glaze, and he bowed his head.

"I couldn't find Furu anywhere and my suit was starting to freeze so I…"

"I know Cole. I understand. You can go, go get some rest." With that order, Cole turn and headed for the door. As it opened, he turned to his Captain and gave a salute. The Captain responded with a nod and Cole left the room.

Captain Dietrich slumped back into his chair. He leaned back clutching his forehead. He gently swayed in his chair for a moment before lunging forward and shaking off whatever he was thinking. He spread the palm of his right hand on his desk and a fingerprint scanner illuminated in the table and verified him. Then a keyboard display lit directly in front of him. He pushed a single key, and it beeped once. He stared down at the keyboard. There was a second beep and a voice sounded in the room.

"Yes Captain?" The replying voice was smooth, sensual and southern. The Captain leaned forward.

"Annabelle, I need to locate Cole's suit from the Charon mission and take it to be analysed," Stefan told her.

"Yes Captain. Anything in particular I should ask?"

"I what to find out if any crystallised ice was on it in the past twenty-four hours. And keep it quiet."

"I'll get on and fix that, Captain," Annabelle replied and Stefan closed the call.

Annabelle rose from her desk chair in a room much like the Captains office. Her room was smaller, and she had placed a rearing horse statue on her desk and artificial flowers on each end of a shelves upon the wall to her left. She stepped out from the desk and brushed off her lavender, body cone dress. She was easy on the eyes with her rosy skin, heart shaped face, large blue eyes, soft curved lips, and long crimson hair. Annabelle was slim at the waist with a prominent behind and an unusually large bust. The kind of body only a glamour girl could brag about. She looked completely out of place amongst the crew outfits of varying flight suits.

Since her early development Annabelle Brooks hated being labelled as a gorgeous country girl. She worked extremely hard to be remembered for her brain's not her boobs. She fought tooth and nail through high school and college. Now she worked aboard one of the most famous A-class ships in the U.S.C. directly for the ship's Captain.

She slipped off her short black heels and stepped into a pair of Velcro grey shoes that all the crew wore. She took a hair tie from her desk draw and ponytailed her hair before heading out of her office. Although her office was on a lower deck than the Captain's office, she would still have to take one of the many express lift's down to the docking bay seven decks below. She made her way through one of the white oval shaped halls of the upper decks to an express lift. She thumbed at the control panel and waited as the lift whistled up to her. As she waited two Technicians were heading toward her, she spotted the two men and smiled.

"Hi Bebe, where you heading?" One asked as he approached.

"I'm heading down, Tom," she replied politely with a glance.

"Oh, going down to join the riff raff again are we." The second man joked.

"Definitely, you know I love to learn, Paul."

"I could give you a technical lesson if you'd like," Tom taunted.

"Aww bless your heart. I doubt I'd learn anything new Tom." She threw back as the lift doors opened. Paul burst into laughter shoving Tom.

"Hey, fuck you man," Tom snapped back at Paul. "Even Bebe knows you'd be shit in bed," Paul mocked as they walked. Annabelle stepped inside and pushed the button. She was grinning extensively as the two men berated each other as they left.

After a few seconds, the elevator stopped two floors above the one she'd chosen. She took a step back as the door opened. Three engineers were standing at the door. They had blocked the doorway with toolboxes and machine parts.

"Oh, hi Bebe…Grab this." One of the male engineers said handing her a toolbox. She took it without hesitation and set it down beside her. The second two, one man and one woman shuffled in with a box and a part in each hand. The first man handed in another two parts to his colleagues, then followed in himself with the last two machine parts. They shifted round a little to spread out. The second man pushed a number for a lower floor than Annabelle was heading, and the doors closed.

"How's the Captain today?" The Woman asked addressing Annabelle.

"He's okay Mian. Considering."

"Yeah…Horrible what happened." The second man said.

"Yeah, you need balls of steel to be an Astronaut." The first man added.

"Or boobs of steel. Isn't that right," Mian said nodding at Annabelle.

"Is it?" The second man asked.

"What?"

"Boobs of steel? Or something else." The three looked at each other and shrugged.

"I'd go with orbs. Work's for everyone," Annabelle suggested.

"Yeah, orbs of steel, I like that." The woman agreed.

"Balls or orbs, you gotta be tough as hell." The first man finished. The elevator stopped again.

"This is me," Annabelle said, and they all shifted round again.

"Bye y'all," she said stepping out. The three said byes together as they disappeared behind the door.

Down at the lower decks it was like another ship entirely. Not a single spec of white. The walls were rustic and damp looking. There were no flat panel lights in the ceiling like above. The lights where round spotlights that hung loosely from the ceiling. Either side of the ceiling was exposed ducting and piping. The wall opposite the elevator was bent inward allowing for more piping to run along that wall. The flooring was not a white smooth finish like above either. All the flooring throughout the bowels of the ship was grated with electric ducting beneath that would also power the lights on the deck below. Annabelle looked down and could just make out movement beneath but heard no voices.

She turned left and headed toward the docking bay. The lights began to flicker, and she slowed her pace. They flickered again before going off completely.

"Great." she said reaching to the vertical left-hand wall. Running her fingers along she stepped slowly forward. As she rounded a corner, she could see small block lights set above closed doors. *Oh, thank you so much. I hate dark places.* The light came back on behind her and she turned. Hands slapped her shoulder.

"Oh Lord!" She yelled as she cringed with a shudder bringing her elbows up to her chest, her hands to her face. She looked back to see a tall man with short blonde hair and a strong jaw smiling sinisterly at her. She spun round and slapped him upon his chest.

"Oh, you son of a…" Annabelle continued to slap him. "Why the hell would you do that. Damn it, Ellis." He began to laugh as she hit him. Ellise coward down slightly as she smacked the back of his head. She stopped and Ellis glanced up at her still sniggering. Annabelle smirked and began to giggle with him.

"You are a dick you know that," she said smacking his arm.

"Aww." He mocked.

"I'm sick of telling him." A young woman in the same engineering suit Ellis wore said stepped into the hallway. Her hair was short and dark brown, and her hazel eyes seemed tired. She was roughly the same height as Annabelle and had good cheek bones beneath her fair skin. Her suit seemed to be too large for her. *Maybe she'd been unwell recently.*

"Do you know Chelsey?" Ellis said changing the subject.

"We haven't met," Annabelle confessed, "Hi sugar," Annabelle added. Chelsey gave a quick wave before yawning into her hand.

"Oh, I'm sorry it's been a long day," Annabelle waved back. "It's okay, I have to get going anyway. And you…" She slapped Ellis's arm again. He mocked agony again as Annabelle headed off down the hallway.

"You're an ass." Chelsey told him.

Annabelle made a right to the docking bay. The hallway was sectioned into stretches of five metres with a bulky airtight door with a thick frame that looped the walls ceiling and floor. As each door opened, she had to step over the solid frame. Each section would close behind before the door ahead would open. Reaching the seventh and final door she entered a large cubic room that had been laid out like a departure lounge, the small yet comfortable seating laid out in rows. There was a long reception desk on the right. The desk had four chairs along it each with a console protruding from it's top. The room was also a rustic brown but was very well lit with lots of low hanging lights. Annabelle approached the desk where one man with African features sat. His face was thin which made his lip's look much larger than they were. His eyes were grey and friendly, and his hair was cornrowed in a directional design.

"Hi Briggs. Are you busy?" Annabelle asked. He looked up from his console wide eyed.

"Not anymore my Goddess," Briggs said standing. He leaned forward over the desk getting close to Annabelle's face.

"Have you finally given in to your animal desires and came to me for reproduction?" Briggs said softly. Annabelle smiled and leaned into his ear.

"Oh, ya sugar. You're as pretty as a peach. I can't hide my feelings anymore. I want you. I need you, Elijah." She whispered sensually. Briggs moved back slightly.

"You're just toying with me aren't you."

"Who? Me? I would never." She smiled maliciously. Briggs moved round the desk. Annabelle arched her back extenuating her backside and stretching up at the desk.

"Oooh, uh, please, take me now." She groaned convincingly.

"Okay, okay I submit," Briggs said with a shudder and Annabelle laughed.

"What can I do for you Bebe?"

"I need Coles suit from his mission," she said changing to a more serious tone.

After a moment of thought, Briggs returned to the desk and tapped at the keyboard of his console. He scanned the screen. Annabelle moved to the end of the desk and glanced over.

"Anything?" Annabelle asked.

"Got it. The suit was logged in on return. And sent to be decontaminated…Before cleaning."

"Sam Hill!" Annabelle said stepping back. "Get on to Laundry. Don't let 'em clean that suit," she said moving away.

"Yeah, you like it dirty," Briggs jested. She spun back. "Now Briggs!" She growled before disappearing through the door.

After ranting at the slow doors of the corridor, she ran to Laundry, her boot's clanging on the grated floor. Her chest hurt and she held her arms across her bust as she ran. Crewmen lunged as side as she charged down the hallway. She reached the elevator and thumbed the panel several times before the door opened. She went up one floor and squeezed out as the elevator doors opened. She growled as she caught her chest on one edge of the doors. *A gift and a fucking curse.* This floor was loud with machinery echoing through its narrow halls. She was breathing heavily when she came through the door to Laundry. As she walked in, one of the staff pointed at a metal table to his right without looking at her. He studied a monitor that displayed clothing inside the decontamination chamber behind. Annabelle spotted the large bulky suit resting on the table. She approached the table looked at the suit then at the man.

"Just decontaminated…No cleaning," he said still holding his gaze. Annabelle bundled the suit up the best she could and lifted it. It was heavy but manageable. *Bad back tomorrow. Like every day.*

"Thanks," Annabelle said leaving again.

Chapter 6: Luna

The soft glow from the moon's surface began to fade as the shuttle craft got closer. The craters from its millions of years of beating seemed to change shape as the sun light adjusted in their shadows. The silent expanse of the surface began to reveal its blanket of softness as the shuttle got closer. As the Sphere turned, large orange domes with thick grey lines came into view. From the largest dome in the centre white tubes ran from it, connecting to smaller domes like a spider's web. There were twelve smaller domes at the most outer edge with six larger domes between them and the largest central dome. At its north-eastern edge, Kara could see a giant hole which could be mistaken for another crater, at first glance. The void was clearly deep with large machines dotted around it and seemed to have lit cabins attached to them.

"What are they doing?" Kara asked spotting a plume of dust erupting around one of the machines. James glanced in the direction of the cloud before answering.

"Oh that. They are mining rock for the printers."

Kara looked again.

"That's how the station was built? 3-D printing?"

"Yeah, how did you think it was built?"

"Well, its old so I just assumed it was sent up in-sections," Kara confessed.

"Oh, right you're talking about the original base, not much left of that now. You see the lines in the dust over there," James explained pointing to the west. Kara scanned the area and saw the lines, interlacing lines of curves and angles.

"I see them."

"That's the foundation of the first structure built on Luna. Once the printers were up and running, they began expanding…really fast, their amazing machines," James finished talking as the shuttle came down to surface level, throwing the snow dust all around them.

Pulling level's back and flicking switches again James brought the shuttle forward across the surface leaving a shallow trench in its wake. James positioned the shuttle inside a cube like chamber attached to one of the smallest domes. He pressed a red panel on the console and a roller shutter of carbon deposit and metal ores came down behind them. The panel turned green, and James shut the console down, laying the shuttle on the deck. As James uncoupled his harness two rectangles of metal ejected from the far wall and moved apart revealing a doorway.

"And there's your welcome party," James said pointing toward the door from the cockpit. As Kara pulled of her restraints, she saw a man who was a little overweight with long aging hair in the doorway. James opened the shuttle door and waited for Kara to step out. She glanced around the bright reflective room as she stepped on to the metallic floor. James opened an invisible compartment just behind the door and fumbled at a metal case inside. Kara watched him pull a block of hardened form from it and laid it on the bench inside. Then out came Kara's case that had been secured inside and he set it on the floor beside her.

"Good luck," James wished her, stepping back inside the shuttle. Kara turned to him.

"You're not coming with me?"

"I've got to do my inspections ready for my return trip," James explained sliding a clip board from the ceiling of the shuttle.

"Oh okay. Well, Thank you J.J."

"You're welcome, Kara. Any time," James said before turning quickly inside the shuttle and leaving her view.

Kara pinched at her shirt adjusting it before running her hands easily down her back and over her bottom, removing any creasing. She bent her knees and took hold of her case handle pulling it up for dragging. She made her way across the room, her short heel's echoing through out. The man waited patiently as she approached. His Light grey jump suit had been marked with moon dust and grease that had fused together like icing or glue. He offered his hand and Kara excepted.

"Karabina Farion. It's a pleasure."

"Sabastian Armstrong. Security." He replied, his accent strongly Scottish. Kara smiled sincerely shaking his hand.

"Nice to meet you Mr Armstrong."

"Ha, just Sabastian. I'll avoid formalities when I can."

"Very well Sabastian. No point asking where you're from."

"And I was expecting you to be another dumb lass," Sabastian quickly replied.

"I'm far from dumb sir," Kara retorted.

"Good to know. Idiot's don't last long up here. Follow me." He added leading Kara into one of those connection tunnel's she saw on the way in.

"You Russian?"

"Ukrainian."

Sabastian nodded in acknowledgment.

The tunnel was narrow but well lit, it seemed to gradually bend to the left with small control panel's every ten metres. The disc shape lights from the ceiling mirrored off the black flooring. The wheels of Kara's case clunked over the tunnel's section seal's ever five metres as they walked quickly.

"I don't like being in these tunnel's too long you no. I always think one's gonna blow out on me," Sabastian confessed marching quickly in front of her. Kara scanned the seals quickly as they walked.

"They've all been stress tested though, right. I mean, they wouldn't really blow," Kara suggested.

"Be fucked if I know. I'm no engineer lass. I keep people safe from people not what's out there," Sabastian blurted out.

"Do you get many disputes up here?" Kara asked keeping pace.

"It doesn't happen much anymore. No body want's a fat Scot sitting on them…Ha, ha, ha," Sabastian said with a fake laugh.

At the end of the tunnel, they enter the second dome. Exposed piping and cabling ran along the walls and sections of the floor. They led in all direction to the engineering equipment of pumps, valves, and fans. With three connecting to large computer terminal that could run a power plant. Two men were pulling on a huge spanner at one pipe connection while another took notes from a read out being printer at one terminal. There was humming and hissing all around and Sabastian waved Kara to stop. He stepped over a pipe section half a metre thick and approached the nearest terminal.

The man that sat there was balding heavily with large thick glasses on his face. He stared wide eyed at a tiny computer screen fiddling with his huge spectacles. He stopped and glared up at Sabastian, his eye's looked enormous behind the frames. The two men began talking but Kara could not hear. The seated man looked at Kara and adjusted his head, so his eyes were fully behind his specs. They spoke a little longer before Sabastian returned.

"We're going through to that tunnel there. Shall I take your case lass," Sabastian offered. Kara agreed and lowered the handle for carrying.

Sabastian lifted the case to rest upon his hip and stepped cautiously over the lower and smaller piping and lose cabling. Kara followed. They moved to a tunnel on the right of the current dome and Sabastian heaved the case off his hip to the floor. He proceeded to extend the handle again.

"Thank you I've got it," Kara said reaching into extent it herself. Sabastian led her down the next tunnel. It was almost the same as the last apart from it being large and bending the opposite way.

"Your Supervisor is in Hydroponics' right now, so you can meet him there," Sabastian explained, walking at his speedy pace. They entered a door at the end of the tunnel into a glass box with a large camera lens at either side. There were small coils of tubing heading up around the box to vents at the top.

"Hold on to your hair lass, it's gonna get blowy," Sabastian stated reaching for a red panel on the opposite door frame. Kara reached behind her head pulling her hair into a ponytail and held it as He pushed the button. A powerful blast of air jetted into the room like the hose of a fire extinguisher. Sabastian looked back and burst into laughter seeing that Kara's short jacket had blown upward to her elbows.

"Come on Lass." He giggled as she lowered her arms from her hair. The opposite door side open with a gentle hiss.

Warm humid air washed over Kara's face as she stepped in behind Sabastian. The room was lush with green plant life. Plants lined perfectly through square planters that were caged at a metre high. Fruit trees grew high with caging guiding their trunk's. Vines twisted tightly around the domes seven supports. There were shelves on the west side that curved around with the dome. The petite plants in each tray upon the shelves were tended to by people in white overalls and gloves. A man strolled along a narrow path between two large planters spraying them with liquid from a pump bottle. A gentle hum echoed around the room for large fans in the dome ceiling. Sabastian pointed to the group of people at the shelves where a man was dressed differently. He wore a flight suit much like Sebastian's, but it was a mat black with two gold bars upon the shoulders.

"Xander!" Sabastian shouted toward the group. Kara felt naked as the whole group turned to face them. Xander regained their attention for a minute more before tapping one on the shoulder as he left the group.

Xander was tall and cleanly shaved. His light brown hair was tied in a bun behind his head. Kara almost grimaced at the long thick scar that ran down his tanned face through a pale left eye.

"What is it Sab, I'm very busy," Sabastian shot a hand at Kara's face and she almost flinched.

"Farion. She just arrived, apparently Miss Farion is under your charge," Sabastian explained.

"Ah. Karabina Farion right? You come highly recommended. I am Xander Savas. Superintendent of Luna. Welcome to…Mare Imbruim. Do you have your documents?" Xander said shaking Kara's hand.

"Oh yes I do," Kara said crouching down and thumbing her case lock.

"Right, I'll be off then," Sabastian said quickly disappearing amongst the foliage of hydroponics. Kara pulled her folder from an inner pocket of her case and handed to Xander from her squatting position before locking her case back up and standing. Xander quickly flicked his fingers through the folder of paperwork for a moment before setting it under his arm.

"I'll tell you what. Why don't we get you bunked in first then you can join me at the control centre later? This way Farion." Although everyone had been pleasant enough so far, Kara was beginning to feel annoyed by being passed around from person to person and following them like a lost puppy. As she began following Xander through Hydroponics she mentally counted to ten, tearing the urge to scream from her mind.

When the pair reach the central dome, the inside seemed like any normal office block back on earth. They were straight partition walls, rectangle door's, potted plants scattered the halls and there were even pictures hung on the walls. Kara expected the framed pictures to be photographs of space but strangely they were sea view's, waterfall's, and forests. Kara glanced at each picture as she followed and almost laughed aloud when she saw someone's family portrait.

"Through the door to your right just ahead is our canteen, you can check it out at your own leisure and this door here…" Xander stopped touching the door to his left.

"Is the habitation quarters and recreation lounge," Xander continued pushing the door open gently. The door seemed weightless possibly carbon fibre, Kara thought.

"Get yourself settled into room twelve, which is down the hall to the right, and I'll see you in Control later. Okay," Xander said stepping back into the hallway allowing the door to slap Kara's backside. She jumped at the impact before looking angrily at the innocent door. She looked out into main Hallway as Xander made off further into the dome.

"How do I find control?" Kara called down the hallway. Without stopping or turning Xander said.

"A navigator should find it easily Miss Farion." *I'm definitely sick off smart arses who try to test me.* Kara said to herself before shoving the door with her behind and turning into the narrow hallway before it closed again.

Kara struggled to walk with her case catching on doorways behind her. She stopped and hoisted it to her front and began pushing it in a hunched position trying to keep it going straight. As she approached the T-junction a woman in a light blue flight suit went sprawling over Kara's case. Kara dropped the case and covered her mouth in horror.

"I'm so, so sorry are you alright," Kara pleaded bending down to the grounded woman. The woman laid flat on her back. Her head was shaved on the left side around her ear, the rest was a rainbow of pink, purple and red hair spread around her head. Her face was short and oval. The woman opened her eyes and stared up at Kara. Her eyes were bright hazel and alluringly large.

"What the fuck!" The woman shouted before sitting up. Kara reached out to aid her but had her hand shoved away.

"Don't touch me you clumsy cunt." The woman snapped whirling up onto her feet. It sounded so strange hearing her soft Danish voice shouting at her. Almost harmless sounding.

"I said I'm sorry. I didn't do it on purpose," Kara shot back. The woman thrusted her head toward Kara but didn't connect. She pointed her thin finger in Kara's face still almost touching noses.

"Doesn't change the fact you're a fucking moron!" The woman shouted. Kara held up her hands.

"It was an accident," Kara replied loudly. A room door opened behind for a moment then slammed shut. Then another did the same. A third door opened at the left side of the T-junction. The woman stared past Kara.

"What the fuck are you looking at Seth?" She yelled at the occupant as she stepped toward him.

"Shut...The...Fuck...Up...Jennifer." Seth demanded before slamming his door shut in her face.

"Yeah, fuck you," Jennifer shouted kicking at the door.

She turned back to Kara, but she was moving down the hallway. Jennifer stared at her bewildered.

"Hey!" She shouted marching after her. Kara found room twelve and opened the door. Jennifer's reached across the threshold blocking the way.

"Where the fuck, do you think you're going?" Jennifer barked. Kara put her case down in the doorway. Rolling her eyes, she turned to face the bitch.

"Into my room you fucking idiot," Kara insisted.

"Your room? This is my room," Jennifer told her.

"That bunk is mine, that desk is mine, this room is mine," she continued. The room had a double bunk set up laid into the wall with a white pull-down shutter on each. The opposite wall housed a mirrored desk with a door next to it that Kara assumed was the toilet room. The far wall had a large flat screen that looked like a window but was blacked out.

"This case is mine," Kara told Jennifer shoving it into the room with her foot.

Jennifer lunged inside after the case. As she bent to grab it Kara charged into her shoving her across the room past the case into the flat screen. Jennifer threw her elbow around with her body, but Kara telegraphed the move and dodged, quickly locking her grip back into Jennifer with an elbow against her throat. Jennifer roared pushing Kara across the room into the shelves on the entering wall. Kara squealed as the middle shelf broke and splintered against her back. Jennifer forced her forearm against Kara's cheek pressing her deep into the shelving.

"I'm gonna kill you bitch!" Jennifer screamed. Kara threw her hand up shifting Jennifer's elbow up over her head, sending Jennifer on a turn. Kara followed up with a push, sending Jennifer headfirst into the panelling between the bunk beds. Jennifer squeezed her forehead as she came away from the panelling. Jennifer kicked her boot out behind her robbing the air from Kara's lungs. She wheezed highly as she dropped to her knee.

People began to stand in their doorway's as the two women fought.

"We should do something." One woman suggested.

"You go ahead." A man threw back. Jennifer stood over Kara pulling at her hair. Kara grabbed at her hand's getting to one knee. Jennifer swung wildly with her hand slapping Kara around the temple. As she connected Kara launched upward taking Jennifer's legs from under her into a tackle. Kara reached for Jennifer's face scratching. Jennifer wrestled Kara's hands and threw her thighs around her head in a choke hold. After a few second, Kara pushed up onto her feet rolling Jennifer onto her shoulder's. To her shock Kara lifted her of the ground and fell forward, dropping Jennifer on the back of her head.

"Aww Fuck!" Jennifer yelled rolling into a ball on her knees, holding the back of her head. Kara slowly struggled to her feet almost breathless. She was leaning back with her hands on her hip's trying to get more air in when Jennifer launched up herself. Grabbing Kara under the cheek's the pair turned and fell toward the desk. Kara landed on the desk in a sitting position, she threw her legs around Jennifer and squeezed. She grabbed at Jennifer's hands as they came up again.

Jennifer's hands let out to palm the wall either side of Kara's head. They stared at each other breathing deeply for several seconds. Still being held by the wrists Jennifer came closer. *This is unexpected.* Kara studied her lips. Their eyes met. Jennifer leaned in further. She studied Kara's lips has her tongue ran along the top. She leaned in further, opening her mouth slightly. She could feel Kara's breath on her mouth now. Suddenly she felt pain in the back of her head as Kara pulled sharply on her hair locking her gaze at the ceiling. She tried to look down, but Kara held the grip on her hair.

"I like your hair by the way…Jennifer," Kara whispered. One man from the hallway looked inside. They both threw him a glance, as much as Jennifer could at least and the man drifted out of view. Leaving them in their suggestive pose.

"I'm Karabina, you can call me Kara if you like." She explained slowly releasing the grip on Jennifer's hair. She lowered her legs allowing Jennifer to step back. The pair examined the room for a moment. They looked at each other again. The two smiled. That smile became a laugh.

"We should clean up," Kara suggested.

"Yeah, I think so too," Jennifer agreed.

Chapter 7: Sample

Rajiv Mody thumbed the panel. It beeped with a green light and the white door slid upward. He stepped inside lab room one and all the flat panelled lights came on. He sipped at his thermos cup and walked inside, past tables with microscopes and glass beakers and containers. He reached his desk and picked up a Cyber Station. He laid his cup down and thumbed the screen, unlocking the display. He turned and stepped round a large shelve unit filled with glass vials and containers. Behind it was a wall of small wired and glass cages. Each one had varying mammals, reptiles, and amphibians. Rajiv Mody had a small build with mopped black hair and dark skin, he had a button nose and mousey ears. He wore a clean white flight suit that represented his science sector class about the Euphoria. Rajiv studied each animal in its cage. Watching them closely he added notes to his Cyber Station. Rajiv was born in Ramgarth, just south of the Damodar river in the Jharkhand region of east India. His father had been an in-house servant that travelled to Delhi for months at a time while he and his mother barely scraped by. What Rajiv didn't know then was his parents lived harshly to guarantee his future out of the poverty struck region. To give him a chance to be somebody and there was no way he was going to let them down.

After inspecting each one, he reached the end and placed his open palm onto a panel there. Another beep filled the room before food pellets, tiny pieces of meat or several insects dropped into their designated cage. He waited for a moment before quickly checking over each animal again and added more notes. He walked back around and sat at his desk where a larger display screen stood. He laid the Cyber station behind it and pressed a button and all the information leapt to the large screen. A digital keyboard lit on the desk. He continued to sip his cup while reading the notes he'd just made. Spotting errors in his writing he'd edit the information or added additional. Several beeping tones began, and he glanced to his right where a smaller display of digits lit with a slider. He slid it with his finger.

"Good morning, Rajiv," said a soft southern belle voice in a playful tone. He glanced at the digits and smiled widely.

"Good morning, Bebe." He returned the playful tone and focused back on his work.

"Do you have good news for me?" she asked.

"Yes, all done. You can collect it when you're ready."

"Oh sugar, I love you. I'm on my way."

"Okay see you soon," he said before she ended the call at her end.

"Who was that?" Another voice asked and Rajiv turned.

In the door stood Rajiv's boss, Martha Green. She was a woman of fifty years, her hair was dark brown, shortened to jaw length and had started to grey. Her hazel eyes were sharply shaped. She was thin at the top, yet wider around the hips, backside, and thighs. Her suit was also white, but she had black insignias on her shoulders.

"Only Bebe, Ms Green." He said. Green sniggered.

"Bebe. Brooks you mean?"

"Yes, Ms Green." She marched past him and took a seat at her desk near the corner to Rajiv's left. Green turned on her screen and began negotiating through her files and folders.

"Well…What does she want this time Mody?" Green asked frustration in her voice.

"Just the analysis on the Astronaut suit."

"Oh, the suit you wasted a day on." She jabbed. Rajiv rolled his eyes and huffed. Green turned to look at him.

"Did you say something?" Her eyes like lasers.

"No Ms Green."

"You know she's only nice to you, so you do things for her," Green remarked. Rajiv didn't respond.

"She flirts with everyone you know, the using slut," Green continued. Rajiv gritted his teeth and scrunched his eyes, still fixed on his screen so Green didn't see. Green left her desk and went around past the cages. She headed to a second area of the laboratory that had been closed off with more shelves. Behind it was large glass containers with gloved holes set in them. Beside the large container's she examined smaller cubes of glass. One had laser cut sections of the core drill attachment from Charon. She shifted attention to the large boxes. Each one had thick sliced sections of material that was previously inside the core. The first was brown and dusty, the next was a grey rock like section but the last was odd. It looked like a softer sediment with thick black tar woven through it.

"Mody come here…Bring your Station." She called. Rajiv rolled his eyes and stood. He took his Cyber station over to Green.

"Yes, Ms Green?" He said trying to hide his inpatients.

"Look at this. Was it like that yesterday?" Rajiv looked closer.

"Uh, no it wasn't um." He tapped at his Cyber Station.

"Lower section…a soft earthy texture with a black tar like substance. Stuck at one end. Additional: Ice crystal formation receding," Rajiv recited off his notes and looked at the section again.

The sound of the laboratory door opening pulled them out of their stare.

"Rajiv?" Annabelle called from the other side of the room. Rajiv stepped away and Green glared at him before shaking her head. He returned to his desk where Annabelle was waiting. Rajiv struggled to keep his eyes from bulging, sighting Annabelle in a red vest top that was baggy at the waist yet struggled to contain her bust. She also wore a pair of navy-blue leggings. Her hair was tied back but slightly tangled at the end like she had slept that way.

"Hey, you," Annabelle said sweetly as she turned and spotted him. Rajiv smiled, slight embarrassment on his face. They heard Green make a loud tutting noise. Annabelle looked over narrowing her eyes. Rajiv shrugged and moved to his desk. Sitting down he began tapping the keyboard. Annabelle placed a hand on his desk and the other on arm of his chair leaning into the screen. Rajiv looked to his right, her bust millimetres from his face and looked up at her. She studied the screen for a moment. *Oh, dear god.* She noticed him and regarded him.

"Are you okay? Am I in the way?" Annabelle said moving back straightening slightly.

"No, it's fine I was just wondering how you are."

"Aww bless your heart, aren't you sweet." She responded levelling her chest near his head again before he turned quickly back to the screen.

"I am very well, thank you for asking. I'm a little worse for wear this morning hence the outfit," she said drawing Rajiv's attention to those things again.

Control Rajiv. Please god give me control. "There it is," Annabelle said pointing at the screen before pulling back her finger.

"Sorry," she said looking down at him. Rajiv refused to look again. *She'd see you crack, control Rajiv.*

Rajiv slowly moved his hand toward his Cyber Station so Annabelle would notice his attempt and move. *But she hasn't moved. She knows I'm reaching for it.* He continued to reach out, his upper forearm gliding across the smooth surface of her top. As he gripped his Cyber station, he could feel the weight of her breast pressing against his arm.

"Uh hum," Green said loudly, and Annabelle looked back at her, straightening fully.

"Hi, Ms Green. How are you?"

Green folded her arms. "Better than you it seems. Is that night wear?" Green assumed.

"Oh no. I just threw this on to collect the data, I haven't dressed yet," Annabelle said politely.

"I can see that. Mody, are you done?" Green asked impatiently. Rajiv glanced at Annabelle as she mouthed the words 'sorry'. Rajiv smiled. "Your Cyber station?" he asked.

"It's right here," Annabelle said lifting her top slightly at the back and slipping the Cyber Station out of her leggings. Rajiv took hers; it was warm with her body heat. He laid it at the right side of the desk where his had been. He set his on the left and linked with the screen. The data leapt from his to the screen then straight to Annabelle's station. He scooped it up and gave it to her. She held it like a romantic present.

"Thank you, Rajiv you're the best." She leaned forward and kissed his cheek. He gave a smile as her soft, warm lips touched his cheek. He also tensed his groin like he'd grabbed himself.

Annabelle hastily made off out the door like an embarrassed girl that had given her first kiss. Rajiv leaned back in his chair running his fingers through his hair. He let out a long breath. He sighed. *Oh, my sweet Annabelle what could have been…*

"Are you planning on swooning over that tart all day? Or are you going to do some work?" Green ranted reappearing from behind the shelves.

Rajiv rose from his desk, mentally strangling Green before he returned to her. She had loaded a scalpel and a hooked scaler into a draw attached to the box.

"Get the camera," she said pushing her arms into the gloves attached. She took hold of the tools inside and Rajiv brought a small tubular camera on a thick cable. He pushed buttons on its body.

"We're rolling," Green moved her hands to the section slowly and started to push the blade in and pull the soft earthy substance away with the scaler. It took a bit of effort, but she started to break it apart.

"Did you see that?" Green said, pulling a piece away causing the black tar to retract from the open air.

"Oh my god. Is it alive?" Rajiv asked taking the camera closer. "I'm not sure. You can say that plants and bacteria are alive. But what is this?" Green said as she started again. The more she broke up the further the tar retreated into a small puddle until she had completely spread the earth. The Tar arced to the far corner of the box and re-puddled there. Green dropped the tools and pulled her hands out of the gloves, turning one inside out. She backed away.

"This is incredible. We need to get everybody up…Not only is this mass alive…It has intelligence."

It wasn't long before an additional ten members of the science section were in the room. All watched the tar in amazement, some taking notes on their Cyber Stations or using them to take images. Two were moving around, the rest recording every movement.

"This is amazing," one said.

"Amazing? This is historical," said another. Another looked round studying the faces of his colleagues and the tar inside the box. He turned quickly and approached Green at her desk. She pulled a wireless earpiece off her head and set it on the desk. Green looked back at him and shook her head. He was much older than she was, and his grey hair was styled in a slick back. His eyes and skin were light brown, his skin freshly pampered. His white suit had black lapels with gold insignias.

"What did the Captain say?" he asked.

"The same thing Hassan…It's too risky given that we lost two astronauts on that moon."

Hassan shook his head. "I'll have to see him in person."

"And say what? What can you say that I haven't already said?"

"I'm going to remind him that the Euphoria is a science vessel." Hassan said heading for the door.

"Did you see that?" A scientist said, getting Green's attention.

"It reacts to sound." Another woman said turning to Green as she approached. Green pushed in and stared at the tar puddle.

"What did you do?" Green asked.

"Watch," said the man to her left. He slowly lifted his hand, making a point with two fingers, and jabbed at the glass making a dull thump. The puddle balled up and needle spikes formed around its body for a moment before returning to puddle form.

"That's a lot more than a reaction to sound, Pamala. That is a reaction to a threat."

"A defence mechanism." Pamala agreed.

"Is it defensive or aggressive though." Another suggested. Green looked round the faces surrounding the box. She peeked over the crowd and saw Rajiv cataloguing sealed beakers on the shelf behind.

"Mody. Bring me a mouse," Green said before looking back at the tar.

"What? Why?" Rajiv asked. Green glared at him. "Get me…A mouse."

Rajiv set his Cyber station on the shelf and went round to the cages. He stopped at a glass cage with several white mice inside and rubbed his head. He unclipped the top of the box and reached inside scooping one up. He brought it up to his face and stroked it gently.

"Sorry my friend," he whispered before returning to Green. She opened the draw and nodded at it. Rajiv reluctantly put the mouse in and slowly closed it making sure not to catch its tail or head.

The mouse sniffed rapidly and searched around the draw before popping its head up. They all watched in silence flashing back and forth at the mouse and Tar puddle. The mouse continued to investigate, raising to its hind legs, its nose twitching wildly. It scurried forward and stopped halfway across the box. The tar puddle slipped tighter into the corner, its back part creeping up the side slightly.

"It knows the mouse is there." One whispered excitedly. The mouse bolted again straight to the black liquid formation. It stopped at its closest side and sniffed. The black gel did not move. The mouse stepped back and sniffed around the box in front. Then the tar moved. It slowly extended out like an arm across the floor of the glass. It crept toward the mouse and stopped beneath its face. The mouse sniffed at it again. The back end of the Tar contracted into the front, re-puddling where the mouse stood. They watched anxiously. The mouse stood tall again, sniffing. The mouse then darted away to the far corner. The puddle remained still. Several of the team glanced at each other, other's tutted unafraid to show their disappointment. Rajiv made a sigh of relief.

"Can I get the mouse out now?" Rajiv asked and instantly regretted it. They all glared at him. He backed away and returned to his cataloguing.

"Stupid boy," Green spat, shaking her head in disappointment.

Chapter 8: Uncover

Annabelle pressed the panel with her thumb. It did not change colour, the panel simply beeped. She waited, pulling any creasing out of her dress skirt. Today's body cone dress was straight across the chest, her breasts up like a shelf. It was a mixture of black and white with thin red straps. The red line extended down the body of the dress lining up with her exposed knees. Her hair was down, and all pulled over to her right shoulder with slight curling at the end. The panel on the door turned green.

"Come in." Captain Dietrich said, after allowing access. The door opened and she went inside, striding quickly to the desk.

"Good afternoon, Captain," she said stretching over the desk and placing her Cyber Station at his fingertips. Stefan laid his hand on it.

"What's this?" he asked her as she lowered into the chair opposite.

"It's the proposals for the funeral arrangements I'm fixing Sir."

"Yes of course," he said taking a look.

"Lilies and chry-san-themums in yellow and white?" Stefan enquired. Annabelle got comfortable in the chair and crossed her legs.

"Chrysanthemums, Yes Sir…For Kasumi Furukawa. It's traditional."

"Where did you find them?"

"Oh, we're having them made. I put in a special order between science and hydroponics', and they managed to create some."

"That's good. Very good. Anything special for Grey?"

"Brett is American so…The Flag."

"The flag?" Annabelle shrugged. "It's what we got. Our Nation's flag is still a big deal."

"Alright, how long do you need?"

"Two days tops Sir."

"Good, get on it," Stefan ordered handing her the Cyber Station. She stood and excepted it.

There was a beep at the door. Annabelle stepped toward the door.

"Anna, come over here."

"Captain?" Stefan directed her to stand at his right. "Help me out with this," Annabelle approached the table. She stood beside him.

"Be, firm." He said, she looked puzzled, but she straightened, her chest popping from her dress.

"Come in," Stefan said leaning back in his chair.

One man stepped in wearing a light grey suit with a padded chest plate. He was average in height with a short militaristic hair style. Behind him came David Cole. *No, I really don't need to be here for this.* Annabelle started to feel uncomfortable but held her posture. A second Security officer entered. Both men stood to attention at Cole's sides.

"David Arthur Cole, Captain." The first officer said as both men saluted.

"At ease gentlemen," Stefan responded giving his quick salute. Cole glanced at the Captain, then at Annabelle and back. Annabelle looked to the Captain, and he returned the look.

"Take a seat Cole," Stefan said gesturing at the chair. Cole casually took the chair.

"Do you have anything to say?" he asked Cole, his face turning to disappointment.

"Captain?" Cole said confused.

"I was under the impression you wanted to change your statement," Stefan said, Cole still looking confused. *Like a lost puppy.* Annabelle thought.

"About Charon," Stefan added.

"I stand by my statement Sir. That is what happened," Cole replied.

"Oh, right my mistake. And you handed in your suit to back up your story yes."

"I didn't think it was necessary Sir. I had it cleaned," Cole explained.

"Oh well it doesn't matter. We suspected you'd forget so I had Annabelle here…Uh, you know Annabelle?" Cole looked at her again, his eyes immediately dropped and raised again. Annabelle had become a master at spotting this general mistake. *Oh, you have got to be kidding. This is why I'm here.* She noticed every single time someone looked at her body, although she'd never pulled anyone on it before, she knew she had to use it now. She directed a glare at him, showing her disapproval and Cole looked down at his feet.

"Yes Sir, I know Ms Brooks."

"Yeah, Well Annabelle managed to recover your suit before it was cleaned…Isn't that lucky," Cole skin began to redden slightly.

"She also had the science lab do a full analysis on your suit," Cole looked at her again, this time his eyes darted to her waist or hips.

"Do you want to know what they found," Cole re-focused on Stefan. He slid a Cyber Station across the desk to Annabelle.

"Why don't you tell him Anna," Stefan said, and she gave a curious look. *For fuck sake.*

"Go ahead. Tell him," Stefan said pointing at Cole. Cole looking even more on the spot than she felt.

Annabelle reached for the Cyber Station and stepped forward. She raised the Station.

"The analysis of astronaut suit registered to David Arthur Cole. Minor deposits of dust from Charon. Minor deposits of earth from Charon. Nil deposits of ice…"

"No ice?" Stefan interrupted. "That's very strange considering you told me verbally and in your report. That you searched for Furukawa for as long as you could. But again, no ice deposits on your suit. Care to explain," Cole's skin was shining now, a single bead of sweat rolled down his temple.

"I can't explain that Sir. Maybe all traces were gone after ascending from the surface," Cole said. Stefan nodded.

"He's right, that could be possible." He directed to Annabelle.

"Is that all it says?"

"No Captain."

"Well get really close so he can hear," Stefan suggested, she looked at him, briefly closing her eyes. *You want me to strip too?* She engaged Cole again and stepped closer. She was standing in front of the lead security man now.

"Nil deposits of ice. Minor deposits of…Cable grease." She was closer still.

"Still nothing to say?" Stefan added again. Cole said nothing, he kept his stare fixed on the desk in front. She looked at Stefan. Her Captain flicked his head, and she stepped closer again. Her body close enough to Cole's face he could smell her skin. Annabelle was looking down at him.

"And finally, minor deposits of plasma…Human plasma…From Astronaut…Kasumi…Furukawa."

"Anything to say Cole?" Stefan asked him. Cole held his blank stare.

Stefan had enough. He launched from his chair. His fists clenched.

"Come on Cole! What did you do to that poor woman!" He shouted. Cole said nothing, his head still turned.

"Come on Cole! The woman on your right must arrange their funerals! What happened?!" Cole glanced at Annabelle unable to catch her eyes and looked away again.

"Fuck this get him out of here! Throw him in the brig!" The two-security officers gripped Cole's shoulders and ripped him from the chair as Annabelle stepped back. The door was opened, and they bundled him into the hallway.

"I'll get to the truth Cole! You can count on that!" Stefan yelled as they left.

Stefan took a deep breath and huffed. Annabelle stood in silence. *You, fucking bastard.* He returned to his seat. He rubbed his hands through his hair. He looked at Annabelle. She was staring back at him.

"What?" he asked, Annabelle's mouth was tight. Her brows were down.

"What?"

"What was that. What in the Sam Hill was that?" She said. Stefan was stunned, she had never cursed in front of him, let alone at him.

"Hot women make men feel uncomfortable," Annabelle glared at him.

"Not cool Stef. You used me. You of all people," Annabelle ranted before storming toward the door.

"Anna, come on I wanted to rumble him. Throw his focus, his control that's all," Annabelle stopped mid stride and marched to the desk. She slapped her palms onto the desk and leaned in, making Stefan recoil into his chair.

"I've fought every day since these things appeared." She grabbed her own breasts. "For everyone to see me. Not them! I have never. Never! Used these or this." She smacked her own behind. "To get ahead. It would have been so much easier to screw my way to the top. But I didn't Stef. That's not me," Annabelle barked.

Stefan held up his hands. "Alright I'm sorry…I wanted to make him feel uncomfortable. That's all." He repeated.

"And in the process, you made me feel uncomfortable. I swear if you do that again…I resign," Annabelle told him before storming out of the room.

Annabelle stopped outside the door. *I expected so much better from him.* She held her mouth and squeezed her eyes, but it was no good. Her skin beamed with heat, tears began to leak, and her hands shook uncontrollably. She hurried off down the hallway and into the elevator.

Rushing out on the habitation deck Annabelle kept her head down as she moved past crew members.

"Bebe?" One called spotting her upset. She kept going. "Bebe, are you okay?" Another called after her. A woman twenty years her senior in a green medical suit stood in front of her and took her by the shoulders.

"Anna? What's happened sweetheart?" she asked softly. Annabelle shook her head wildly, holding her gaze down. She side stepped the woman and made off around the corner into habitation.

"Are we going to medical Doctor Lancaster?" A young man in his early twenties asked at her side.

"Uh? I'll meet you there later Johns…I need to see if Anna is alright," she said. John's nodded and they parted ways.

Annabelle launched into her quarters. The room was circular with white padded walls and a curved couch along the left side. The back of the room had a small kitchenette area and beyond was a bathroom door. She slapped the door lock panel, charged toward her bed on the right side of the room and face planted the thick red duvet. And she exploded into tears. She felt sick. She felt dirty. *I am not a slut! This is what I get for being nice. Being playful. It's just teasing. I'm not a fucking slut!* Annabelle threw her arms around her head and continued to cry. Her sadness was slowly turning into anger.

The door to her quarters beeped.

"Go away!" She yelled, burying her face again. It beeped again.

"Anna? Sweetheart? It's Grace." She glared at the door for a moment.

"Just a second." She got off the bed to the kitchenette. She washed her face at the sink, smearing her eye shadow and eye liner. *Grrrrrr! Now I look like shit too!*

"Come on Anna open the door," Grace ordered. She unlocked the door and returned to the bed. The door slid open, and Grace came in and sat beside her. She offered her arms and Annabelle embraced her. She began to tear up again.

"Tell me what's happened sweetheart," Annabelle shook her head. "I don't want to talk about it."

"Come on now. It'll help, you know that. Talk to Auntie Grace."

Doctor Lancaster had become Auntie Grace to several of the younger crew members. Although she had more opportunity to be there for the girl's rather than the boy's, since the young men always tried to hide their feelings, they still regarded her as a mother figure aboard the Euphoria. With her calm English accent that always held attention she gave more therapy to the young ones than the actual therapists did. Her face was small with thin lips, her skin was tight over her cheek bones. She had comforting blue eyes and her dirty blonde hair was neatly squared away in a low bun.

"I was just thinking about your first day. You remember?" Grace spoke softly, holding her. Annabelle nodded. "Before the Euphoria set out on its trip two years ago, we met during the leaving party. And I knew immediately that you were far too young for the position and had lied about your age on the application."

Annabelle nodded again.

"Do you know why I kept quiet?"

Annabelle shook her head.

"I was impressed. I was impressed that, an eighteen-year-old girl had managed to land the job of assisting the Captain. A job that was usually reserved for more experienced candidates. Not only that, but she had achieved this with effort and brains, not her looks," Grace stroked Annabelle's hair.

"I never saw an attractive bimbo who got there on look's alone, unlike other members of the crew at the time. I saw straight through to the real Annabelle. And I see her right now."

Grace lifted Annabelle's head.

"Look at me…Wipe your face," Grace ordered firmly. Annabelle did so and forced a smile.

"That's better. Now, tell me what happened."

"I don't want to get him in trouble." She whimpered. Grace rolled her eyes. "I knew a man would be involved. Did someone touch you?"

Annabelle shook her head.

"It must be something big Anna. Come on spill."

"Doctor's confidence?"

Grace smiled softly.

"Doctor's confidence."

"The Captain used me to…un-stabilise a crew member."

"Ah, and you feel used and mistreated?" Annabelle nodded quickly as she clenched her eyes as tears came again.

"I understand how you feel sweetheart, and I know it hits you harder. Stefan is a good Captain, and a good man. Do you think he meant to upset you?" Annabelle shook her head still blubbering.

"Trust me when I say, if you were not there, he would have used another tactic. He's a military man that deals in scenarios. Use what you have to win you know," Grace explained. Annabelle was attempting to wipe her tears away.

"And think of this. He believed you could handle that pressure. And if he had a better card to play, he would have played it…You were his top trump honey. You were his bomb," she finished a movement of head bobbing and hand waving, like a girl with attitude. Annabelle laughed at her impression and finished wiping her wet eyes.

The door beeped and both women stared at the door. Annabelle looked at Grace for guidance. She gestured at the door.

"Hello normally works," Grace mocked. Annabelle gave an obvious glare.

"Hello? Who is it?"

"It's Rajiv," Annabelle went wide eyed. "He's never come here before." She whispered. Grace smiled.

"Maybe he heard you were upset and has come to see if you're okay."

"With a ship so large, you'd think it would take longer," Annabelle rolled her eyes.

"News travels. What's done is done. Now you wash your face properly and I'll go let him in. Then I'll leave you to it," Grace said standing. Annabelle grabbed her hand.

"You can't leave," Grace held her hand with her free one.

"Annabelle sweetheart, he hasn't come to see me. I don't think he's into older women," Annabelle's jaw dropped. Grace approached the door.

"Remember good men are really hard to find…Now wash your face. You look like…what's that word you use, a ragamuffin," Grace said before firmly pointing toward the bathroom. Annabelle darted for the bathroom as Grace tapped the panel.

Rajiv was taken a back.

"Oh, uh Doctor Lancaster. I was uh. Looking for Annabelle's room," he said glancing down the hall thinking he was in the wrong place.

"Hello Rajiv. This is Anna's room, she's in the bathroom. Why don't you come in and wait for her?"

"Oh, uh, I can come back some other time," Grace rolled her eyes and gripped his arm. And pulled him inside.

"Let me give you some advice. It doesn't hurt to be strong as well as sweet." She winked at him and walked out leaving him alone. Rajiv looked round the room and nodded his head, seeing Annabelle's quarters for the first time. Immediately spotting the multitude of bras scattered around the place.

In the bathroom Annabelle was freaking out. She was staring into the mirror breathing heavily. *Why are you feeling like this now? Yeah, you flirt with him, you tease him, do you fancy him? He's really sweet, he'd do anything for you, but do you fancy him or pity him? No, we are friends, does he want more.* She took a deep breath and splashed her face again, she towelled off and investigated the mirror one more time. With another deep breath, she stepped out.

Rajiv leapt up from his uncomfortable position on the couch, he approached her and took her hand.

"I heard you were upset. I come to see if you're okay, or if I can help in anyway," Rajiv said softly.

"Don't worry about me Rajiv, I'm alright," Rajiv laid his other hand on hers.

"But I do worry about you. I worry a great deal."

"Really Rajiv. You're adorable. But I don't need protecting."

"I never said you needed protecting Anna but that doesn't mean I can't care."

"Of course, you can care Ra…You've never called me Anna before."

"Huh?"

"Anna. You called me Anna." He wants more than friends.

"Is that okay?"

Annabelle gave an innocent smile in response.

"Why don't I get us a drink?" Annabelle said taking back her hand. She entered the kitchenette space. And opened the fridge there.

"Do you drink alcohol or would you rather coffee?" Annabelle asked, bending to the fridge. Rajiv admired her behind until she glanced over the door. Rajiv refocused.

"I'm easy whatever you decide."

Annabelle glared at him.

"Alcohol is fine." He finally said. Annabelle brought a bottle of Tennessee whiskey and two glasses. She set the glasses down on a side table beside the couch and poured half full servings. She handed Rajiv his glass before downing hers in one gulp.

Rajiv looked at the drink, closed his eyes and down the liquid. He immediately started to cough. Annabelle glanced away hiding her smile.

"Are you sure I can't get you a coffee?" Annabelle asked pouring a second glass for herself.

"No, no it's nice…I'll have another," he said tapping his chest. Annabelle rested one hand on her hip and held the bottle up with the other.

"Rajiv, you are the last person who needs to impress me." She admitted.

"I'm not trying to impress anyone." *Liar.* Annabelle added more whiskey to his glass.

"May I ask what it was that upset you today?" Rajiv asked holding his glass with both hands'. Annabelle threw back another whiskey.

"It was just a miss understanding with the Captain," Annabelle said pouring for the third time, she gestured the bottle at Rajiv, and he downed his second. She poured him another.

"I'd speak to him if you like," Annabelle choked on her mouthful and wiped her mouth with her arm.

"Why would you even think such a stupid thing? He's the Captain Rajiv, our Captain. You'd never fly again. Not to mention never see another Lab."

"I know but I still do it for you, Anna," he said softly. Annabelle's heart melted.

She took his glass, left it on the side table and sat next to him. She grabbed his hand tightly and stared at him.

"Now you listen to me. I appreciate the idea. But your career is far more important than my happiness. You need to pursue your own happiness. Think about your future," she told him firmly.

"If anyone upsets you, they'll have to deal with me."

"I don't want you to deal with anyone, it's my problem to fix," she said angrily, looking away. He kissed her cheek. She stared at him. Shocked.

"I'm sorry. I…sorry," he said embarrassedly. He stood. "I'll go." He turned for the door, but Annabelle grabbed his hand and pulled him back. She stood and gently directed him to sit. Slowly and smoothly, she straddled his lap. She gazed into his eyes, lent in, and kissed his lips. She sat back and touched her mouth, thinking about his taste and texture. Rajiv ran his hand along her neck, up to her cheek and pulled her in to kiss again. This time the kiss was prolonged and enthusiastic.

Annabelle sat back again. She reached behind and unzipped her dress. She gently pulled down the straps. Rajiv marvelled at the unfolding event. She lowered the dress to her waist, revealing her red bra that could not contain her. Her breast's bulged over the top. Rajiv admired her body for a moment before looking up at her. Her erotic gazed excited him just as much as her astounding cleavage.

"You can touch me if you'd like," Annabelle whispered sensually. He reached slowly and touched the cup of her bra. She took his hands and guided him over the cups and onto her smooth skin above. He dabbled a finger into her cleavage. She kissed him deeply again. And while doing so she led one hand inside, making him caress her aroused nipple. She moaned with sensuality into his mouth as they kissed vigorously.

Chapter 9: Spreading

Rajiv lay on Annabelle's bed, his arm around her. She had cuddled into him after she had pleasured him with her hand. To his disappointment she had not done anything else that night. His fantasies getting the better of him. Still, he could not complain. It had been the most enthusiastic hand attention he had ever received. And Annabelle had not pushed for anything in return. This surprised Rajiv. He thought she would have insisted on a return gift.

The sound of Annabelle's waking alarm sounded pulling him out of his thoughts. He reached for the control panel above her bed and tapped the alarm off. Annabelle stirred and he gently kissed her forehead. She saw him and smiled. Closing her eye's again she gently rubbed his toned chest.

"Good morning handsome." She whispered.

"Morning beautiful."

"I wish we could stay like this."

"Why don't we stay?"

Annabelle smiled innocently and rolled on to her front to her elbows. "You know we can't."

He pecked her lips. "Sure, we can. I'll log a sick day."

"Well. I can't."

Rajiv gave a childish growl.

"You need to get moving Mister," she told him pushing him to roll off the bed. She rose to her hands and knees. From the floor, Rajiv studied her erotic position and smile. *I want you so much right now.* She glanced at herself and realised her error. She saw his hungry smile.

"Rajiv, we have to get ready for work. Stop it," Annabelle slid of the bed. Backside first.

"Aww Anna, you're killing me."

"You need to shift it, Rajiv, get going," Annabelle threw his shirt at him. Her unzipped dress slipped from her shoulder flashing one breast. Rajiv instinctively grabbed his groin. Her jaw dropped as she covered her breast. A moment later she removed her hand giving him a good look before smiling innocently.

"Get going Rajiv. I'll see you later," Annabelle edging him toward the door. He resisted.

"When?" He stroked her bare breast.

"I don't know. Find me in the Cafeteria for lunch…Now get out of here." She ordered turning him and tapping his bottom.

Rajiv stepped out of the room. Peeking back as the door began to close, he saw her dress drop around her ankles. Getting a brief view of red over her peachy backside. *That was a thong! Bloody doors*. Shaking his head, he cleared his mind and headed quickly to his quarters at the other side of the habitation deck. After a five-minute walk, he was there. He rushed inside and threw off his flight suit and basin washed in the bathroom. He leapt into a fresh suit and darted for the door. He hurried to the cafeteria. He collected his daily coffee thermos from Loo. Or Latino Loo, as she was affectionately known being Columbian. Who was head chef during the morning rush. Loo hair was straight and long. Her hair looked longer with her body being small and she always tucked it into her catering jacket. Hair nets were not her thing. Her eyes were dark and deep with wide lips but a small mouth. He stressed his lateness and got going. He moved quickly, almost being toppled by larger crew men when bumping into them. He'd make his apologies and continue.

Rajiv stepped into the Laboratory and froze. He was not the first to arrive this morning, despite only being minutes late. A group of scientists gathered near the cages and a second group was at the tar box. Strangely two men from security were present. They stood amongst the first group and Rajiv approached. Looking into the crowd he saw why their attention was drawn. A small section of the floor had been closed off with a tiny puddle of white, pink, and red gore in the middle. His heart sank. Green whirled when she saw him.

"I told you to leave it in the box!" She snapped.

"I did. I never went near it." He immediately responded.

"Someone let it out!" She bit back looking back at the mess. Another scientist began scooping the remains into a beaker.

"Well? What happened to it?" Rajiv asked.

"Brooster stamped on it." A security man said bluntly.

"Why?"

"He said it bit him. So, he killed it," said the second security man, also bluntly.

How the hell did it escape?

Rajiv moved around the crowd to the second and studied the box. The draw was still inside and to his surprise, the Tar like substance was on the side wall of the box closest to them.

"Green?" The man studying the beaker called. Everyone turned to him.

"What is it?" Green asked approaching the table of microscopes where the man was bending toward the glass beaker. He pointed.

"I don't recognise that," Green looked closely. There was a tiny patch of black amongst the mushed-up mouse. Green lurched up staring toward the box.

"The mouse must have swallowed some of the organism," Green swung back. "Get that sample sealed right now." The man moved quickly and set the beaker into a small glass box. He opened the lab's refrigerator and pulled out a spray can. He blasted the top of the beaker and sealed the box shut.

"Ladies and gentlemen…This is, no longer a new discovery. It is a quarantine issue," Green began, the rest becoming shocked and uncomfortable.

"I suggest you all return to your designated lab's immediately." She added before turning to the colleague over the box. "Take that to be decontaminated and have it quarantined." She ordered and the man bolted for the door. The rest of the room filed out, leaving Green and Rajiv.

"What do we do now?" Rajiv asked. Green threw him a look.

"We do nothing."

"Surely we should warn…"

"This is on you Mody…Ergo this is on me. And I'm not risking my career, for your mistake." She interrupted.

"I didn't cause this," Rajiv insisted.

"Yeah, but who would believe you!" Green fired back. Rajiv said nothing.

Annabelle would.

Rolan Pavlov tapped his foot impatiently. He was late again. Third time in a row and he was pissed. Someone had dragged the closest elevator down to the lowest depths of the ship and was holding it there.

"Damn inconsiderate grease monkeys." He began to consider running to another elevator although he could then miss this one. The numbers began to change.

"Aw finally." He growled as the elevator rose toward him. He glanced to his right hearing someone running down the hallway.

"Don't think for a second you'll be having this elevator." He mumbled. The scientist came into view as the lift door's opened.

"Look out let me through!" The scientist yelled, still running.

"Fuck you!" Pavlov called with a gesture. He made a step for the door but leapt to the side. A Large hydraulic strut appeared through the elevator door. The runner ploughed into it. The glass box he carried. Exploded over the strut. The glass littered the hallway, including Pavlov. Then the gunk hit his neck and chin. Even his mouth. Pavlov spat and coughed.

"Ты глупый, блядь, придурок! Посмотрите, что вы сделали!" Павлов вытер лицо. "Что ебать это дерьмо в любом случае! Это кровь? Это кровь! Боже мой!" Pavlov yelled charging into the elevator and shoving the out the two engineer's that carried the strut.

"Ooops." An engineer sniggered.

"What'd he say?" Asked the other.

"Don't know. Don't care," replied the first as the pair walked off down the hallway, leaving the scientist shell shocked by what happened.

Annabelle arrived at her office. She set her Cyber Station on the desk and moved to the shelves. She tugged at the burgundy knitted jumper she'd dressed in. It was way too large, but that was the point. It made her look several sizes larger along with oversize jogging trousers, but she didn't care. She was making a statement. *I'm not a slut!* She pulled three folders from different locations on the shelves and sat in her chair. She opened each folder and spread them across the desk. She palmed the I.D. scanner, bringing up the number display. Glancing over a document she keyed in a number. She waited during the beeps until a woman replied.

"Olla? Loo speaking."

Annabelle instantly smiled hearing her excitable voice.

"Good morning, Loo."

"Oh, Olla Bebe girl. How are you today?" Annabelle brushed her hair back with a bare hand.

"I'm good Loo. Thank you."

"Oh no, are you sure Bebe girl…I heard you were upset yesterday."

Yeah, everybody did.

"Yes, I am fine. Thank you."

"Okay, good, good, what can I do for you?"

"Catering for the wake after the funeral needs to be decided. Especially with Kasumi's heritage."

"Oh, yes, sushi and rice are the obvious choice."

"Yes, that's great, I'd also like sliced pork pieces," Annabelle flicked through pages.

"Yeah, sure."

"There seems to be a kind of cone wrap, they put rice and sushi in and arrange it like a bouquet. That would be perfect."

"Yeah, sure. I've found the recipe for Japanese potato cake's too. Breaded chicken is also a thing."

Annabelle grimaced.

"Oh no, forget the breaded chicken. We may have southern fried on Brett's spread. But it seems underwhelming for Japanese culture."

"What of American culture?"

"The only thing that makes our food cultural is it's fast food." Loo broke into a laugh.

"I guess you're right…So what else for Brett?" Annabelle pondered the thought for a moment.

"I've got it! Barbeque."

"Excelente. I can do a Picada." Now Annabelle laughed.

"An American barbeque Loo."

"Okay, okay."

"I'll leave it at that for now…See you later."

"I see you for lunch?" Loo asked. Annabelle smiled again.

"Yes, I'll be there for lunch." The called ended with a beep. Annabelle scanned through the folders and started dialling again.

The door beeped. Annabelle glanced at the door.

"Who is it?" She called, cancelling her dial.

"It's Stefan." *Oh, fucking hell.* She cleared her throat.

"What can I do for you Captain?" She replied professionally.

"You can unlock the door. I am still your Captain aren't I?"

Annabelle said nothing. "Come on let me in," Stefan said sadly. Annabelle reached to the left and brushed her hand across the desk. A red light beside the door became green.

"Alright, come in."

He entered the room with his hands raised. "If I had a white flag, I'd be waving it?"

Annabelle looked at him confused.

"Never mind. I forget how old I am."

"You're not that old," Annabelle said bluntly, studying the folders.

"Does that mean I'm forgiven." He forced a smile.

Annabelle simply glanced at him.

"Is this outfit for my benefit?" He gestured at her loose clothing.

"Not just yours," she said scornfully. Stefan's face changed to regret.

"Oh Anna, I am so sorry. I didn't realise it would upset you."

"It, would upset me? You upset me," Annabelle interrupted now looking at him again.

"If I had known that I would upset you, I wouldn't have even considered it," Stefan approached the desk.

"Listen, you are the last person I'd ever want to upset. When you left yesterday…I." He paused and glanced down.

"Don't tell anyone but I got upset. I mean I actually cried," Stefan confessed. Annabelle was surprised. *The Captain of the damn Euphoria cried over me?* "You, cried? Why would you over me?" Annabelle asked. Stefan dropped his head again.

"When I look at you…I see Eva," Annabelle was no longer surprised. She was stunned. Her jaw dropped. *Eva Dietrich was the Captain's young daughter who was tragically killed in a car accident six years ago.* Annabelle's eyes began to well up. She sniffled and broke into tears.

"I'm sorry, I didn't know," Annabelle's eyes puffed up before they began to leak. She began to cry in her hands. Stefan looked up and rushed round to her. He turned her chair and crouched in front of her.

"Why are you sorry? You didn't do anything wrong…I was the asshole."

"I overreacted. I thought you were seeing me in a sexual way." She lifted her head to speak.

Stefan looked up around the room.

"In a way I was."

Annabelle glanced up again, this time with a scowl.

"I imagined what I'd feel like with you stood over me during an interrogation."

Annabelle's tears had stopped, and her scowl was becoming sharper.

"Maybe you should stop talking."

"From his perspective. Not mine. This is coming out all wrong…I."

"Promise me you'll never do that again."

Stefan took her hands.

"I promise. I'll never treat you that way again."

"Thank you, Captain. I accept your apology. I better get back to work."

Stefan stood quickly.

"Uh, yeah. Me to, back to work," Stefan marched toward the door but paused and turn.

"Lunch?"

Annabelle still wiping away her tears.

"Pardon Captain?"

"Have lunch with me today. We can make amends properly," Stefan asked awkwardly. Annabelle smiled.

"That be nice, thank you Captain."

Chapter 10: Grease Monkeys

Deep inside the bowels of the Euphoria. Three members of the engineering section, all in the orange flight suits worked on a large engine block that powered a cargo crane. The lower deck floors always seemed damp. The walls were cloaked in that rustic brown. The room was the size of a hanger with a track that ran through the middle. The track managed to keep its shimmer with its tram's and cargo flat bed's rolling through daily. At each end of the track, inside the room were steel doors over a foot thick. The doors had to be opened before either track vehicle could come through. There were smaller doors for personnel at each end too with a railed catwalk on the walls with no large door. These catwalks help the engineers reach the rolling mechanics of the huge door's and the crane arm's, to a degree. Ellis slopped his gloved hand into a tub of black grease. He scooped up a blob and bend into the side door of the crane where the engine block sat. He squeezed in as much as he could, reaching over piston heads.

"Can you see it Luca?" he asked and a man with a deep new Zealander accent responded.

"Yeah mate, go ahead and drop it," Luca said, and Ellis rotated his wrist slowly. The grease plopped from his hand into Luca's palm, four feet below.

Despite his six-foot eight bulky frame Luca had climbed under the grated flooring and crawl to the underbelly of the engine. Luca began to spread the grease over seals, bolt threads and cogs.

"Alright mate. Let's give this a try," Luca said moving away from the under belly and putting large orange ear defender's on. Ellis wrenched out of the compartment. And scanned the catwalk ten metre's up.

"Hayes? How we looking?" Ellis called.

"Not good," she replied. "Huh?...Chelsey?...Did you say not good?"

Hayes appeared between the dual bars of the safety rail. She wore a harness with screw drivers and spanners that were laid out like shotgun shells. She hung over the side holding a hydraulic tube. She tapped it with a spanner.

"This Ram is screwed. We need a new one."

"A new one?" Ellis was confused. Hayes turned the part.

"It's bent! Look at it! It took me twenty minutes to pull it out!" She shouted down.

"Alright calm down," Ellis said before leaning back into the block.

"Luca? Luca!…Luca!"

Luca looked up.

"Huh?" He said pulling the ear defenders off.

"Hydraulic arm is fucked. We need a new one," Luca looked down for a moment. He looked up again.

"If Hayes can tighten the seals enough, we can still see if it starts," he explained.

"Yeah," Ellis directed to Hayes. "Tighten the bolts at the seals of that arm!"

Hayes spread her arms. "What's that gonna achieve!"

"We can assess the engine!"

Hayes gave a long-annoyed growl before slipping back through the bars.

Using the scaffolding reddish frame of the crane arm Hayes climbed on. She stepped closely to where the hydraulic ramp had been. Taking a small drill with a socket from her rigging she tightened the bolt at the top, then squatted for the bottom. She awkwardly climbed back on to the platform.

"Okay give it a try." She called impatiently. Ellis gave a thumb to Luca below and pushed a large green mushroom cap button. It chugged slowly along with its belting and roared into life.

"Yes, we got it," Ellis called out.

"Turn it off! Turn it off!" Hayes yelled out of sight. Ellis did so and stared up at the catwalk. Hayes appeared again. Pure rage on her face accompanied by oil. Her short hair was thick with oil. It was in her ears, down her suit. It even dripped off the tips of her fingers.

Ellis howled into laughter.

"I'm going to kill the both of you!" She whaled.

"What did she say?" Luca called from below.

Ellis explained what had happened and Luca joined the laughter. Hayes pointed her drill and spun the socket pretending she was shooting Ellis. He broke out laughing again.

"Come to the ladder I'll help you down," Ellis said moving toward the ladders base.

"Fuck you Ellis," Hayes snapped heading toward the top rung. She slung round the top railing of the ladder and slid down. Near the bottom she slipped off. Launching backward into Ellis's body. He managed to keep his stance and laughed again. She turned quickly and splattered a handful of oil onto his head. Now she was laughing.

"Aww come on it wasn't my idea," Ellis blurted as he bent, the oil dripping on the floor.

Luca popped his head out from an open grating panel, they'd opened for access.

"What happened?" He smirked; Hayes gave him a dirty look.

"Does this mean the shift is over?" Luca mocked.

"You can't be down here alone, and we need to get this stuff off," Ellis nodded. Luca lifted himself out of the flooring and stripped his gloves. They made their way through the pedestrian door and Hayes led the way. The two men began laughing again watching Hayes's legs akimbo walk.

"Fuck you both." She bit as she swayed down the corridor. Hayes reached out for the elevator panel and second guessed it. Luca laughed as he stepped to the side of her and pushed the button.

The door opened instantly, and Hayes launched backward.

"What the fuck?" Luca and Ellis looked in.

"Is that Pavlov?" Luca asked. Rolan Pavlov was sat in the corner of the elevator. He was hunched over; vomit drenched his lap. Ellis crouched to look at his face. His face was blood stained over his mouth and throat.

"Is he dead?" Hayes asked coming away from the wall.

"No but he's looking really bad. We need to get him to medical," Ellis said standing again and moving inside. Luca stepped in behind Ellis and crouched.

"Pavlov? Can you hear me mate?"

Ellis glared back at Hayes.

"Come on let's go."

"We don't know what's wrong with him. I'm not coming in there."

"Fine," Ellis said angrily, slapping the elevator panel. The doors closed leaving Hayes behind. As the elevator rose to the upper decks Luca touched Pavlov's forehead with the back of his hand.

"His skin is on fire mate," he said looking up at Ellis. Luca lifted an eye lid.

"Fuck me," he said quickly. Pavlov's iris was black and slowly spreading into the white of his eye. The elevator stopped and opened. They both took

Pavlov under the arms and hauled him up. They stumbled toward medical, shouting for onlookers to move aside. Pavlov's feet dragging along the floor.

They barged into medical bay two. Two nurses in green suits saw them and rushed over.

"What happened to him?" One asked quickly gloving her hands.

"We don't know. Found him in the elevator," Ellis said.

"The elevator?" The second said taking his arm from Luca. Taking his shoulders and feet they laid him onto a collapsed bed before stamping a pedal at its side. The bed gently raised to waist height.

"Follow us." The male nurse ordered as they began wheeling the bed to an area with monitor's and drip tubing set into the wall either side of a large screen. They moved the bed into place. They clipped a bio-monitor to his hand. One turned Pavlov's head before checking his heart and lungs with a stethoscope.

"Heart is slow. Lung's sound wet." He announced. The female nurse began feeding a nasopharyngeal airway into his throat.

"You found him this way?" she asked the engineers. They both nodded in silence.

Dark blood lurched up the tube and spurted out the end. The nurse removed the tube. Her skin turned white as she dropped the blood thick tube on the floor.

"Doctor!" The male nurse called while pulling a dental suction vacuum off the wall. Pushing a button. The sound of suction began, and he gently lowered it into Pavlov's mouth. The obstructing gunk was sucked from his throat before the male nurse removed it.

"Try again," he said and the lady nurse inserted a new airway tube down his throat. No blood or bile came through. She connected the tube to the ventilator and began feeding Pavlov oxygen.

"What happened to him?" The female Doctor asked approaching from behind the male nurse. He glanced back.

"These two men found him in one of the elevators." The Doctor approached the bed.

"Scan." She ordered. The male nursed lowered what looked like a large light on the end of a robotic arm.

"Was he out when you found him gentlemen?"

"Yeah," Ellis said.

"His skin is like a furnace. And his eyes, damn," Luca added. The male nurse began the scan process, and the robotic arm guided its light down over his head, scanning down to his feet and back again. Each pass added another layer to a projection screen above. The Doctor took a pen sized light from her green coat and opened an eye.

"What in god's name?" She checked the other eye. Both blackening.

"What's that stuff all over you?" she asked Ellis.

"Hydraulic oil…It's from earlier."

"Oh." She nodded. "I'll need blood samples from you both."

"Why blood samples?" Luca asked. The doctor glared at them.

"Because you've been exposed gentlemen," she said turning to the large screen.

"Exposed to what?"

She studied the image of Pavlov's internals. "I don't know yet…Josephine take care of it." The doctor said.

"Yes, Doctor Lancaster." Molly replied, slipping away from the bed. She removed her gloves and washed her hand's.

"Over here please gents." The men reluctantly approached her.

The male doctor leaned into Doctor Lancaster's shoulder.

"What are you thinking Doctor?" She glanced back for a second.

"I'm just playing it safe…What is that around his lungs?" she asked studying the image on the screen.

Chapter 11: Bonding

Annabelle had changed into something a little more her. She could not stand that jumper anymore. She wore dark grey leggings and a vest top. Both dawned the Euphoria symbol. They could be used for cadets or for working out. She stood beside Loo at the back of the serving area in the canteen. Loo had laid out several test samples for the funeral the next day. Annabelle laid her hand on Loo's shoulder and smiled.

"You've out done yourself yet again Sugar."

Loo waved it off like it was nothing.

"Try this one. I wanna know if I got it right." Loo said pointing at the Cone wrap.

"Oh really, I'd hate to spoil it. I mean it looks incredible. It really does look like flowers."

"Oh no bull shit. Come on try." Loo demanded waving her hand at the dish. Annabelle rolled her eyes then smiled. She took up the cone with both hands and bit into the top. She instantly smiled again.

"Perfect," she mumbled; mouth still full.

"Yeah, she likes it." Loo announced to the serving chiefs. Annabelle swallowed hard and set the wrap back down.

"Good morning, Captain. What can I get you?" Loo called out spotting him at the counter.

"I'll have a steak please Loo. Fillet. Medium rare. And Annabelle."

Annabelle swallowed hard again. The raw fish going down this time. Loo grinned at the Captain with a cheek glare.

"I can't put Annabelle on a Plate Captain."

Annabelle blurted out a cough as she choked for a second.

"That's not funny Loo. Sorry Captain," Annabelle said approaching the front side of the serving area. Stefan laughed.

"It's fine Ms Brooks. Are you able to join me?"

Loo glanced up at Annabelle. She glared back.

"Uh Yeah, Yes. I'll have the same thank you Loo."

"I got this no problem. Go. Go." Loo said tapping Annabelle's backside. She smiled with embarrassment as she came from behind the counter. Loo marching toward the back.

Annabelle stood in front of the Captain. Hands together but her elbows were bent not to emphasise anything.

"Sorry about that Captain."

"No need to apologise for someone else's actions Ms Brooks. Shall we," Stefan replied directing with his hand. Annabelle passed him; he studied her leggings around her backside for two steps before following patiently. She moved between the occupied tables and chose a table halfway down but near the back wall.

"Okay here Captain."

"Perfect," he said pulling a chair out and gesturing at it. Annabelle smiled and almost curtsied but settled for a gently nod before sitting in the offered chair. Stefan closed his eyes as she bent to sit. She glanced up at him as he moved round to the seat opposite.

"So?" Annabelle said.

"Yes, huh," Stefan re-seated in the chair, Annabelle noticed his eye line drop. Not subtle enough Stef.

"I need to say again how sorry I am."

"Forget it. You're forgiven."

"Okay. Okay. Good," Stefan smiled and glanced round the room. Annabelle leaned forward and clapped her hands together. Her bust now resting on the table. Stefan glanced again. Annabelle smirked.

"What?"

"I was meaning to ask about what you said earlier. About Eva."

"Oh right. Okay ask away."

"Well. Why do I remind you of her? Is it just my age because you've shown me a picture and I look nothing like her?"

"She had driven. I see the same determination in you. I think it's also the way you react to me."

"How so," Annabelle lifted off the table and leaned back. She loosely folded her arms beneath her chest.

"When I. Screwed up and you laid into me. I saw my little girl then. Telling her dad how it is," Stefan confessed.

"I never expected my outburst to have a positive outcome."

"Neither did I." The pair laughed.

"Look. I've seen the same traits in you for a while. But it was the temper that confirmed the feeling."

Annabelle smiled.

"It is nice."

"What is?"

Loo reached their table with a tray with two plates with steak and two bowls with fries inside. She smiled sweetly and set the tray down.

"Thank you."

"Thanks Loo."

She nodded quietly and walked away. Stefan began sharing out the tray's contents.

"What is."

"Well, this. Having the father figure vibes from you."

Stefan froze, staring at her.

"I mean you do look at my tits but."

Stefan dropped a bowl, several fries bouncing out. Stefan stared down at the table, frozen with embarrassment. Annabelle leaned forward and took his hand.

"Stefan. I've had to deal with men looking at my boobs since I was thirteen. It doesn't bother me."

"A dad would never do that."

"Well, mine did," Annabelle blurted out. Stefan stared straight at her.

"It wasn't like that. He didn't do anything. It was more. This is something you need to handle. Except the fact that everyone is going to look. Even girls. Did you tell your daughter to dress more appropriately?"

"Of course."

"Yeah, I never took the hint. If you like what you see good. If your jealous, fuck you. If you touch me, I'll bust your nuts."

Stefan laughed; Annabelle scowled.

"I'm not laughing at you. There she is again. My Eva taking no shit," Stefan explained. Annabelle smiled.

"We better make a start on this," she said gesturing at the food. They both began to eat.

Rajiv stepped into the cafeteria and joined the lunch line. As the que moved swiftly, Rajiv scanned the room between movements. He eventually spotted Annabelle's auburn hair tied in a low ponytail. He then saw who she was sitting with. The Captain?

"What can I get you?" A voice said. Rajiv turned to the man serving at the counter.

"Huh?"

"What do you want?" The man said gesturing at the menu card on the counter.

"Oh yeah, sorry. I'll have two slices of today's pizza please."

"Spicy beef today," the man explained walking down the counter toward the pizza under the hot counter.

"Great thank you," Rajiv said glancing back to where Annabelle and Stefan sat. Annabelle threw her head back in a dramatic laugh and Stefan giggled behind his hand with a mouth full of steak.

Rajiv accepted his tray of pizza and turned to face the tables. He scanned the room for a minute between glancing over at Annabelle. He walked straight from the lunch line across the cafeteria and found a table two rows back from the wall. He ate slowly and watched Annabelle's movements. He also watched other crew members who continued to glance at her. Especially during her laughing moments as her bust would bounce against the table every time she leaned forward again. Rajiv continued to eat alone. He would smile softly to himself every time a group looked at her. *Yes, I've seen what is under those clothes.*

Chapter 12: Mare Imbruim

Kara and Jen stood silently in Xander's office set in the near corner of the Control Centre. They stood at attention; their eyes fixed on the wall ahead. They were both in light blue flight suit's, clean and pressed. They had been escorted there by Sabastian who stood purposefully beside Xander's desk. The desk was composed of a reflective black top with a murky glass frame. Xander paced behind the girl's in the white panelled room. His reflection casting a shimmer across his desk. Kara's strength had abandoned her. She felt like a child, half expecting her father's palm to cross her tushy. She peeked at Jennifer on her right, who looked irritated more than anything. She glanced up at Sabastian who seem to have wondered off in his own head.

"I'm not surprised by your involvement Kruse, but you Miss Farion. I expected much better," Xander finally said.

"I paired you both expecting some good to rub off on you Jen. How wrong was I? Damn it," Xander continued moving around to his seat at the desk. A Brown leather office chair that had been sent up from earth. He shifted papers on his desk and reached for a silver pen in a holder.

"I have no choice but to put in a formal request for your immediate departure…Jennifer Kruse," Xander announced. Sabastian peeked at Xander before quickly returning to attention.

Jennifer was completely stunned, Kara was also.

"I've served here for two years; you can't just throw me out!" Jennifer snapped. Xander glared up at her from his writing position.

"I can, and I will…All you do is cause argument's and fight's Kruse," Xander snapped back. Jennifer looked at Kara then at Xander.

"In a few weeks, I'll have the required space time. If you kick me out, it's back to earth," Jennifer pleaded, her voice starting to break up. Kara lowered her head with guilt. *I must do something.*

"That's on you Kruse. Not me," Xander said, starting to fill in the transfer paper. Jennifer lunged forward slamming her fist's down on the desk. Xander slung back in his chair as Sabastian shifted forward to restrain her.

Suddenly Jennifer was upright. Kara's hand pulling her hair again. The two men stared in shock as Kara leaned into Jennifer's ear.

"Stop you bitching. You're acting like a child," Kara whispered, aggressively but smoothly. Jennifer went limp like a puppy in its mother's jaws. The men looked at each other, shook stricken. Sabastian raised his eyebrows. Without moving his stare Xander said.

"Jennifer…Get out of my control centre." As he spoke, Kara released her grip keeping her hand up and Jennifer turned at once and left without making a sound. Kara waited for Jennifer to disappear before lowering her hand. The two men stared at Kara.

"What the fuck was that?" Sabastian blurted out. Xander raised a hand to silence him.

"I'll deal with this Sab…What the fuck was that?" Xander repeated. Kara stood to attention again.

"Me rubbing off on her sir," Kara stated.

"That's not what I…" Xander paused.

"Well fuck a doodle do," Sabastian added. Xander leaned back in his chair rubbing his hands over his head and exhaling hard.

"I think we have Jenny's leash sir," Sabastian stated.

"Yeah, I think so too. Okay Kara, take Kruse to the scouting dome, compile all their data and re-map the area…Understood," Xander told her. She nodded.

"Understood sir."

"Go on get moving. Let's see where this goes," Xander added, and Kara left the office.

The control centre was literally built in the centre of the largest dome. It had two upper platforms' than run circular around control. Each platform was built on black shaped panels much like the tunnel layouts. There were no grated walkways of any kind in or around the central dome. Printing read outs and computer terminals littered the upper areas and the ground section looking like a replica of mission control back on earth in Huston. Kara assumed the isled lay out that match was to simply mimic orders more efficiently. No body looked up from their working stations as Kara walked through the room. Reaching the double door, the only way in or out of the control centre. She set her hand upon a security panel. This was the largest she had used, being familiar with thumb scanners only. The door's slid open with a hiss and Jennifer was waiting a few steps away leaning against the hallway wall. As Kara got closer, Jennifer moved off the wall.

"How did it go?" She grinned parting her arms. Kara clutched her shoulders and drove her into the wall and leaned in close.

"You owe me, big time," Kara insisted before biting onto Jennifer's top lip. Jennifer winced. Kara worked her mouth, pressing her lower lip into Jennifer's mouth. After several seconds of violent kissing Kara relented, revealing the teeth mark's she had left behind. Jennifer winced again as she tried to close her mouth. Kara gently took her hand and led her down the hallway.

The pair walked hand in hand for a while telling each other about their home lives and comparing lifestyles. Jennifer grew up in Maribo city, a popular tourist town on an island southeast of Denmark called Lolland.

"It sound's wonderful," Kara began as they walked.

"I've always wanted to live on an island. What's it like?" she asked. Jennifer thought for a second.

"Very yellow."

"Huh?"

"The houses, most are yellow. Painted Yellow," Jennifer explained. Kara smiled in response.

"What's the island like I mean?" Kara corrected.

"It's an Island in the Baltic sea…It's Fucking cold," Jennifer said before the two laughed aloud. Jennifer pointed ahead.

"Scouting Dome," Jennifer said moving ahead and thumbing the entry door.

With a Hiss and a gently pulse of air the door slid open. They stepped into the Scouting dome. The dome was sectioned off in front of them with a huge glass screen running the full length of the room. The glass was high and thick with Cameras scattered along the expansive computer console below. Five men and one woman worked at various parts of the long console.

"Hey guys. This is Kara," Jennifer said pointing to her left. The six workers turned in their office style chairs that had oddly large rubber wheels at the bottoms.

"Hello Kara." They all said and five of them turned back to the console. The man still facing them was very small indeed. Not dwarfism but close. With his scrunched-up face, he looked like an upright hamster in the chair he occupied.

"How are you doing Jen? I heard you've been to the Super again," the man smirked.

"Oh, don't worry about that. We need the latest maps," Jennifer explained walking toward him. Kara walked with her and glared out through the glass. Outside the room were six Scout vehicles lined in parallel. Four had at least one of their huge wheels removed with other parts peppered around the giant dome space. Men and women worked together out there, some trolleying equipment round.

Others working on electrical panels. A pair was attempting to fit a new side panel onto another. One man drove a fork truck carrying, what Kara assumed to be a new heating system. Kara refocused her attention on Jennifer and her colleague tapped away on his console.

"I'll send it all to the end console for you," he told Jennifer pointing to his left. Jennifer leaned in and kissed his cheek.

"Thanks, Dario…You're the best," she finished, tapping his shoulder, and moving off with Kara. They approached the end of the stretched room and Jennifer offered Kara the chair.

"Okay…How are we going about this?" Kara asked sliding into the seat. She looked back waiting for a reply while Jennifer stepped away. She came back rolling a chair from the corner to the console.

Settling into the seat on her left, Jennifer uploaded image files onto one of three screens across the console. She transferred the files to the left-hand screen.

"Grid references, S.O.S. data base," Jennifer said, and Kara rolled her chair in slightly and began to type on a small matt like Keypad. Jennifer began to catalogue images into separate folders.

"Okay grid is up," Kara said.

"Great. Now I'm guessing these areas based on similarity, it's quicker," Jennifer explained.

"Right?"

"I'll throw half over to the end screen and we can start cross referencing each image with L and L, then build the puzzle on the grid in the centre," Jennifer explained. Kara slid her chair across to the far-right screen of the console unit.

"That's it?" Kara asked.

"That's it. Great huh," Jennifer smirked, still separating images.

"This isn't a Navigation assignment. This is doing the donkey work for their Navigator's…In a 2-D space. I haven't done anything like this since I began my course," Kara complained, typing her way through grid's and images like a machine. "Sea of Storm's right. More like sea of sod all," Jennifer said. *Damn it. I am too good for this place. There is nothing of significance here. Nothing that stimulates me.*

When the Luna 6 p.m. came around, the console operators of the Scouting Dome had begun filtering out as the D.O.M. was quickly approaching.

The two young women had re-mapped seventy percent of the images they had been given. Kara rubbed at her eyes for the eighth time that, as we would call that afternoon. Six empty paper coffee cups lay strung across the console where they worked.

"Jen?" Dario called from across the room. Both looked at the same time.

"We're shutting down for dom. You girl's coming?" Jennifer gave him a high wave as she began shutting the console down. Kara leaned over toward her.

"Domme?" she asked, provoking a smile from Jennifer.

"Dom. As in Dark of the Moon. We can't really cull it night-time," Jennifer explained. Kara blurted out a short laugh.

"I don't know about you but I'm so hungry, and tired," Jennifer admitted, standing from her chair, and stretching. Kara stood also but squeezed her arms around herself.

"Still cold?"

"Yeah, it's going to take some time to adapt," Kara confirmed.

The two headed out of the Scouting Dome back toward Habitation where they joined forty or so co-workers in the canteen. They got themselves a dinning tray and merged with the dwindling que. There were so many different discussions going on it was hard to hear Jennifer explaining what different meal types to expect on each day. When Kara got close enough to the food trays, it was clear that Jennifer did say something about oriental. There were rice and noodles of mixed vegetables and assorted meats to add. There were radish cakes stir fried tofu and a variation of soups of meat and bamboo. There was even a Hot Saki area set up, but Kara decided against it. In the end, she chose a chicken and bamboo soup with a bowl of rice and pork to mix in herself. She turned and spotted Jennifer taking a seat at the end of a table near the rear of the canteen. Kara reached the table and Jennifer stopped her idol chat to introduce her. Kara said high to everyone at the table and sat opposite Jennifer. She spooned her soup as the occupants started talking again. There were two from hydroponics, four from engineering and three technicians all discussing each other's fields of expertise.

"Kara, right?" One technician asked her. "Yes, that's right. You are…?"

"Donald, one of the Techy boys," he said and Kara nodded in acknowledgement as she finished off her soup.

"I bet you can't wait to get on a ship am I right?" He said. Strangely it did not seem like he was mocking or teasing her, his expression was genuine.

"By the looks of things, I'm going to be here a long time," Kara told him before making a start on her rice mixing.

"Now who told you that? Flight crew are never hear long, a couple of weeks' if most," Donald added. Kara stopped mixing the meat.

"Well. Nobody I just assume because…" She halted her train of thought. "Aww, no. Jennifer is special. Aren't you Jen?" Donald threw in.

"Aww here we go." A hydroponics worker declared. Kara was eating her rice and pork, looking at Jennifer. Her head was down, embarrassment colouring her cheeks.

"Special? How do you mean?" Kara finally said throwing him a look of disgust. Donald was grinning extensively.

"The reason she is still here is because she a liability, She hyper emotional and short tempered," Donald continued.

"And yet you have to provoke her." Another indicated slapping the back of his hand across Donald's shoulder. Donald laughed as he cupped his shoulder. He held his hand's up in apology.

"Your right, your right I mean…It's not her fault she has daddy issues," Donald roared into laughter. Jennifer launched across the table toward him and froze mid clamber. Kara had her by the wrist.

The canteen was silent. And all eyes were on Jennifer, half mounted on the table. Kara tugged gently on her wrist leading her off the table. Kara gently touched her chin and looked her in the eyes. There was a raging inferno inside them.

"Let's go, come on," Kara said gently guiding Jennifer to her front with one arm. She began walking Jennifer out of the canteen and Donald giggled with his back to the girl's. Kara stopped and launched a palm around the back of his head.

"Aaah," he said covering his head, still sniggering.

"Ass…Hole!" Kara yelled into his ear before continuing to escort Jennifer out of the canteen.

In the hallway, Kara held Jennifer by the shoulders. The redness slowly leaving her skin.

"Are you okay Jen?"

"You should have let be at him." She insisted, still anger in her words.

"In front of all those people? In front of the Supervisor?" Kara let her word's set in.

"Your right. I don't think, I just…"

"React," Kara finished the words for her. "A friend once told me. If they are bigger than you, don't fight harder…Fight smarter," Kara quoted.

"A friend huh?" Jennifer questioned. Kara smiled. "Yes, Jen a very good, friend."

The two walked slowly down the habitation hallway back to their room. Going inside Kara sat on the lower bunk and tapped the cover's, inviting Jennifer to sit. She put her arm around her.

"Does this happen a lot? The ridicule?" Kara asked cradling Jennifer's head.

"All the time. I lashed out once and ever since…it's like a game for some," Jennifer explained. Kara was taken a back. "Donald's not the only one?" Jennifer looked up, her eyes turning glassy.

"No, there are a few guy's here that push me…But Donald…Fucking Donald…He's never stooped so low."

"I got the impression he wanted to see my reaction too," Kara suggested. "He did get under your skin then. Really. Did you…have trouble with your father?" Kara asked quietly. Jennifer did not reply, she just held on to Kara tightly. Kara gently leaned back, bringing Jennifer down with her until they were lying on the bed together.

Chapter 13: Funeral

Two golden frames, hand painted sat side by side on the table laden with white silk and flower arrangements. Inside were blown up I.D. profile images of Brett and Kasumi. Chrysanthemums, Lily arrangements were laid on every other table. Bouquets of red, white, and blue roses had been set on the tables between. The mess hall was surprisingly quiet as crew members filed in. Some wore their uniforms, coming straight off a work shift. While others wore moaning suits and dresses. Captain Dietrich greeted everybody as they entered. Each one was handed a glass of beer or a wine from the catering staff. Almost a third of the crew were unable to attend through shift patterns although thoughtful messages had been handed in to Annabelle for their families. Everyone gathered in the middle of the room as the tables were spread near the walls.

Crew whispered quietly or sipped at their drink while the Captain welcomed. The food was hidden under cloth along the canteen's food counter. Loo standing guard. Annabelle moved round the outside, inspecting the arrangements. She had styled her auburn hair in a tousled loose curl and wore a black dress that hugged her waist but flowed loosely to her knees. Her upper body was hidden under a black shoal. She examined the tables until she reached the food counter on the far side. She spoke to a member of the catering staff, and they handed her a glass of beer and a red wine. She walked past the crowd on the outside, smiling and nodding as she passed. The last of the arrival's came in. After Captain Dietrich had greeted them, Annabelle spoke to him for a moment while handing him the beer glass. They walked together halfway along the food counter before he stopped, and she continued to the far end again.

The Captain took a deep breath and addressed the crew.

"Good afternoon, Euphoria Crew," raising his glass. They all gestured the raise in response.

"Today is a special day for two reasons. Today we celebrate the lives of Brett Grey and Kasumi Furukawa. Two incredibly brave astronauts who lost…No who gave their lives in the name of exploration, and the advancement, of humankind. Brett and Kasumi will not, go down in history as astronauts we lost in space. But as two pioneers, that changed the world, and our understanding of the universe. They will go down in history as the astronauts that found life, on Charon."

The crew began to whisper about this unprecedented news.

"Yes! Brett and Kasumi discovered a biomaterial on Charon. Which will not only extend the mission life of the Euphoria but ensure that their names…Will live forever." He raised his glass.

"To Brett and Kasumi, may our descendants, sing your names."

"Sing your names." The crew chanted back.

"Now secondly…Or the second reason to celebrate I should say, is that in 8 hours…we will reach…Earth orbit." The crowd erupted into cheers and raising they glasses high.

When the cheering had calmed, the food was revealed and everyone began eating, drinking, and having conversation. Annabelle was alongside Captain Dietrich among the section heads. Hassan Tousi was pressing his outline for further trips to Charon even though the Captain had already agreed to the venture. Lazar Markov the head of engineering and Emmett Shriver, head of technical were talking amongst themselves. Something about making the ship go faster Annabelle thought. She turned her attention to Andre Dumont the head of security,

"Mr Dumont, any word on Doctor Lancaster joining us this evening?" she asked.

"I do believe she will attend at some point she's getting Pavlov into an incubation chamber or something like that."

"How is Flight navigator Pavlov?" Hinting for a little more respect for the man.

"Still no change for our navigator Ms Brooks." *You got half the hint.*

"And what about your man…The one who was bitten, Brooster was it?"

"Michael Brooster yes. Last seen in his quarter's I heard complaining about his hand being like a balloon or something…Lazy little…" He smiled politely before finishing his sentence.

Annabelle spotted Ellis and Luca talking between themselves, looking over and laughing. She liked the men, but they sure acted like little boy's sometimes. Annabelle slipped an arm behind Andre and gave them a finger, both men broke into laughter noting they had got her attention. Ellis gestured for her to come over. She rolled her eyes.

"Excuse me Mr Dumont." Andre nodded as she left him. She turned her head slightly and squinted at the men. *What are you pair up to now*? She reached the men and pointed.

"If either one of you boys ask me: where would you be if you hadn't called. You'll both get a knee in a low place." She whispered so nobody would notice the unprofessional remark. Ellis made a shocked face.

"Bebe, I would never, I wouldn't do that," he said sarcastically.

"Yeah, you would," Luca said stepping back. Annabelle gave a tut before turning to leave them.

"No, no this is important," Ellis said taking her hand. She glared at her held hand and glared at Ellis.

"Back away slowly," Luca whispered as if Annabelle had become a bear.

Annabelle flashed her teeth and made a quiet growl. Ellis released her hand quickly. She slapped her hands to her hips.

"You were about to say something important," she said impatiently.

"Yeah, has the Captain chosen a replacement Navigator?"

"No…Why?" she asked suspiciously.

"I know one."

"You know one…and?" Annabelle held her palms out.

"I was hoping you could ask the Captain to consider it."

"Why me?"

"He listens to you," Luca said bluntly. Ellis gave her puppy eyes, Luca followed suit smiling. She rolled her eyes again.

"Alright, hang on," she said before walking back to the Captain. The two men watched as she approached him and touch his arm. She apologised to Hassan for the interruption. She spoke for a moment before pointing at the men. Their faces dropped.

"What is she doing?" Ellis asked.

"She's…Throwing you to the wolves…See ya," Luca said dashing away.

Annabelle waved at Ellis, then she invited him over. Ellis rubbed his hair and took a breath before walking sheepishly toward the group. Annabelle stepped away and approached him.

"What have you…" Ellis questioned as she gripped his arm cutting him off.

"You own me big time," she told him before pushing him toward the Captain. She smiled deeply as Ellis extended a hand and Captain Dietrich excepted. She realised Luca had abandoned his position and scanned the room. He wasn't hard to find given his size. She slowly moved through the crowd giving smile's and hello's before reaching him. She stood behind him.

"For such a big man, I didn't realise you were a coward," Luca turned quickly.

"I didn't ask for anything did I? Why should I get involved?" Luca explained.

"Uh huh," Annabelle nodded.

Luca invited her to stay amongst the engineer's and relax, rather than stay with the section heads and follow etiquette. She made light conversation with many of the light-hearted crew and had a hysterical conversation with Chelsey Hayes about her idiot co-worker's. Shortly after a mixture of rock music and pop had begun. Between talking with colleagues and rejecting dance proposals, she was having fun among Luca, Ellis, Hayes, and the other engineer's around her. The music went quiet, and crew began looking round. The Captain was back in front near the food counter.

"What's this?" Hayes asked in a whisper.

"I don't know," Annabelle replied. The Captain waved his hand to silence everyone.

"I thought that now would be a good time to say…What a brilliant turn out we've had today. Thank you all for attending." The crowd clapped.

"I also thought now was a good time to mention how well organised this event has been." *Oh no.* "Everything here, the deco, the food, the music, even my…Brilliant speech." The crowd laughed. *Oh please no.*

"None of this would have been achieved in record time…Without Annabelle Brooks." The crowd clapped again.

"Where is she? Where's Annabelle?"

"Right here," Luca called out pointing down. Annabelle bowed her head and covered her face. The Captain shifted trying to sight her. The crowd parted, revealing her location.

"Ah. There you are. Anna. You have done a fantastic job arranging this day. And the only way I could show my appreciation for your efforts. Is to invite you to dance with the Captain." He finished offering his hand. The crowd roared and began clapping.

Annabelle peered through her fingers. Although a dance with the Captain is considered a great honour, Annabelle's skin was on fire. She could feel sweat on her neck and her lower back. She bowed her head and lifted again, her hand's covering her mouth. The clapping turned into a chant. They were chanting her name. The Captain waited; hand still extended. She looked over the crowd. All eyes were on her. And there to the left of the crowd, near the door she saw Grace smiling back at her. Annabelle smiled back and noticed she wasn't chanting; she was saying something. *Top Trump*?

Those two words blew her out of embarrassment. Those two words told her. *This is your moment. Own it.* She slowly reached to her shoal and open the clasp. The shoal fell from her shoulder revealing the strapless Skater dress beneath. Members of the crowd whistled in baritone and soprano. Annabelle smiled shyly as she emerged from the crowd. A soft melody began to play, and she laid her hand in the Captain's. Stefan gently laid his hands on her waist and made a pouting wide-eyed face at the crowd. Annabelle embarrassedly palmed her face. The crowd reacted with laughter. She laid her arms around his shoulders crossing her hands loosely. The pair began to move, swaying from side to side as the crowd looked on.

"Thank you for this," Stefan said quietly. Annabelle smiled and dipped her head.

"Don't, you'll set me off." She whispered.

"I mean it. This means so much more than…"

"No. I completely understand what it means. Thank you too."

"What are you thanking me for?"

"This means a lot more to me too," she told him smiling sweetly. They both hugged tightly, and the crowd erupted again.

Friends and couples began to add to the dance space until many of the crew were slow dancing in pairs. Annabelle directed Stefan's glance. The pair saw Luca leading Ellis in their own mocking slow dance, and they laughed. After a few moments of laughter, Stefan's face stiffened.

"I know I shouldn't ask this of you."

"Ask me what?" She said still amused by the two idiots.

"I want to ask you to stay," Annabelle looked puzzled.

"I know I shouldn't pressure you, but I want you to continue with us when we head back out. To stay with me," Annabelle began to tear up. Panic in Stefan's eyes. He hugged her tightly.

"I'm sorry you don't have to say yes." She pulled back and looked into his eyes.

"Yes…I'll stay. You said I remind you of your daughter. Well, you remind me of my daddy," Stefan's eyes began to glaze. *Rustlers killed Annabelle's father when she was fourteen.* The pair embraced tightly again. The music began to fade. Stefan hid Annabelle as she cleared her face of tears.

Just as quickly the music flared up again. This time with much more of an energetic dance beat. The couples in the dancing space began to separate and dance more wildly. Hayes moved out of a congregation of people.

"Bebe. Come on," Hayes called out getting her wiggle on. Annabelle smiled over her shoulder before addressing Stefan.

"Go get 'em," he said releasing his hold. She perked up and kissed his cheek before heading away. Since Stefan's confession and the long talk, they'd had at lunch, Annabelle had fully embraced the daughter role and he knew that it was a little more for him than her. But what she had said to him was real and he knew that too. He watched her until she reached Hayes and the group before moving off the dancing area and re-joining the section heads.

"Grace. You made it. How is Pavlov?" he asked.

"Not great to be honest. He will get all the care he need's when we get back." Doctor Lancaster assured him.

"I saw you two dancing." She smiled, directing her first glass of wine in Annabelle's direction. He looked at her while she and Hayes had begun moving together in a mirrored dance.

"Yeah. The highest point of my trip I think," Grace agreed and smiled as they both watched her like proud doting parents.

Chapter 14: Party

Rajiv rubbed his eyes. Then rubbed his head. He looked across the laboratory toward a digital clock mounted on the wall. 18.37. *I'll Miss it at this rate*. He glared across the room at Green who was once again watching the black organism inside the glass box. He looked down into the biological microscope again. Inside the petri dish was a tiny drop of red liquid. In the microscope lens, it seemed huge. Rajiv gently tapped on a keypad at the microscopes base increasing the zoom and clarity of his vision. Beside him to his left was seventeen closed petri dishes and twenty-two on his right. Everyone had a spec of red liquid inside and he was checking them all. He leapt back and threw his arms up.

"Yes, I've found it." He turned and smiled at Green while she turned and approached him.

"Took you long enough." She scowled as she investigated the lens.

"You see it has enveloped the cells," Rajiv said happily, Green glared at him.

"I do have eyes." She spat before taking a step back.

"On the big screen Mody." She ordered, folding her arms.

Rajiv tapped keys on the desk display and an image two metres squared appeared on the wall above. The pair studied the image. Tiny black discs, half the size of a mouse blood cell, slowly encircled the one of five remaining cells. Lines jetted out of the circles into the cell fading its Scarlett colour until it was completely black. Almost every effected cell looked out of shape and jagged, with those tiny black disc's leaking out. The next batch of invading cell's encircled another healthy cell. Then nothing.

"Why did they stop?" Rajiv asked. Green shrugged.

"Maybe it's dying, or the cells are fighting back…Check another." After a moment she looked at Rajiv, he hadn't moved just looked at her.

"It's almost seven. Ms Green."

She tutted. "I don't see why you want to go anyway; you didn't know them."

"My friends are there."

"Ha, you have friends. Now that's a joke." She sniped looking at the screen. She looked down at him.

"Oh, get out of here before you start to cry...Damn baby." Before Green could insult him anymore, he was up and heading for the door.

"Give my regards to the riff raff." He heard her call as he raced through the door.

Green studied the screen for a few more moments before looking into the microscope.

"What are you up too?" She whispered. There was a bang and Green stood straight and looked at the box. The organism was on the glass spreading like spider legs. She watched it for a moment. The petri dish under the microscope shattered. Green leapt back, hitting her back against one of the animal cages. A rat leapt at the wall of the cage with a screech and Green launched away toward the box. She stopped her momentum three feet from the glass and turned. Her face dropped. The thing had gone. Her head jerked back and forth searching the floor for the organism. She looked back at the box. It was not broken in anyway. She approached cautiously. Scanning the box, her face touching the glass she saw a thin black tail disappearing into the glove that was hanging outside. Panicking she quickly grabbed the glove tightly. Then realised her mistake and rammed the glove back into the box. She screamed in pain. Her hand was stuck to the glove. She pulled back violently.

The organism now hooked around her finger's stretched from the glove as she pulled. She wrenched backward into the animal cages again, this time hitting many at once. Before Green was able to fall away from the impact the organism spread rapidly. Latching onto the cages and spiking the occupant's with needle tentacles. The mammals, reptile and amphibians let out their own screeches of distress and pain as the black tar like mass spread over Green's face and lurched down her throat.

As Rajiv came up in the elevator the sound of beating music began to reach his ears. The doors opened and he quickly moved toward the sound. He stopped and looked down at his white lab coat. Rajiv undone the buttons and whipped it off his back, then balled up the coat and stuffed it beneath his arm. He looked down at his appearance again. *Should have got changed.* He took a deep breath, smiled, and strolled casually into the mess hall. Rajiv stepped in behind a crowd of people and discreetly hid his coat on a chair. He strolled up to the food counter where the staff were handing out drinks. He excepted a glass of beer. He leaned over to the male caterer.

"Have you seen Annabelle?" The Caterer held his hand to his ear.

"Huh?"

"Annabelle?" Rajiv repeated and then the caterer nodded and pointed across to the dance area. His smile faded away. Dancers closely surrounded Annabelle. Male dancers. Young male dancers. And Annabelle was dancing sexually. She mixed Kizomba and Jamaican wine dance together. She was squatting with her legs parted. She was laying her hands between her legs making the loose skirt she wore tighten around her thighs. She swung her hips slowly and sensually. By simply swaying her shoulders, most of her movement was around her hips, legs, and ass. And the men around her were loving every erotic second.

"Rajiv?" Grace appeared in front of him.

"Oh, hello Doctor Lancaster," he said quickly, shifting to keep his eyes on Annabelle.

"How are you doing sweetheart?"

"I'm fine. Thank you. And you are good?" He half-heartedly asked while mentally fighting the men off Annabelle.

"Oh yes, I'm very well. I tell you what. This has been a very good turn out."

Doctor Lancaster tapped his arm as if to refocus him.

"How are you arriving so late?"

"Ms Green kept me behind to work." The Doctor stopped and glanced back, following his eye line. She gripped his face at his cheeks.

"Hey…Listen to me very carefully Rajiv…If you catch a lady like that…let her fly…And she will always come back to you," Rajiv glanced at Annabelle working her body and nodded.

"I understand Doctor Lancaster."

"Good. Now, enjoy your drink. Relax, mingle, you'll know when it's time to go to her." She smiled softly and tapped him on the shoulder before leaving him.

Rajiv drank his glass quickly and took another before moving around the dance area to the chatting crowd's. He stopped behind a large man and waited, the man was energetic with his arms and was heavy in conversation. Rajiv tried to squeeze past with no avail. He waited longer.

"Excuse me please," the man gave no response.

"Excuse me sir," he said louder. Still nothing. He tapped the man on the shoulder. The man spun round.

"What?" Luca snapped looking down at him.

"I can't get past," Rajiv said quietly.

"Yeah, go somewhere else," Luca turned his back on him. Rajiv looked round and tapped his shoulder again. Luca turned round slowly.

"What did I just say mate. Go round," Luca said angrily pointing a way round with his finger.

"Or you could just move for a second," Rajiv jerked backward as Luca gripped his shirt. Another man touched Luca's arm and nodded toward the Dance area. Luca looked over for a moment. He released Rajiv and stepped aside, extending a hand into the crowd to move the others.

"Thank you. Was that so hard," Rajiv said smugly and walked by.

He joined a group of young men and women from the science section. Undergrads like himself. They looked at him wide eyed.

"What did you say to that guy to make him move?" One asked.

Rajiv shrugged, "I told him to move so he did." His colleagues were extremely impressed with his statement, and they spoke amongst themselves about their work and their insufferable bosses. Then one of the men shoved the other playfully.

"Nah, it's me she want's not you."

"Yeah right, she's looking at me pal."

"Who are you talking about?" A third interjected.

The two men nodded out to the dance area. The third looked and laughed.

"In your dreams guys," Rajiv looked also. Annabelle was still dancing sexually, but she was lowering her gaze and tilting her head. She was moving her shoulders more and softly bobbing, her breasts bouncing. But with every move she made she did not take her eyes off him. He felt his heart rate increase and almost instinctively looked behind to see if she was looking at someone else. But she was not. She was looking at him. Looking at him like she wanted him right then and there.

Rajiv made his way back through the crowd. His colleagues watching him, wondering what was up. He reached the edge of the talking crowds. Annabelle slowly stretched out her hand. The men around her watched her. She reached between them. Rajiv walked to the circle and took her hand. Still dancing she moved forward and slowly laid her arms on his shoulders. She kissed him smoothly and threw her head back. Bringing her head back down, she smiled. She pulled him closer, her chest pressing against him. She took hold of his hips and guided him to move with her. Rajiv smiled widely seeing the shocked or disappointed faces of the men who had been attempting to dance with her for so long. After the next song begun, she moved to the side bringing her lips to his ear.

"I want you to come back with me tonight." She whispered.

"Okay. I'll come back with you." She glanced down and smiled. She went to his ear again.

"I Mean to stay," Rajiv looked at her.

"I'm ready," she said softly staring into his eyes. Rajiv smiled deeply and they held each other, their sensual dancing becoming a slow-moving embrace.

Chapter 15: Stirring

The laboratory was quiet, the animal cages were bent and distorted. Tiny animal remains lavished in blood splashed through them. Green's body was sat hunched over at the base. Her shoulder's dripping with the animal entrails. Her crotch was wet and muddy after her bladder and bowels had relaxed. Her body jerked, and again. Tremors ripped through her limbs. Her chest thumped as though being shocked with a defibrillator. Her head lifted; her eyes opened; gooey black oil trickled from her tear ducts. Her eyes were completely black, soulless, dead. She slowly raised her arms above her and gripped the cages behind. She pulled with her arms, her backside lifting off the ground. Her arms continued to pull, her back continued to arch. She kept crabbing upward. There was a crunch. Her spinal column ripped and tore.

She turned, throwing her right leg to the left. The crunching unrelenting as her lower half twisted round. She used her hands to turn her upper body the same way as the lower. Her hands climbed the slick gore riddled cages. Her body straightened with a deep crack. She was statue still for several seconds, then her body jerked again. Her body moved sharply, deliberately. Her head and arms lurched, moving like a concerned squirrel. Her jaw dropped suddenly, then slowly closed. Again, the jaw dropped and closed slowly. Her head wrenched back and flung forward, jaw dropping again. Her hands raised to her face. Her fingers slipping into her mouth. Her hands parted fast, ripping the cheek flesh from her face. A wave of blood and saliva fell from her mouth. Small black rods extended from the upper and lower jaw where her cheeks once hung. They coiled and latched together forming a new support for the jawbone. Her mouth wrenched open again, three times as wide.

Rajiv held his arm around Annabelle's tightened waist. He was smiling vigorously, the proudest man alive. Annabelle dipped her head shyly stroking her hair behind one ear.

"How long have you two been a thing?" Captain Dietrich asked, mild shock still present across his face. Annabelle peeked at Rajiv, urging him to answer.

"A few days Captain. That's all," Rajiv said sheepishly. The Captain nodded with a downturned lip.

"You're in the science section, aren't you?"

"Yes, Captain as an undergrad."

"An undergrad." The Captain frowned. "When do you become a graduate?"

"After the next trip out Captain."

"Oh, good. Okay. Have you guys…You know?" Rajiv was struck with bewilderment. Annabelle turned her head attempting to hide a smirk before tipping her head to the side and glaring at the Captain.

"Well, uh, we have…"

"I didn't really want to know, boy…" He cracked laughing. "This guy, Anna, really?" He sustained his laughter.

"Yes Captain…This guy," Annabelle said seriously. The Captain coughed, killing his laughter.

"Don't worry boy. I'm just screwing with you." *No, you're not Stefan.*

"Yeah, well. Enjoy the rest of the evening, take care of my girl," he said pointing at Annabelle.

"Big day tomorrow Anna, orbit day. Bright and early, yes?"

"Yes Captain," she replied before he moved away to speak with other crew members.

Rajiv stood motionless. *I'm not good enough for her. What was I thinking? Anna can do so much better than me.* The sound around him was muddled. People were talking but he had no idea what they were saying. *Are they talking about me?* He turned sharply as Annabelle touched his chin.

"Did you hear me or what?" Annabelle asked him.

"Huh?"

"I said are you ready to go?"

"Oh, yeah sure," Rajiv nodded.

"Hey?" Annabelle said turning him to face her.

"Are you alright? Do you want to come back with me?" The gravity of her words took the wind out of him. *She's asking for reassurance from me.*

"Yes, yeah of course I do," Rajiv broke into a smile. He felt her hand slide into his.

"You take your sweet time." She whispered. Rajiv took this as move your ass and be lined for the canteen exit with Annabelle in toe.

The pair moved quickly through the corridors and hallways toward the habitation deck. They reached the entrance to Habitation and Rajiv tapped the button several times impatiently. Annabelle made eye contact with him and they both giggled. The entrance door opened, and Annabelle stepped in and jumped as Rajiv smacked her behind. She peeked over her shoulder; her mouth open. That surprised but impressed look that men love to see. This excited him so much more and he leapt in behind her, forcing her roughly into the hallway. Annabelle was turned to her left and pressed firmly against the side wall, chest first. She let out a sensual gasp followed by another shocked look.

"Am I going to pay for that?" he whispered. Annabelle turned quickly in the restricted space he'd given her.

"Damn right you are." Her breath in his ear. He kissed her roughly. He felt her hand on his groin, rubbing. Rajiv grunted hard as she grabbed him lower. She let out a louder gasp while squeezing gently as they kissed. Annabelle adjusted her hold and began rubbing him again. Annabelle let out a long pleased mmm as he began throbbing. The pair heard talking back through the entrance and hurried away, giggling.

Annabelle skipped past him and ran down the hall toward her quarters, Rajiv gave chase grabbing at her behind. Rajiv almost ran past when she thumbed her door. The pair fell in as Rajiv pushed against her. Annabelle turned and they were kissing again. She pulled his shirt up over his head. Dropping it on the floor she kissed him again. Rajiv moved to pull her dress down.

"Aww, the zip, at the back." She warned and Rajiv reached behind her, grabbing, and groping but then he got it. Annabelle stepped back, un-sleeved her arms and gently lowered her dress. Rajiv gaped at her hulking breasts clambering out of her bra. She slid her dress off her hips and stepped out. She kissed him again, this time she began kissing down his chest, his slim firm stomach. Annabelle was on her knees now removing his belt and opened his trousers hungrily. She gasped seeing his impressive penis, although she had already seen him. And gazed up at him. She was like an actress in one of those movies doing all the right movements and making the right sounds.

She took him in her mouth. Rajiv felt like he was transcending. He closed his eyes and threw his head back groaning while she pleasured him. She was gentle at first and then continued more vigorously using her hand. After coordinating her mouth and hand expertly for a few minutes Rajiv's member began to pulse. She stopped and looked up at him.

"I'll keep going if you want me too." He looked down at her sweet features as his body jerked. He shook his head. She guided him to her bed and sat him down. Undoing her bra, her breasts burst free. Rajiv immediately took one of her small but firm nipples into his mouth and she gasped and groaned. He fondled and massaged her orbs. She slipped her thin underwear down and urged him onto his back.

Annabelle crept up his body like a cat before lowering herself onto him. She leapt up slightly, letting out a wince at his impressive reach, then lowered again. Rajiv laid there, wide eyed at her lips holding him tightly. *I love you so much.*

"Is there anything about you that isn't perfect?" He said quietly. She smiled innocently as she began a rocking motion. Rajiv grunted constantly in a state of pleasure while caressing her breasts. She began to grind rapidly on him and lowered to tongue his mouth. Rajiv felt himself edging closer. He began to pulse again. Annabelle slowed for a moment, breathing heavily. She waited for a surprising thrust that did not appear.

Rajiv gave it his all not to waste this moment and Annabelle knew it. She smiled sweetly and kissed him again. She repositioned herself into a squatting pose. *Holy shit she's going for it now.* She lowered her body all the way down, her mouth springing open. She rose to the very end then slid to the lowest point again. She continued to use every inch of him as she rapidly moved her posterior up and down. Annabelle's hips went into overdrive as she ploughed down on him. Rajiv held her furiously moving breasts as she hammered his nail.

Annabelle squealed, then screamed as Rajiv erupted. She arched back, her body jerking violently as Rajiv felt her returning the favour. She slumped over him.

"Oh my, she likes him," Annabelle blurted out. "I mean that was amazing."

"Wow, you are incredible...I've never been ridden like that before," Rajiv smiling. Annabelle smile innocently again. Nothing innocent about that. That's for sure. Annabelle moved to his side and slid off the bed and went into the bathroom. Rajiv stared at the ceiling.

"Rajiv you lucky bastard."

Chapter 16: Moon

The following morning Kara woke to the distant sound of voices in the hallway. She checked on Jennifer who was now facing the inner wall of the bunk. She gently pulled her arm free from Jennifer's sleeping head and wondered into the toilet. She relieved herself and washed her hands at the basin, before splashing her face. She came out of the bathroom and stood against the doorway, watching Jennifer sleep. *Aww. I wish I had eaten that rice yesterday…But knowing what I know now, I think it was worth it. She needs me. She needs protecting. Speaking of which.* Kara heard Donald in the hallway and stepped out there. She looked left, nothing. She looked right and he was there, a few yards down talking to another man also in a technician's flight suit. Kara straightened herself and marched toward the pair of men. She considered waiting for his colleague to leave. *Fuck it…double the lesson.* Kara continued on her trajectory moving with purpose.

"Donald?" Kara said sharply. As he turned Kara stepped into him launcher her foot into his groin as hard as she could. As her foot crunched into his testicles all air leapt from his lungs. His legs snapped shut as he bowled backward onto the floor.

"Aww fuck." The colleague announced seeing Donald curling up on the ground.

"I can dish out low blows too!" Kara shouted pointing down at him. She glared at the on looker and he took a step back.

"If any of you, asshole's bully Jennifer again. I'll cut them off! Understood?" The standing man nodded. "Understood Don?" She demanded. Donald barely managed a nod, tucked up tightly on the ground. Kara straightened quickly and stormed away as the standing technician crouched down to help his colleague.

Kara returned to her room shutting the door behind her and leaning against it. She took several deep breaths trying to slow her heart rate down. Jennifer rose to her side in the bunk.

"What's wrong?" she asked.

"Nothing wrong, it's fine," she replied stepping away from the door and heading into the toilet. She leaned onto the wash basin and stared into the mirror. Jennifer followed into the room.

"What's happened?" she asked appearing in the mirror behind her.

"I don't think you'll have any more trouble Jen," Kara stated splashing her face with water again.

"What did you do…I've fought before it doesn't change anything," Jennifer explained.

"Yeah, well I'm pretty sure I broke Donald."

"You didn't?"

"Oh, I think I did. I kicked him…really fucking hard," Kara explained nodding into the mirror. Jennifer covered her mouth for a moment.

"Holy shit," Jennifer smirked. Kara turned to face Jennifer.

"Pretty sure I'm fucked now. That wasn't the plan. I just…"

"Reacted?" Jennifer finished.

Kara decided to shower alone, despite Jennifer's suggestion to save water. She washed herself quickly and washed her hair half-heartedly. Inside the shower cubicle she pressed tiny rubber buttons on a circular control panel. Warm air began to envelope her, and her hair began to dance around. The full body drying appliance was loud but efficient. Within moments her skin was completely dry. Stepping out she found Jennifer waiting, standing there as naked as Kara was. Jennifer was incredibly toned, especially around her core which helped to elevate her bust. Kara smiled and tilted her head.

"We can't be late, can we? I think we're in enough trouble as it is," Jennifer stepped close and embraced her, her breasts pressing against her own.

"Jennifer. We cannot do this now," Kara said softly, feeling Jennifer's heart-warming heat on her skin.

"Your hair smell's really nice," she replied after taking a deep breath. After another few seconds Kara split the embrace, straightening her arms upon Jennifer's shoulders.

"Your hair will smell just like mine in a few minutes Jen. So, drop the seduction tricks and get your ass into the shower," Kara moved past her, quickly smacking her behind. "Your firm ass into the shower." She added leaving the room. Jennifer smiled deeply glancing over her shoulder. She focused on the floor at her feet and smiled deeply again before climbing in to wash.

Kara began to dress, listening to the shower water. She clothed in thick socks, comfortable knickers, taking note of the tight flight suit she would soon don and a supportive under shirt. Taking her suit of the dresser's chair she opened her case and took out a perfume bottle. She scented the suit with a strawberry fragrance before stepping into it. She was tying her hair into a ponytail as Jennifer joined her. Simply exchanging smiles, Jennifer began to dress while Kara added the strawberry perfume to her flight suit. She then revealed her hair straightening brush and used it on the unshaved side of Jennifer's hair. When they were both ready, they headed out. Kara took note of the fact, nobody was in the hallway, thankfully that meant Donald was okay. At least she hoped he was.

Joining the breakfast que in the canteen the pair scanned the room.

"I don't see Donald anywhere," Jennifer whispered.

"Yeah, but I do see Xander over there," Kara nodded, pointing with her eye line.

"Is he looking this way?" Jennifer asked handing Kara a serving tray.

"No, I don't think he's noticed us yet."

"Maybe he doesn't know?"

"Yeah, maybe," Kara began to feel nerves and struggled to focus on the breakfast menu, constantly looking around the canteen as if she was about to pull off a heist. Kara eventually chose a bowl of mixed tropical fruit and yogurt while Jennifer had bacon and eggs. They found an empty table. Kara ate quickly, still feeling the hunger from the evening before. Jennifer ate slowly, cutting eggs and bacon and stacking mouths of both before eating them.

Kara kept an eye on Xander, praying he wouldn't spot her. She saw a man with a drawn face and greying hair in a suit of flight crew colour approach him. He leaned in, whispering in his ear before looking straight at her. *Oh, for fuck sake.* Now Xander was looking over too. Xander spoke more with the man a little longer. He looked puzzled at first, then concern set in with a hint of stress. The messenger then made a bee line for their table.

"Someone's coming over, that's it I'm screwed," Kara whispered, and Jennifer swung round to look.

"That's Joshua. He's our communications guy," Jennifer said calmly.

"He was just with Xander," Kara said bluntly, panic setting in.

"Miss Farion?" Joshua asked.

"Yes, that's me," she said reluctantly.

"Hi, Supervisor Xander has asked that you head to his office when you have finished your breakfast," Joshua announced before quickly heading away. Jennifer turned back to Kara.

"Alright. Maybe you are in deep shit."

"I'm going to be charged…Or worse, kicked off the station."

Kara rocked gently in a swivel chair in front of Xander's desk. Her eyes had reddened from a fountain of tears minutes before arriving at the control centre. She picked at her nails, something that she had never done before. She had been sat there for fifteen minutes at least and she had begun to feel nauseous. *Her four years of study and challenging work were about to be undone by one moment of anger. Surely the slap would not be considered too, would it? The scuffle with Jennifer, although played down had been addressed. No this was definitely a result of kicking Donald in the nuts. It's all his fault if he wasn't bullying Jennifer. Fuck it, I hope I did hurt him. Asshole.* She heard Xander voice outside. Issuing tests or inspections or something. Xander strode into the room closing the door behind.

"I'll cut straight to it Karabina…" He began moving to take his seat. "You are being reassigned with immediate effect," Kara dropped her head in shame. Xander slouched down to look her in the eyes.

"Are you all right, I thought you'd be pleased," Kara raised her brows.

"This isn't a punishment?"

"Why what have you done?"

"It's nothing, it doesn't matter," Xander leaned forward resting his elbows.

"Nothing would not get anyone reassigned. What have you done?" Xander pressed.

"I…I hit Donald, one of the technicians," she confessed keeping her head bowed.

"Yes, I saw. I had the understanding that he was being, what was it? An asshole."

"It was after that."

"Just spit it out Kara, I got other matters to take care of," Xander snapped impatiently.

"I…I kicked him between the legs," Xander rubbed his forehead.

"Why would you do that?"

"He and many others have been bullying Jennifer…I made a statement they'd all understand," Kara explained.

"Ah for fuck…Kara. Jennifer is a troublemaker. She's always arguing or fighting with someone…"

"And there's a reason she reacts that way," Kara interrupted. "And they know that. It's why they continue to push her…You've seriously never wonder why they do it. Would anyone pull a lion's tail, after they've been bit," Kara ranted. Xander leaned back in his chair, hands behind his head.

"I see what you mean. But I don't think you have the right to pass all the blame."

"Look…Sir. I'm not passing the blame for my actions. I should not have done…that. Punish me if you must. But I'm telling you Jennifer is…damaged," Kara began to explain.

"Nobody is born with the need to be controlled," Kara continued. Then it all came together in Xander's mind.

"Oh, fuck me," Xander threw his head into his hands.

After a minute, Xander stood and starting pacing. Kara watched in silence. He stopped, staring out to the command centre.

"She goes too." He finally said. Kara leapt up.

"She'll be crushed."

"No, she won't. She'll go with you."

"Well, where am I going?"

"The Navigations officer aboard the Euphoria has been grounded due to…medical issues. And a personal request was made for you to replace him," Xander explained.

"Personal request?"

"Seems so. A shuttle is set to dock with the Euphoria when she head's back out tomorrow. You, and now Jennifer will be on that shuttle," Xander relaxed slightly and sat again.

"Before you find Jennifer to give her the news. You should check in with medical and see if Donald is there," Kara bit her lip.

"Yes sir."

"And beg for an apology Kara."

"Yes, I got that part." She retorted getting up and leaving.

Kara did as she was told, catching anyone she could on her way to ask for news on Donald. It was floating around the base that he had been injured, but details leaned more toward an accident involving an electrical malfunction. *Didn't think a wiring panel could do that to a man's groin.* But she kept that to herself. She reached medical and inquired about his location and was directed to one of the recovery cubicles. She knocked gently.

"Come in," Donald replied and instantly regretted it. He was sitting in a bed with his legs parted. He almost leapt out when Kara walked in.

"What do you want? I haven't even seen her," Donald snarled. Kara raised her hands in surrender.

"I've come to apologise. I didn't mean to hurt you," she said calmly.

"You must think highly of yourself if you think you hurt me. I'm here because of an electrical explosion," Kara almost laughed aloud.

"We both know an explosion would not be directed at your junk Don. Although describing my kick as explosive is truly kind of you."

"Get out!" He shouted raising a little in the bed.

"I'll keep it to myself don't worry. It's the least I could do," Donald looked away ignoring her statement.

"I do mean it Dom. I am sorry and I hope you're better soon," Kara continued softly. She turned to leave but Dom responded.

"Who sent you? Xander?"

"Yes, he did. But he doesn't know I'm here now. I came because I wanted to say I'm sorry and to let you know I'm leaving tomorrow…"

"Good."

"And I'm taking Jennifer with me."

"Even better."

"Well, if they do work…" She said nodding at his area. "I hope you children aren't bullies too." She remarked before walking out.

Outside the room Kara took a deep breath.

"Asshole." She muttered before heading out of medical to find Jennifer. She eventually found her back in the scouting dome, finishing off the re-map from the day before. She approached her and gave her a hug at her seated position. Jennifer stopped and held Kara's hands.

"Everything went well?" she asked keeping her grip.

"Even better than that. We have been reassigned to the Euphoria," Kara Beamed.

"We?" Jennifer said turning in her chair as Kara relaxed the hug.

"Yes…We are going together to join the Euphoria crew," Jennifer leapt from the seat embracing her so quickly they almost fell over.

"Careful," Kara laughed as they held each other. The other worker's in the room turned to look and Dario hooped from his chair.

"What's the big news?" He called. Both girls looked at him, still in a hug.

"I'm joining the Euphoria!" Jennifer announced. They all cheered and clapped. One operator called into the com to the engineers.

"Hey everyone...Jennifer's finally getting off this rock!" He told them and they joined the celebration, some clapping, others cheering and most banging their tools to the rhythm of the clap. Jennifer refocused on Kara squeezing her tightly.

"I'm so happy."

The two girls soon knuckled down and completed their re-map assignment. And since they would be leaving the very next day. Jennifer suggested a visit to the observation dome. They had a light lunch, a bowl of French fries before traveling to a dome to the southwest. Before heading through the door, Jennifer covered Kara's eyes.

"What are you..."

"Trust me." she said as the air gush from the door blew past. The door slid open, and Jennifer shuffled Kara inside. The ground felt soft under foot as they walked. Kara did not like having her sight taken away, but she smiled none the less.

"Jen...where..." Kara questioned as Jennifer shifted her directions. They stopped and Jennifer slowly moved her hands.

"Oh my...Wow," Kara said glancing back at Jennifer. The ground was blanketed with a thick layer of light grey dust. The dust sparkling snow beneath the dome's powerful lights. Artificial pine trees were scattered throughout the dome, floured with they own dust. There were old rustic looking benches placed in a different quarter of the area and...A pond. A pond with a trickling stream which sounded faster than it was.

"Water," Kara said stunned.

"Yeah, a few of the engineer's built it a few months back."

"It's beautiful," Kara marvelled. She turned and kissed Jennifer on the lips before admiring the feature again.

Jennifer pulled her back and began kissing her deeply, passionately, erotically. They were touching each other on the face, then the shoulders and back while they kissed. Without relenting they slowly lowered onto the bedding of Luna snow. Kara lay on her back, Jennifer rubbing a leg along hers. Kara held onto her hair and considered pulling but let go. Jennifer's hand launched up to catch it. She forced it back onto her hair and directed Kara's hand into a grip. Kara pulled, breaking the lock of their lips and Jennifer gasped throwing her head back in ecstasy. Kara pulled again, this time rolling the pair until she was on top. Kara sat on her knees over Jennifer. A handful of snow hit Kara's face. She sat in shock as Jennifer broke into a laugh.

A second later she flipped Kara into the snow beside her. Kara swung a cloud of snow over Jennifer and they both begun to wrestle. Kara got to her feet and ran. Jennifer gave chase, both laughing. She leapt but Kara stopped, ducking. Jennifer launched over her, face first into the snow. Kara fell backward laughing. Jennifer rose to her hands and knees. She turned and leapt on Kara. Shortly after rolling around a little more the couple stopped. Smiling at each other. They eventually made it to a bench and sat, arms around each other watching the water trickle into the pond.

When the pair started to feel hungry, they went back to the canteen. The afternoon menu stuck with its theme of the day. And today's theme was Steak House. Both girls had a tender rump steak with a large side of salad. Jennifer received many more congratulations from the canteen occupant's, even excepting a short, good luck speech from Supervisor Xander. Even though Jennifer had questioned his references to luck, Kara deflected them. They went back to they're room to pack everything up. They started with Jennifer's belongings, her clothing and books that used to sit on the now broken shelf. And several posters that she insisted on taking along.

Kara set out a change of clothing for the next day for them on the desk. A pair of cream leggings, a peach colour shirt and short jacket for Kara, while Jennifer had decided on green cargo trousers and a black T-shirt that Kara replaced with a black shirt. Along with her Hair straightener, the perfume and a makeup case for a light dressing up. Later when Kara had returned from handing in their flight suit's she crashed on the bottom bunk. Jennifer came back from the shuttle bay after collecting the flight roster and saw Kara resting on the bed. She placed the roster on the desk next to the shirt she had not chosen and cuddled into Kara on the bunk. With a couple of gentle groans and slow movements the two lay in an embrace.

Kara woke with her heart racing and her eyes wide. She jerked wildly; her body pulsed. She looked down in horror seeing Jennifer's face buried between her legs. She tried to speak but her head jerked back, and her body bucked.

"Jen..." She managed before her breath escaped in a groan of pleasure.

"Fa...Fuck." She grabbed Jennifer's head, pulling her in. She raised her legs and Jennifer help to push them further. Jennifer's mouth was magical between her legs.

Every micro movement threw tremors through her body. She bucked aggressively and pulsed rhythmically. She felt breathless but was able to groan louder and louder. Jennifer shifted her position, raising her mouth and Kara squealed. She struggled to control her legs as they jerked violently. Jennifer's tongue began quivering like a rattle snake and Kara yelled out.

"Oh, fuck!" Kara began beating the head of the bunk with her fists.

"Don't, don't stop! Oh, please don't stop!" Kara's back arched high, Jennifer squeezed her thigh's working aggressively. Kara's body began to pulse in rapid succession, and she grappled Jennifer's head again holding her there as she erupted. Heat washed over her as she washed over Jennifer. She released her grip, but Jennifer nibbled a little more, making Kara leap with the sensational ecstasy.

"Oh...My...Fuck...I...I...Jen...Wow," Kara struggled to articulate. She bucked and groaned as Jennifer gently took her reward. After a few more tantalising moments Jennifer slid off the bed and went to the toilet.

She came back and snuggled into Kara again who was still breathing heavily.

"Are you okay?" Jennifer asked sweetly. Kara smiled and nodded.

"You were incredible," Kara confessed. Opening her eyes at last she gazed at Jennifer.

"Well. What now?" Kara asked, and Jennifer smiled and cuddled into her blonde hair.

"Do you want to stay like this?"

"Yes, I couldn't be happier right now," Jennifer explained holding her tighter still. Kara gently ran her fingers through Jennifer's hair until they fell asleep.

Chapter 17: Orbit

It jerked and shuddered in the flickering light. It twisted its head scanning. It took steps, stumbling to the left. It wrenched and stepped again. It pricked up sniffing. It squished down and turned, it head leading like a serpent. It lurched forward in the corridor like being pulled by the waist. Torch light flashed across its path.

"Hey...you shouldn't be down here." A voice called. It stormed forward five paces and stopped. The torch light flashed across its face.

"Ms Green?" The man approached her, clothed in a light grey. His chest protected with padding.

"Ms, Green. The power need's recalibrating in this area. Come back tomorrow." It collapsed into a crossed legged sit.

The man jogged toward her.

"Ms Green? Are you okay?" he asked crouching in front. He swept her hair from her face. Shone the light. Eyes glaring black. Her mouth torn apart.

"Holy shit," he said tearing his radio link from his security belt. Both hands gripped his face. Finger's digging into cheeks and jaw. He couldn't move his mouth to speak. It hissed. His body shaking. It shrieked and ripped his jaw away in two chunks. He collapsed onto his back.

The body twitching on the ground. It crouched over him. It's face, close to his disfigurement. A thick, leathery black tentacle wriggled from the mouth. Licking and lapping at the mangled flesh and pooling blood. Its hand touched the body, still twitching. It pulled the padding from the body, slicing through the clothing and piercing the skin. It sniffed again. It's nose lowering to the groin. It hissed again. It sprang and erratically staggered away through the wavering light.

Captain Dietrich squeezed the bridge of his nose. He glanced up while a man in a light blue flight suit took a step up to his red leather chair.

"Oh, you're a life saver." The flight crew member handing him a glass of water with a small silver case. Dietrich took the glass as the man popped the case open revealing small pills.

"Remind me never to drink again will you." He muttered taking two and washing them down.

"Yes, sir, I will sir," the man said heading back to his terminal on the left. The bridge of the Euphoria was curved beneath the nose of the ship. It was teared in three levels. First level had piloting controls at three locations. The second tier supported communication, monitoring and external scanning. The third simply housed the Captain's chair. One chair on the second level to the far right was empty. Pavlov's chair. At that very moment, he was being trollied down to the docking bay ready for the first shuttle launch.

"U.S.C. has relayed our trajectory, Captain." The communication specialist said. Her blonde hair in a sloping bob, her face was long with a prominent nose and brown eyes.

"Thank you, Com specialist…Relay to helm," he ordered. She nodded sternly before tapping at the touch screen display above her chair. She turned her seat toward Saleem Toure the bald African man at the centre piloting terminal on her right. Keeping his eyes front he gave a thumbs-up and began typing information into a large panel of pre-determined instruction and optional keystrokes. The first pilot on the left, Nashi Khan, a slightly overweight Asian woman with a wide nose and the pilot on the right, a younger mixed-race man with a broad back and spiked brown hair named Asher Deshawn said. "Copy" simultaneously and they tapped at buttons, flicked switches, and moved levers.

"Orbital course locked in Captain." The central pilot confirmed.

"Take us home gentlemen," he said before pinching his nose again.

The Euphoria was positioned to catch earth's pull. Huge plumes of air erupted from its left side, locking the craft into its gravity well. The gravity well was a reference to its constant fall around the planet.

"We are in the sweet spot Captain." The central pilot announced.

"Excellent cruising gentlemen as always."

"Thank you, sir." The three-piloting crew said together.

"Broadcast ship wide, Com's specialist." Another acknowledging nod.

"Broadcasting ship wide Captain." She confirmed. Captain Dietrich sat back in his chair.

"This is the Captain speaking. All crew members…We're home. For those of you who leave us today. I thank you for your service and hope to see you again soon. Shuttles are ready to fly. God speed. Captain Dietrich out." He finished taking a breath. He rubbed his forehead. He stood and headed for the exit behind.

"Inform me of any resupply issues Com specialist," he said before leaving.

"Yes Captain," she replied. He stopped and gripped his head with both hands. He then walked slowly down the hallway.

In the docking bay, all shuttle doors where open and crew were loading in their luggage into their side compartments, while the group of pilots spoke together. Six of the twelve shuttles were a clean white, but the others had a variation of brown and green colouring. The Euphoria shuttles were the size of a pair of Tiger 2 tanks from world war two positioned end to end. They were shaped like a stretched turtle shell that had been forced into a paint can. Air jets positioned where the fins would be. The oval section at its rear housed two large jet thrusters that were characterised with scorched cones. A slim man with a long black beard approached them with a blue clip board under arm.

"Good morning, guys and gals, I trust you're all sober this morning," he said looking at the clip board. All twelve pilots confirmed they were good to go.

"Excellent…Okay uh. Briggs?"

"Yes sir."

"You have a special order from Luna. A Ms Farion. The new Flight navigator. Oh, and a Ms Kruse."

"Two ladies. You shouldn't have," Briggs said grinning.

"Yeah, I know I shouldn't, but this is the way it's gone…Shuttle six is yours." He studied the clip board.

"Shuttles one to five…David, Maggy and Roxy you're on Europe. Peterson and Alberto, you're on china and Japan. And the rest of you on North and south America."

"Mr Wells!" A voice called from the entryway. Mr Wells turned flicking through his notes. He glanced up and saw a young man of twenty years with moppy brown hair and pink streaks through it, shuffling toward him with two duffle bags.

"Aww crap…I forgot about those." Mr Wells said as the young man dropped the bags at his feet breathing heavily.

"The condolence cards. Alberto, you shuttle to Japan and Morgan, you take Grey's cards to Washington."

"Where do we deliver the cards?" Alberto asked.

"Leave them with the port manager and they will do the rest. Okay that's it. Get going. Fly by complete in one hour and twenty. Fly safe," he said before walking away with the tired man. All pilots held out a fist, knocking knuckles in a circle.

"Eighty minutes…Let's do this," Peterson said breaking the circle.

All pilot's and crew members got seated inside their shuttles. A green beacon flashed signalling all shuttles were sealed. The huge lengthy docking bay door opened, retracting into the floor and ceiling. The shuttles fired up, their air jets blasting. Each shuttle gently lifted and moved forward from one to twelve. Shuttle six elevated above the rest before turning left. All others turned right. With a bright burst of light, they accelerated. There were small blinking lights running along the ship as a warning of its presence to other ships. Each shuttle now disappearing into the darkness.

Rajiv opened his eyes to a clang. Then a sound of collapsing boxes. He threw his legs from the bed and stood. He stretched high and shook. He scratched his bare ass and stumbled to the bathroom door.

"Annabelle?" There was a mumbling response.

"Are you okay?" A high-pitched mumble. He gently touched the door and shoved it open. His eyes stretched widely by what he saw. Annabelle was in fresh underwear. A supportive bra and thin underwear that showed her rear cheeks. She turned to the right to spot him. White foamy liquid dripped from her mouth. Rajiv couldn't believe what he was seeing.

Annabelle spat into the sink.

"What?" She managed, lowering her toothbrush. Rajiv leaned on the door frame.

"You look so damn sexy," he said rubbing his tackle.

"Annabelle sensually rolled her eyes and continued to brush her teeth. He began to approach her, but she threw a hand up," she mumbled again shaking her head. Rajiv questioned her with his parted hands. She spat again.

"Rajiv, I'm really fucking late this morning." She sounded disappointed.

"Just tell them it was my fault," he said softly. Annabelle glared at him. She seemed irritated.

"We're not kids, Rajiv. I'm in big fucking trouble…Orbit day…and I slept late." She ranted, swilling her brush and storming past him.

"Hey?" Rajiv snapped, angered at her blanking him. She was opening her clothing draw when she slung back a look with another thrown up hand.

"Rajiv…Sugar. I don't have time for this right now."

"Time for me you mean." He pointed out. Annabelle closed her eyes and took a breath. She pulled a black pair of leggings from the draw, and she climbed into them. She jerked back pulled the tight leggings over her bottom. She darted toward a wardrobe door in the wall. She shoved it open. Out came a white shirt and a clip-on tie, short and wide.

Rajiv watched her fumbling at the buttons as she dressed.

"Pass me the jacket," she said scooping up a hair straightener. He glared to his left, where an apricot blazer jacket with chrome clasps hung.

"Rajiv!" She bit brushing her hair quickly. He strode to the jacket, wrenched it from the wall and threw it at her. She caught it against her chest.

"Why are you being like this?" she asked lobbing the straightener on to the couch.

"Why are you?" He threw back.

"Because I'm fucking late…Why is that so hard for you to understand!" She yelled.

"So, I'm stupid now," he said aggressively.

"No. I didn't say that," she said softly, slipping on the blazer.

"You implied it…And we both know you won't get in any trouble."

"What are you talking about? I should have been in the Captain's office ages ago," Annabelle pressed slipping on her heels.

"Oh, I forgot. Wouldn't want the Captain to miss his morning blow job!" Rajiv stabbed, stepping closer.

Annabelle's face dropped.

"What did you just say?" She said quickly but sharply.

"Aww come on Anna. Everybody knows he wants to fuck you," Annabelle launched her hand across Rajiv's face, almost knocking him over.

"Fuck you!" She shouted, bolting for the door. Rajiv lunged toward her grabbing her hand.

"What the fuck…I…" Rajiv words left him as Annabelle drove her knee up. It was an instinctive thrust not an attack. But that didn't change the force of behind it. His jaw dropped as his breath was taken. Annabelle rushed out as Rajiv dropped to the floor cupping himself.

A minute past before Rajiv bothered to move. Shocked by the event rather than the pain. He threw on yesterday's clothes and left for his own quarter's. After a left and right turn through the halls he reached the final corridor to his room. As he walked, he heard a voice. He stopped. The voice was crying. A man's voice.

"Yeah, I know what you mean," Rajiv said to himself before going. Rajiv thumbed his door and went inside. He stripped again and took a shower.

Back down the corridor. The man Rajiv heard crying was security guard Brooster and he was sat on the floor in his room. Tear's streamed down his face as he cradled his hand. It was massively inflamed with black puss leaking from a small bite mark. His legs shook rapidly. He rolled on to his right side, not releasing his excruciating hand. He tried to get to his feet, but his legs just flayed on the ground. Using his shoulders, he began wiggling across the floor toward his kitchenette. He was sweating profusely and gritting his teeth in pain. He reached with his good hand, opening a draw. He fumbled inside before pulling out a knife. He lay on the floor breathing faster and faster glaring between the blade and his swollen hand. He set his hand on the floor, he raised with blade high. He screamed and drove the blade down into his palm.

The blade was now buried, but the pain did not increase. He opened his eyes to see the damage. There was no blood. Just a black tar like gel, oozing from the hole. The shimmering black spread across the floor, it began slipping up the blade still in his hand. His shocked eyes slowly relaxed. His shaking stopped, his sweat fading away. His body began to jerk and twitch erratically. He lurched up into a crouch before looming to full height. He stretched his head back and released a glass shattering screech.

Chapter 18: Reposting

The following morning, the girls rose early, beaming with excitement. After both taking care of their morning essentials, Kara called Jennifer into the bathroom to join her in the shower. Kara smoothly stripped her of the clothing she'd slept in and crouched in front of her to pull her underwear down. She tenderly kissed her there before surprising her with a long lash of her tongue. Jennifer quivered with a groan and Kara stood. She hinted for Jennifer to strip her, although she wasn't wearing much. Kara was nude at the waist from that night. She held Jennifer on her head until she had supplied enough stimulation to make her legs shake. Stepping away she climbed into the shower. Getting the temperature right before offering her hand and luring Jennifer in. They washed each other thoroughly with gel and shampoo. The sensual situation became comical when Jennifer positioned herself near a drying jet for a down stair's blow dry. Kara followed suit and they both laughed hysterically until they were dry all over.

Kara returned to her case and added a second pair of her shape expressing underwear to their planned outfits demanding Jennifer wear them. They both dressed fully and Kara caressed Jennifer's rump explaining that her posterior was way more defined even in cargo trousers. She spun showing what her ass was like in her leggings and Jennifer greatly approved. Kara added a little purple eye shadow to pull out the green in Jennifer's hazel eyes and a pink lip stick to match her colourful hair. She shadowed her own eyes with a rustic bronze that made her eyes glow and touched her lips with a soft red just for fun.

It was time to get moving. They both moved quickly, only briefly saying their goodbyes to people along the way. They shuffled into to the shuttle bay where a tall, thin African man was waiting for them. He stepped away from the swampy green shuttle to greet them.

"I knew I was waiting for something special in my life…Had no idea it was beautiful ladies." The Man said holding out his hand. Jennifer sniggered walking past him and putting her case inside.

"It must be your lucky day," Kara mocked setting her case at his feet.

"Karabina Farion," she said expecting his hand. "And that's Jennifer Kruse." Nodding to the girl climbing into the shuttle.

"Elijah Briggs, at your service," Briggs announced bending to kiss Kara's hand.

"Easy Elijah Briggs." She pulled her hand away. "Stick to the pilot services," Kara said as she made her way past him to the shuttle door.

"Yes ma'am," Briggs nodding watching Kara walk.

"Hey, keep your eyes to yourself buddy," Jennifer warned leaning out from her seat.

Briggs raised his hands and bowed his head. He climbed into the shuttle checking the two women had harnessed correctly, taking a mental note that Kara had sensually crossed her legs when he'd looked at her. Briggs smiled at her with bulging eyes before he took his seat upfront. Briggs fitted his head set and completed his launched procedure and the shuttle lifted with jets of air. He manoeuvred the shuttle round one-eighty and activated the shuttle bay door. The sound of the thrusters became a distant echo as the shuttle glided forward and out into the empty atmosphere. The shuttle skirted the ground to the right three hundred metres before climbing.

"Are you ladies looking forward to your new posting?" Briggs asked.

"Yes, we're very excited," Kara replied leaning forward as far as the harness aloud.

"What's the crew like?" Jennifer asked.

"I don't know everyone extremely well, but their all-good people. I mean there are almost two hundred people aboard." Brigg's explained.

"How so many?" Kara inquired.

"Divisions. We've got a lot going on aboard the Euphoria. R and D projects, science and medical advancements and trials and engineering crews that maintain the ship and evaluate the R and D ideas," Briggs listed glancing back twice.

"What happened to your Navigations officer?" Jennifer asked.

"Honestly, I don't know. He got sick, fever you know. So medical quarantined him until we returned to earth. He's heading home as we speak."

They continued in silence for a short while before there was a mumbling sound through Briggs's headset.

YOU ARE APPROACHING THE USC EUPHORIA. IDENTIFY AND STATE YOUR PURPOSE. A male voice spoke.

"USC Euphoria this is shuttle six on a return from Luna…Transmitting Ident code…Now," Briggs replied.

CODE ACCEPTED SHUTTLE SIX. PROCEED TO DOCKING BAY FOUR…WELCOME BACK BRIGGS. The voice replied.

Lights along a section of the Euphoria came to life. They streamed across the haul toward docking bay to guide the way. There were scattered lighting all over the huge cylindrical hull, but the running lights were much brighter. The strip lighting began to zip around the airlock door and the running lights faded. The shape and size of the ship became more prominent without the glare of light. The upper section of the ship was smooth like the back of a blue whale, but it was a blend of deep green and rustic brown. The underside was more complex with inverted towers and signal dishes. The rear narrowed near the end before opening out too its four monstrous thrusters. The outer rim of the thrusters radiated with a glow of intense heat.

As their shuttle approached the bay door parted like an opening mouth, its huge thick doors interlocking with the hull. Slowing the Shuttle, Briggs used small air thrusts to move inside. Clanging echoed through the bay. The ship cricked like it was straining or even twisting as the shuttle touched down. The high bay walls looked mouldy grey with strategic neon light sources on the ceiling and over the loading doors to the left.

Briggs shut down the shuttle. He removed his headset and harness while the women unstrapped themselves.

"There you go ladies. Welcome to the USC Euphoria," Briggs announced unsealing the shuttle door.

Chapter 19: Meeting

Rajiv killed the shower blower and stepped out feeling brand new. He picked out a change of clothing and dressed. He buttoned up a fresh white lab coat and stepped out. He glared around him since several crew members stood at their doors. One woman stared at him. He brushed his hair with his hand scowling back at her before heading down the corridor. He strolled through the halls until he reached an elevator and thumbed the panel.

The elevator door opened, and Annabelle stepped out on to the Bridge Deck level. She carried a thick folder under her arm and walked quickly toward the Captain's office. She took several deep breaths before thumbing the panel. The buzz echoed with an immediate response.

"Come in." The door opened and she leapt inside.

"I am so, so sorry Captain. It will never happen again I prom…"

"Is that my folder?" Captain Dietrich cut her off. She quickly moved to his side and placed it in front of him. He glared up at her, she leaned in again and opened the cover.

"Everything is on schedule Captain. Resupply has been hard docked, and our Navigational officers are on their way." She explained professionally.

"Officers?" he questioned.

Annabelle shrugged. "Something regarding a package deal."

"Fine. Anything else I should know?" He said formally flicking through the pages.

"Mr Tousi asked to see you again…I told him not today."

"And why did you tell him, not today Ms Brooks." he asked, focused on the pages. *Great he's really pissed.*

"Because today is Orbital, Captain." He spun his chair toward her.

"Today is Orbital. And Orbit is the most vital day is it not?" he said glaring up at her.

"You don't have to do this Stefan? I know I mess…" Stefan leapt from his chair and towered over her. Annabelle squeezed her eyes shut.

The Captain swayed past her. She opened her eyes.

"You think I'd hit you? Is that it," he said pacing.

"Of course not, but I know your angry," she said stepping toward him.

"Angry…I am so far past angry. Everyone makes mistakes Anna, but on this day…Never again…Never." He gripped his temple.

"Do you realise the only late staff on today's roster is you…And that Rave boy," he continued; Annabelle stood straight.

"Are you angry because I'm late? Or because I have feelings for someone else?" she asked sternly. The Captain froze mid stride.

"I'm angry because of the day! Not some piss ant undergrad!" He fired.

"You don't like him do you!" She fired back.

"Why would I…The boy's a pussy."

"Pussies are tough and durable. They can push out a baby and take a beating from a dick! But balls. Big brave balls are weak and fragile. And retreat from danger," Annabelle's statement killed his anger.

"Your way out of his league," he told her moving close to her.

"Spoken like a real daddy," she whispered.

"Don't mock me girl," he said rising above her.

"I'm not mocking you. You are acting like my daddy and not my Captain right now."

"I am always the Captain."

"Well, there's still time…Fire me Captain." She pushed. Stefan stepped back in shock.

"You don't mean that. You don't want me to fire you." He guessed, folding his arms.

"No, I don't…But I don't think you'd let me go if I did."

"Are you done Ms Brooks? Don't you have arrivals to greet?" He said firmly, changing the subject. *Just as I thought.*

"Captain," Annabelle nodded before quickly leaving and marched down the corridor toward the elevator. *Rajiv was right. He's angry because he doesn't have all my attention anymore. He said I'm like a daughter. More like a trophy.*

Rajiv stepped cautiously toward the laboratory doors. The doors were jammed open with the white light of the room blinking into the dark hallway. He moved close to the wall on the door side. He sidestepped quietly toward the edge.

He rolled a shoulder and peeked inside. The computer terminals had been thrown and the desks had been cracked, their displays barely flickering. Droplets of scarlet liquid scattered from the doorway and around to the cages. Rajiv followed the trail with his eyes. *Is that leading in or out*. He closed his eyes and shuddered. He took a breath and stepped into the room. He froze after a single step. He could see the cages had been torn apart and worst still, sullied with the same scarlet liquid. That metallic smell gripped his nostrils, closely followed by the stench of death.

"Green?" Rajiv whispered taking another step. He began to sidestep across the room keeping his distance from the cages. The microscope station caught his eye. Smashed petri dishes decorated the area. The scope had been ripped from its moorings. *Oh fuck no*. Rajiv found what remained of the microscope. It had been thrown inside the box that housed the organism. The floor around the base of the cages was a puddle of blood. *Fuck this*. Rajiv stepped back slowly before lunging for the door. He slipped slightly on the blood splats as he rounded the doorway and ran.

Annabelle sat in the lounge across from the login desk. Mr Wells was sat behind the desk of the departure were Briggs usually sat. Annabelle knew Wells was not the playful type that Briggs was, so she sat quietly watching the man stroke his black beard. He was fully engrossed in the computer terminal he manned. Annabelle had even tempted a response with a fake cough while arching her back to push out her chest. *Not even a glance, boring*. Annabelle was a professional but liked to have fun. Beside she was just bored now. She flicked through the binder on the chair beside her. She scanned the arrival's details for the ninth time keeping everything fresh. She closed it quickly when she recognised the sound of the docking bay doors opening.

Finally. She stood and straightened her skirt and closed up her jacket to just over her bust. *No chance of doing it all the way*. She could hear the thrusters on the shuttle manoeuvring and setting down. She stood at the door to the bay and glanced over her shoulder at Wells. He still hadn't lifted his head. She rolled her eyes, but then Wells tapped a button without looking and the door opened. Annabelle stepped over the frame and walked confidently toward the now open shuttle.

She saw a slender blonde and an almost as fit rainbow. Briggs was bringing out their cases and the rainbow hair girl took one from him before he could put it down. The blonde girl stood patiently, watching Briggs remove the second case and set it down at her feet. He laid the case at her feet and slowly looked up, checking the goods as he rose. *Yeah, I see you Briggs.* Annabelle thought.

"Good flight Mr Briggs?" Annabelle said abruptly breaking his gaze.

"Hey, Be…Ms Brooks," Annabelle nodded in approval.

"Hello ladies," she announced offering a hand. The blonde accepted and then so did the rainbow girl.

"I am Annabelle Brooks. Captain Dietrich's personal assistant."

"Hello." The blonde replied, rainbow smiled.

"Which one is Karabina Farion?"

"That's me. Kara," she said setting the handle on her case.

"And that makes you Jennifer Kruse. Yes?"

"That's me."

"Excellent. Briggs will take your cases to your quarters. This way please," Annabelle said strolling across the bay. Kara left her case on the ground. Jennifer reluctantly dropped hers and followed Annabelle.

"Stop staring Briggs," Annabelle said loudly walking away. Briggs smirked picking up the cases. Jennifer shot him a look.

"Stares at you too huh?" Jennifer said still staring him down.

"Oh, he's harmless. Good as gold in fact, once you know how to work him." She smiled. Kara laughed out loud.

"You know the rules too huh?" Kara suggested. Annabelle smiled continuing forward.

"Every woman should," Annabelle said sending them through to the lounge ahead.

"Well, I don't," Jennifer sniggered as she passed. Annabelle smile politely. *Miserable bitch.*

In the lightless hallway, Rajiv felt his way toward the elevator. Holding both arms out to his right his fingers caressed the white indents in the padded wall. He lurked forward when his hands past a corner of the wall. Regaining his balance, he stared widely in the darkness. In the distance to his left, he made out the faint glow of the elevator light panel. He began fumbling toward the source, reaching out to the wall methodically. He thumbed the panel, he backed to the side wall as the door's opened. He peeked in. Empty. He slipped inside and scanned the floor numbers, while peeking at the open doors. Captain's office, or bridge. Office is on the way. Office first then bridge.

He thumbed the second level and the doors closed. Rajiv slumped back against the back wall, taking a moment. His focus shot up as the elevator screeched. He lurched of the wall, throwing his arms out to steady himself as the elevator stopped with a mucky thud. He glared at the floor, ensuring the elevator wouldn't move again. Cold liquid tapped the back of his head and neck. He slapped at his neck and leapt back to the wall. A trickle of red in front. He studied his hand, smeared with red. This can't be real it…He followed the trickle to an escape hatch above. *No way, he would reach it alone. Why the fuck would you want to. Fuck knows what is up there.*

Annabelle guided Kara and Jennifer through arrival procedure with the help of Mr Well's. Both newcomers slipped into navy blue trousers with matching jackets to convey their flight crew status before leaving the lounge area. Annabelle apologised for the insufferable air seal doors they had to get through before they reached the nearest elevator.

"I'll take you to the Captain's office and he will take you to the bridge," Annabelle said pushing the elevator panel.

"Wonderful. Can't wait to meet him," Kara said happily.

"What's the Captain like?" Jennifer asked.

"The kindest, yet firmest man you'll ever meet," Annabelle said smiling. She scowled. The elevator panel turned red with a beep, beep.

"That's odd," Annabelle said pressing it again. Nothing happened. Annabelle shrugged.

"The engineer's must be preforming maintenance…We'll catch another, this way," Annabelle said before leading them down the corridor.

Rajiv smashed the emergency open on the panel to no avail. He held down the comm.

"Hello? Maintenance? I'm stuck in elevator…five. Hello?" Rajiv explained after checking the elevator number, since he had no sight when he had got in. There was no response. He paced in the cramped space for a moment, His skin warming up, his heart rate accelerating. He leapt at the door and threw his fists against it.

"Help me! I'm in here!" He yelled. A howling screech rang outside the doors and he launched backward. *Oh my god…What the hell was that?* He heard scuttling movement in the hallway ahead. There was a smash against wall panelling with more erratic movement. Rajiv shifted into a corner.

Chapter 20: Confusion

Ellis and his team strolled down a corridor on deck eight, all three of them were tooled up with drill guns, sockets, and spanners. The corridor was dim at their end, but sparks leapt from a control panel ahead. Two Technicians stood at the panel, both men had their faces shielded with face plates. One man was hunched over, guided a blow torch over the panel while the second watched.

"Hey guys?" Ellis called out. Then men stopped and lifted their visors.

"Hey Ellis," the rear man said.

"There's something wrong with elevator eight," he explained.

"And you guys are stumped. What a surprise," Hayes said grinning.

"It's not a technical fault. The controls are fine. We think there's a blockage in the shaft," the torch welder said.

"Jesus Christ. Talk about the shit detail," Hayes complained.

"Alright, alright let's just get in there...Cheers fellas," Ellis said before leading his team to the elevator. Ellis pressed the panel and the doors opened. Hayes leapt in, swung to the number control, and flicked a switch. The green panel in the hall changed to red and Luca stepped inside. He stretched on his tip toes and turned the hatch handle above. The door swung down, and Luca recoiled, covering his nose with the back of his hand.

"What's up with...Holy shit, that's fucking rank," Hayes said as the smell slapped her nose. Ellis took out a torch and Shon the light upward.

"Damn. There must be something dead up there," he said covering his own mouth and nose.

"Like what? A rodent from the lab maybe?" Luca suggested. Luca looked at Hayes.

"No fucking way." She snapped. Ellis turned to her.

"It's your turn Chelsey."

"How'd you figure that."

"We took Pavlov to medical remember," Luca added.

"That wasn't part of our job though."

"It was still a dirty job," Luca pressed.

"Agreed," Ellis said looking up through the hatch.

"Alright. Fine," Hayes said moving to the opening. She lifted her foot and Luca took it. As she reached up, Luca thrusted her up into the opening. She pulled herself in the rest of the way.

"Oh, God. I hate you guys."

"Yeah, you keep telling us," Ellis said offering up his torch. Laying on her stomach she leaned back through taking it. She rolled onto her back and stood. Luca turned on his torch, shinning it up. Hayes set the torch down for a moment before applying her thick work gloves. She moved around the edge of the elevator aiming her torch beam.

"I can't see any obstruction around here."

"What about the cable?" Ellis suggested. She shone the light over it. The cable was more reflective than normal. Hayes ran her hand down it and inspected her glove.

"Yeah, there's definitely blood on the cabling."

"So, where's the source?" Ellis asked. Hayes shone the torch, seeing a far as she could into the darkness.

"I can't tell from here. Don't make me climb the shaft," she said kneeling over the opening.

"Nah, we don't have our rigging for the harnesses anyway," Ellis said, putting her mind at rest. She sat, with her legs through the hatch.

"So, what do we do?" she asked before dropping back into the elevator.

"Take another one up to the top and check wheels?" Luca asked closing the hatch.

"Yeah, sounds good," Ellis said shutting off his torch.

Rajiv slumped in the corner of the elevator. His head resting on his knees with his arms wrapped around. He had been sat in silence for fifteen minutes, the trickling liquid had slowed to a drip. He lifted his head, realising the quiet. He slowly stood and stretched. He regarded the door. He pushed his fingers into the parting the best he could. He managed to pull the doors apart an inch and a half before he let go. *Fuck.* They closed again. Rajiv sat on the floor and pulled off his left shoe. He set it against the seam of the doors. He gripped and pulled again.

As he made the same parting, he kicked at his left shoe jamming it in the breach. He released and the shoe held. He wriggled his fingers to bring the feeling back before fully gripping the doors and pulled again. The doors opened to a foot wide before he stopped. There was no spring back. *Oh, thank god.* There was flicking dim light at his feet, he knelt. A line of light came through the outer door. He looked down the outer door and began removing his belt.

Turning it buckle down, he slowly lowered it. Almost halfway down, he hooked the buckle over a thin lever that ran off to the side. He pulled. Nothing happened. He knelt back on his ankles and squeezed his face. *Fuck.* Rajiv straightened and looked again, tilting his head slightly to the left along the run of the lever. Ha huh. He stretched his whole arm inside and wrenched his arm to the right in a swinging motion and the lever gave a comforting clunk.

Annabelle slammed the underside of her fist on the elevator panel in frustration. The panel flashed red. Annabelle closed her eyes and took a deep breath. Looking back at the two women behind her she smiled.

"I'm terribly sorry about this. It's never happened before," Annabelle said politely.

"Four elevators are down?" Jennifer said bewildered.

"Where are the staircases?" Kara asked trying to find options. Annabelle shrugged.

"We don't have any. We have emergency ladders."

"So, where are they?" Jennifer asked. Before Annabelle spoke, Kara interjected.

"They're in the elevator shafts aren't they."

"Yes, they are," Annabelle confirmed.

"So, what do we do?" Jennifer asked impatiently.

"We need to open the doors somehow. We head back to the Docking bay for some tools, or we get on comms," Annabelle explained.

"Either way, it's back to the Docking bay, yes?" Kara confirmed. Annabelle nodded and the three women began walking back the way they came.

Hayes jerked up through the hatch of elevator seven and stood. She flicked on the torch again and scanned. She turned and dropped to a knee, Ellis came through the opening, and she lurched onto her back pulling him in. He dropped onto her, his head on her stomach.

"Sorry Chels," he said quickly getting up. He helped her back to her knee and they both reached down. This time they pulled together, struggling, and grunting Luca slowly came through the hatch on to his upper body. He wriggled his legs up, the others on their backs breathing heavily.

"If I didn't know you better," Luca laughed, getting to his feet.

"Shut up," Hayes said rolling away to her knees.

"I'm definitely complaining to Markov later. No way all the lifts can be out," Ellis said standing. They scanned their caged surroundings for a moment.

"Alright, Chelsey you go first."

"Why me?" She snapped. Ellis glared at her.

"If you fall, we can catch you."

"Oh, fair enough," she said fitting her gloves. She slipped her torch under the left lapel on her flight suit and started to climb the shaft cable. Ellis started behind, followed closely by Luca. The torch light struggled to penetrate the darkness. Hayes climbed slowly; she pulled her arms in tightly as they shivered.

"Say if you need to stop Chels," Luca called up.

"I'm good. It's fucking freezing in here," she said explaining her pace. The sound of their boots echoed around the shaft.

"How many decks, to the shuttle bay?" Luca asked.

"Five decks," Ellis told him as they climbed.

"Fuck. Can't we get out sooner?" Hayes asked.

"The shuttle bay has a nearest direct line to the bridge," Ellis explained.

Rajiv slowly pushed into the breach. His head peeking into the hallway. He gripped his mouth and recoiled. He heaved but did not vomit. He looked again. The opening was high in the corridor and as he looked to the floor, he saw the lower half of a body, the legs twitching. The intestines stretching toward the elevator. The white walls had been plastered in blood and fleshy clumps of human remains. He could make out limbs from varying uniform colours spread around the corridor and beyond. *This must be the habitation deck. How long was I in the Lab?* Rajiv slowly turned inside the elevator and slipped his legs through. He turned his body halfway through and dropped to the floor. His feet flew from under him as he slammed onto his back in a pool of gunk. He glanced to his left, he grimaced at the half body beside him and rolled away slowly. His breath gone from his lungs. *Again.*

He settled on his hands and knees before taking a good breath. He crawled to the wall across from him and used the padding to get to his feet. He held onto the wall and stepped slowly. He reached a turn in the corridor and rounded it and froze. Blood and entrails had decorated the corridor but that is not what stiffened him. Several metres along was a man that held the head of another person. His left leg had been torn away from the outer thigh to his knee. Two thick black lines occupied the space where his muscle had been.

The bone of the left elbow was protruding through the skin, but he didn't seem to notice. Then Rajiv realised the arm was bending the wrong way, they both were. In fact, the whole body was away from the body it held, apart from the head. It's back, well its chest was extremely inflamed. It jerked like someone fighting for oxygen in water. Thin lashing black tentacles flicked over the head it held rapidly, with an outer ring of larger appendages. These hooked tentacles tore flesh away, shoving them into a gaping hole where it's face had been. The inflated chest burst open with a split from collarbone to navel. Pusy black goo, trickled out like an unravelling tongue.

The balling puss began to shape and solidify. There were spikes forming on its 'back'. The hands flinched and the tentacles withdrew as the head dropped to the floor. It lurched up and shuddered. The tentacled head flung up with a screech. The body lurched backward, or forward toward Rajiv a few steps before it flung its arms around to turn 'It the right way'. Rajiv leapt from the corner as the creature slashed its now elongated fingers at the wall where he'd stood. Chucks of wall padding flung from the wall as Rajiv made off down the corridor.

Captain Dietrich wiped his brow. He stared at his fingers, sweat shining on them. He blew out a breath and unzipped his flight suit to his waist. He rubbed the sweat from his palm on to his thigh. He tapped at his call panel. The beeping began. After almost a minute a male voice responded.

"Yes Captain?"

"Who am I speaking with?" Dietrich asked the responder.

"Romiley, Captain."

"Where's Kwan?"

"Her shift has ended Captain…I'm on Comms now."

"Fine, Fine. Put me through to Page please Romiley," he said wiping his brow again.

"Yes, Captain," Romiley replied. From his station on the second level of the bridge he pushed two buttons on his console.

"What's up?" Page said into the Comm, she was within ear shot at her console the opposite side of the room.

"Captain's waiting."

"Copy that," Page acknowledged while pressing her on controls. She quickly organised her displays, moving each monitoring information blocks on her screen so all where easily accessible. Romiley redirected the Captain's office to her Comm.

"Good day Captain…Page on Monitoring," Page said, sitting up right but patiently.

"Page, I want a diagnostic on environmental's…It's getting Hot in my office," Dietrich told her pulling his flight suit down off his shoulders. Page began working her fingertips on the keys.

"Yes Captain, right away," Page scanned her blocks rapidly, finding the environmental block. She studied the charts and read out there.

"Environmental's are all in the green Captain…Searching for other possibilities," Page quickly told him. The Captain stood and moved round his desk to the right. He waved his palm along the wall. A hidden shelf flipped down; a plume of cool air sailed into the room. The shelf extended.

"Water," the Captain said. After the sound of a working mechanism, a short glass of water was revealed in a steel hoop. He extracted the glass and threw it back.

"Water," he said again after replacing the glass.

"Captain. I've found amber warnings on the Hydroponics block. Several duct ways are showing blockages. Air purity is good through out, but the circulation fans are struggling. I'll inform maintenance and…"

Dietrich spun to the desk.

"And what?"

"Elevators are down," she continued, confusion in her voice.

"Page?" Dietrich called after a few seconds of silence.

"Yes, Captain?"

"How many are down?"

"Huh…All of them," Page said. Dietrich grimaced and swung round to his chair and sat.

"That's not possible Page…What is going on? Do you have a board malfunction?" He insisted leaning on his elbows.

"I've run a full diagnostic Captain. All board is good. We have one elevator locked out on twelve. All others are locked out on three," Dietrich launched from his chair and made for the door.

"I'm on my way. Get everyone on this now," he said before leaving the room.

Annabelle led the new arrivals back to the shuttle bay, when they were back inside the departure area Annabelle scanned the room quickly, but there were no occupants. She moved for the hanger door.

"Wait here," Annabelle said quickly pointing toward the waiting chairs as she moved. She thumbed the door and raced through. Neither woman sat and Kara moved round the desk they had just registered at.

"What are you doing?" Jennifer asked her, approaching the near side. Kara had already began tapping keys at the closest terminal.

"I'm learning how all this works," she said scanning the screen. Jennifer spun from the desk back to the several air seal doors. There was a clung, then a light tapping, and another clung.

"What the hell is that?" Jennifer said shifting to the side wall. Kara looked up from the terminal as the tapping continued.

"Someone could be in trouble," Kara suggested, and Jennifer shrugged. *Fuck sake.* Kara moved from the desk to the doors and began making her way through. Jennifer followed closely behind. They stepped cautiously into the hall, moving toward the tapping sound that would temporarily get louder. They moved further down the hall from their arriving direction.

"I think this is a bad idea," Jennifer whispered behind. Kara rolled her eyes.

"If someone needs help. We help them right. Let's make an impression."

"Seems you already have," Jennifer sniggered. Kara stopped and turned.

"What's that supposed to mean?" Kara questioned; her eyes wide.

"You know that pilot guy," Jennifer said sheepishly.

"Are you kidding me…"

A loud clung startled Kara as the elevator door beside her, jolted open. She stepped back toward the piped wall, as did Jennifer. They looked through the gap and downward to spot a woman looking at them. She had a bewildered look on her face for a moment before throwing out a dirty hand.

"You mind giving me a hand?" Hayes asked. Kara and Jennifer shifted from the wall and assisted her ascend into the hallway.

"Fuck me what a climb," Hayes said, her torch light flashing in their eyes. They watched the girl turn and bend back to the opened doors. She glanced back at the pair.

"Come on, help me here." She gestured with her head. The girls stepped in again and saw the man Hayes was attempting to pull up. Kara took the left hand of the man and heaved. The man stood straight, and Kara stepped back in shock.

The Man paused for a moment. He smiled at her, then turned away to help Hayes pull Luca in.

As Luca stood, he saw Jennifer staring up at him. He couldn't tell if she was amazed or terrified. Hayes spotted the stare off and intervened.

"Don't worry miss. This mountain of a man is Luca. He's harmless. And this is…"

"Nathan?" Kara interrupted. He smiled happily at her. Hayes and Luca realised who the girl was.

"How are you?" Ellis asked, his face reddening.

"So, this is the famous Karabina," Luca said, putting Ellis even more on the spot. Ellis gaze darted downward; his skin bright now. He looked at her again and stumbled slightly as Kara launched her arms around him.

"I can't believe this. I thought I'd never see you again," Kara admitted, her eyes filling. Ellis squeezed his arms around her, tucking his head to her shoulder.

"It's good to see you," Ellis said softly. Hayes and Luca turned and pressed against each other, both cocking a leg.

"Awwwww." They mocked in unison. Ellis glanced at his colleagues.

"Yeah, Yeah…Who's your friend?" he asked catching Jennifer's unimpressed glare. Kara released and stroked her hair shyly.

"This is Jennifer Kruse. We met on Luna a few days ago," Kara explained.

"How come you're down here?" Ellis asked Kara.

"Elevators don't work," Jennifer said coldly looking him up and down, making it painfully obvious that it in her eyes it was his fault, being an engineer.

"They're all down," Hayes threw in thumbing back at the open shaft.

"They were all out when you arrived?" Luca asked surprised.

"Yes, we came back to the shuttle bay to contact the bridge," Kara explained.

"Where's Bebe?" Luca asked glancing round.

"Bebe?" Jennifer said sarcastically.

"Annabelle," Hayes corrected.

"Oh, she went into the hangar…Why Bebe?" Kara asked. While Luca was raising his hands to display large breasts, Hayes elbowed his ribs.

"Because she buzzes round the ship like a Bee," Hayes said, eye balling Luca.

"You said the hanger?" Ellis checked.

Chapter 21: Chaos

Rajiv ran through the corridors; his breath was short and shallow as he ran. The high squeal of the creature behind gave urgency. But not control. He turned for a bend in the corridor and missed. He flung forward into a dive and slammed his rib cage into the far corner of his turn. He crumpled to his knees, clutching himself around the mid-section. He glanced to the right. The creature was stumbling and shuddering toward him like a drunken monkey. The body was still moving in a backward motion, its arms flailing in the air. The only thing that seemed to have full control was the tentacle filled face. Its mouth limbs stretched and tugged at the air, never touching each other.

All Rajiv thought about was the pain. The lack of air in his lungs. *Three fucking times now*. He tucked his head in for a moment. *Stay there and let it kill you*. He gritted his teeth and growled. *The most important person in your life…Is you!* His feet slipped on the blood slick floor, but he moved. The creature lunged at the corner where he lay. Its face opened widely and split its self-open upon the corner of the wall. It let out a gargling squeal as black oil splashed outward from the corners of its mouth. The tentacles shook violently as it slumped to the floor.

He sat on the ground clutching his ribs, staring at the creature. Black liquid oozed from its cave of a mouth. Slowly but steadily, he climbed to his feet. He bent slightly, he coughed. His own blood joined the rest. He wiped his lips across his sleeve. The creature lurched up, reaching for him from its prone position. It's razor claw like fingers tearing into the floor at his feet.

Rajiv hobbled down the corridor, moving as quick as his ribs would allow. The creature stumbled and wrenched it's self on to its feet as it continued to lurch forward. More black bards extending and attaching. Repairing and extending its jaw size. The parade of tentacle fingers increase in the opening. With his slower pace, he was able to round a second corner without falling. He quickly chose a door and slapped the panel. As it opened, he fell inside.

Annabelle stepped slowly across the shuttle bay. There was nobody around that she could see.

"Where is everyone?" she said aloud scanning around crate stacks from the earlier re-supply. She paused. Looking over toward the shuttle, she could see a large grey duffel bag on the ground near the nose of the shuttle. She scanned again before moving toward the bag. *Oh no.* She broke into a run toward the front of the shuttle. *Oh god no.* Annabelle quickly realised her mistake. There was no bag, there were legs in grey trousers. *No, a grey flight suit.* She reached the front and rounded it. There was a large man on the ground, blood oozing from the back of his head. She crouched and pushed at his shoulder, turning the large frame slightly she realised it was Mr Wells.

"Mr Wells? Can you hear me?" she asked touching his cheek. She released him, covering her mouth. Her eyes began to weep. His skin was freezing to touch, and she knew Mr Wells was dead. Then her face dropped as another realisation set in. *Someone has hit him…Someone has killed Mr Wells.*

From her crouched position, she erratically searched the room for the attacker. One of the smaller crates toppled from its spot to her one o'clock direction. She shifted into the nose of the shuttle, being careful not to stand over the body of Mr Wells. After a moment, a man emerged from the crating area. *How the hell did I not see him?* He was wearing a dirty flight suit and was carrying a rectangular silver box by a fixed black handle. Annabelle's eyed went wide. *COLE!* He approached the shuttle at its side door and thumbed the control. The door slid open, and Cole climbed inside. Annabelle quietly slipped off her shoes. Keeping one as a weapon, she began tiptoeing toward the opening. *How the fuck is he out of the brig?*

Just short of the opening now she considered climbing in behind him. *No, I need to?* She launched her shoe across the bay, it hit the stack of crates where Cole had come from. Almost instantly Cole stuck his head out of the door glaring toward the crates. Annabelle leapt at him and threw her left arm around his neck. Keeping her legs up, she pulled him down into a crouch.

"What have you done! You son of a bitch!" She screamed into his ear. Cole grabbed her around the legs and lurched back, slamming her head and shoulders into the side of the shuttle. She slumped to the cold floor onto her right hip. Cole reached down, grabbing her at the collar of her jacket he wrenched her to her feet and pushed her into the shuttle wall again.

Annabelle drove her knee up into his groin. Cole's hips shot back from the force and releasing her with one hand. Cole quickly raised his fist and punched her face. His knuckles ploughing into her mouth. Both her lips split against her teeth as her head smashed hard into the shuttle wall. Blood fell from her mouth. She felt dazed and tired. She slumped to the floor, this time on her backside.

"Bitch!" Cole yelled down at her before throwing his own foot into her crotch.

Annabelle let out a deep groan and dropped onto her right side. Cole grabbed her left arm and bottom of her jacket and jerked back sharply. Annabelle was flung across the bay floor into a slide on her right shoulder. Cole stepped back into the shuttle. On the threshold, he stopped. He turned to face her. Annabelle was slowly rolling on to her front and pushing up.

"Aww for fuck sake!" Cole growled storming toward her again. Annabelle slumped down again. Cole grabbed her left arm and tugged her onto her back. He grabbed her throat. Annabelle threw her arms and legs up around his head. She squeezed with all she had. The pressure broke his strangle hold. He pushed his other arm into her vice grip and gripped her jacket with both hands. He jerked his body up with a roar. He lifted her to chest height before rammed her into the floor. Annabelle let out a howl as the air escaped her lungs and she went limp.

A large boot sole rammed into Cole's face. The tremendous force knocked him unconscious, and he launched backward onto the ground. Annabelle opened her eyes to see a large man march past her before Hayes appeared over her.

"Anna? Fuck. Anna, can you hear me?" Hayes said quietly, kneeling beside her.

"Luca don't!" Ellis called out running to the front of the shuttle where Mr Wells lay. Luca was standing over Cole. Blind rage in his eyes. He was going to kill the unconscious Cole.

"Kara!" Ellis shouted, pointing toward his huge colleague. Jennifer joined Hayes at Annabelle's head. Kara ran to Luca and grabbed his muscular arm.

He turned sharply; Kara stepped back.

"Don't. We need to know what happened," Kara said calmly. Luca glared back at his victim before roughly nodding a response. After a second, Luca took a calming breath. Kara nodded back, thanking him for his control before joined Hayes and Jennifer.

"Is she alive?" Kara asked getting on the floor too.

"Yes. I don't think anything is broken," Hayes said, feeling around her limbs. "But she definitely hurting."

Annabelle coughed, blood lurching from her mouth. Jennifer and Hayes helped her to a sitting position as the blood ran down her chin. Annabelle slowly moved her hand and gently touched her mouth. She winced.

"Fuck," she mumbled opening her eyes.

"Are you okay?" Jennifer asked rubbing her back.

"No…Where's Cole?" she replied quietly.

"He's still out."

Annabelle glanced up to see Luca crouching at her feet.

"Are you alright Bebe?" Annabelle tried to smile but winced instead.

"We need to get her to medical," Hayes said addressing Luca. Then Ellis returned, his head low.

"What is it?" Kara asked, everyone waiting.

"Wells is dead," Luca turned sharply to Cole, but Ellis grabbed his arm.

"The Captain needs to know about this," Ellis explained.

"Yeah, so he can kill him," Hayes added looking at Annabelle's busted lips.

"Okay. Okay. Luca take that piece of shit back to the brig and find out what's happened over there," Ellis began. Luca nodded stepping toward Cole.

"Hayes and Kara, go with him."

"Sure."

"No problem."

"Huh. It is a problem," Jennifer said looking at Kara, then glaring at Ellis.

"Hey. We don't have time for this Jen. I'll be fine."

"I'm going to need you to help get Bebe to medical," Ellis finished.

"Okay. Fine," Jennifer said now glaring at Kara. Ellis moved round and took Hayes's position and he and Jennifer slowly helped Annabelle to her feet.

Before Hayes and Kara were near Luca, he had Cole over his shoulder. Standing like the man weighed nothing at all. Kara was taken aback and smiled.

"He's a bear," Hayes threw in and they started to head out behind the other three.

Captain Dietrich waded into the command centre, the heavy blast door closing behind him. All crew turned in their chairs hoping for leadership. He scanned the faces of his crew from left to right.

"Romiley? Have you called in the engineering teams?"

"Yes Captain. The team's I was able to reach are investigating the elevators and hydroponics," Romiley replied. Dietrich looked at him puzzled.

"The one's you could reach?" He pressed. Romiley shifted nervously in his chair.

"Yes Captain. We have several crews missing," Dietrich spun round to glare at Page at the Monitoring station on the right side of the room.

"Page? Info?" Page was a mid-thirties woman with dark skin, thick lips and brown eyes. Her hair had been tied back, bringing all her dark braided hair together.

"Yes Captain. I pulled up the bio-monitors and we have many offline. We have Ellis's crew near the shuttle bay, but the off duties should be around the Hab…but their gone," Page explained turning back to her screen as Dietrich barrelled toward her.

"People don't disappear. Or go offline. Faulty connection?" The Captain asked her bending toward her terminal. Page brought up the bio-monitor screen and maximised the view.

"If there was a fault, we'd be showing offline too. But were all in the green." She looked up at him.

"There's only one active bio-mon on the Hab deck…Rajiv Mody," she continued, concern deep in her eyes.

He thought for a moment. *Annabelle!*

"Locate Miss Brooks," he barked and Page quickly tapped the keyboard.

"Shuttle bay. Bio-Monitor…Anna," Page scanning the screen. "She in distress. Her breathing is below normal. Endorphins are high. She's in pain," Page announced looking up at him again. Dietrich rubbed his forehead.

"Captain…We have Nathan Ellis on comm," Romiley called out. The Captain ran across the room. The sound was distorted but understandable.

"Wells has been killed. We believe it was Cole's doing. He attacked Bebe. Heading too Medical. All elevator's down. Working on a patch job. Elevator seven," Ellis rampaged over the comm.

"Understood Ellis. I have the Captain here," Romiley explained offering a headset up to Dietrich. He slipped the headset on.

"What happened to Anna?" Dietrich snapped.

"We found her and Cole in a fight. Seems he may have been attempting to take the Shuttle."

"Is Anna alright?" Dietrich shouted, causing Romiley to flinch away.

"Injuries to her face and…" Ellis's voice went silent.

"Ellis? Ellis respond?" the Captain barked.

"We've lost connection Captain," Romiley said quietly. Dietrich slammed his fist down on the desk before ripping the head set away.

"Romiley divert all shuttles to Luna. I don't want Cole getting more options," Dietrich said hurrying toward the exit. Romiley looked afraid and confused but followed the order.

Dietrich raced to his offices down the hall. He smashed at the panel.

"Come on…Come on." He shouted before the door gave access. He moved fast and thumbed the desk draw on the right side. Sliding open smoothly it reveals, a padded layout that contained a small torch, a chrome cased USB drive, a gun holster and a pistol with two magazines and a torch attachment. The handgun although pristine was old. It was a black USP forty-five military grade pistol with a twelve-bullet capacity. He took the pistol first and slotted in the first magazine. He took the torch next and locked it onto the bottom mount of the weapon. He chambered a round and laid it on his desk. He secured the holster onto his belt before adding the pistol magazine. He took the USB in his left hand and picked up the pistol in his right and left the office.

Dietrich turned left, heading back toward the bridge, and stopped at an elevator on his right. He put the USB in his teeth and pressed the panel. Its response was a red light, with a dull access denied tone.

"Captain's override: Stefan Dietrich…7 8 6 4 5 8 5." He spoke methodically. The light panel slid upward to reveal a port. Dietrich inserted the USB and the elevator doors immediately opened. He retrieved the tool, slipping it into a pocket just below his belt. He flicked the torch attachment with his index finger, turning it on. Pointing the weapon down over the side he peeked over behind it. The dark abyss of the shaft was not comforting or inviting. *No shaft lighting.* He tweaked the torch aim around the shaft and the beam extended down two decks to where the elevator had jammed. He focused his sight, spotting what seemed to be a security officer laying face up on its roof.

Moving the light more he caught the light reflection off the person's face guard. *Security for sure. Fuck you, Cole.* He tucked the gun into the holster and crouched onto his knees and reached into the right, grabbing the ladder inside. *Not as spry as you once were Stef.* He clumsily got a foot onto a rung and lurched onto the rail. Holding on tightly and closing his eyes.

"Fuck. Fuck," he said aloud, angered at his own fear. Dietrich shook off his distress and began his descent into the darkness.

Chapter 22: Calm

Briggs stopped in the hallway. He took another deep breath. He glared at the two cases he'd abandon almost an hour ago. He wiped his brow with the back of his hand and settled his hands on his hips. *How the fuck do I get to the Hab deck now.* He approached the cases in front of the elevator door and kicked one over with a grunt. Brigg's was still on the shuttle deck. He'd thought he'd heard a voice, or banging from time to time, but every time he investigated there was nothing. He began his journey back to the shuttle bay. *I must get some engineering boys down here.* He walked slowly and at times just stopped and rubbed his thighs. He was sick of walking now but continued on. There was a new bang sound to his right. In the wall maybe. But he kept moving.

The lights above him flicked in and out of life and another bang echoed though the corridor. Above me. He instinctively crouched for a moment glaring up at the grated ceiling above. The collection of pipe and ducting making it impossible to see if anyone was there. Especially with these shitty lights.

"Hey! Anybody up there!" Briggs shouted. His skin began to leak heavily as the response came.

A high-pitched whaling called back, echoing all around. He took short but quick steps to the nearest door. He tapped the panel and stumbled backward into the side room. He stood motionless in thick darkness. Well done fool. Now your truly blind. There was a clang and he fired to his left, hitting metal. A light blinked into life. He studied the room he was in. *A storage room.* He looked at the steel shelf he'd thrown himself against with a tut. He moved backward, deeper in when the whaling became a screech. There was movement above yet again. *No clambering. Crawling.*

He shifted through the equipment across the shelfs, just three rows in all. It wasn't a large room, although he would crouch to the bottom shelves and stretch to the top. The piping and ducting above began to shake, Brigg's ducked behind the third row of shelfs. He pulled a compressed cylinder from a mid-level shelf to the floor and inspected the label. Flammable. One of the largest pipes dropped slightly from its ceiling straps. Briggs dragged the cylinder back toward the door end scanning the shelves as he moved. Blowtorch. A long, thin blade of black tore through the piping above. The smell of stale water filled the room as the liquid began to spray from one of the cut pipes. Briggs grabbed for a bundle rubber hosing. The black glistening blade came through again, this time in a stabbing thrust.

Briggs struggle to keep his grip on the torch as he attached the hosing. He dragged the cylinder further back toward the door. He hastily attached the hosing to the cylinder and turned the valve. The torch ignited. Briggs set the nozzle upon the blade.

"Fuck you bitch," Briggs said as a second blade stabbed through the piping. Electricity erupted from the freshly cut piping. Above the piping the attacker screeched and squealed. The wiring inside the pipe flung around whatever was up there and the thing barrelled backward in the piping. Briggs kept the nozzle fixed on the opening. A sparking cable touched the water. Current raced through the soaked room. Across the shelves, along the floor, up Briggs' legs. His back and arms locked in an unnatural pose as he screamed. The current took the cylinder and exploded. Briggs disappeared in a red mist of bone fragments and flesh. His remains being propelled around the room in a red water show.

Hayes stopped clasping the harness she'd fashioned around Annabelle. Staring down the corridor as it shook.

"What in the fuck was that?" she asked glancing at Luca, who had a knee across Coles back on the floor behind.

"I think…something exploded," Luca said smugly looking down the corridor.

"Thanks for stating the obvious," Hayes mumbled continuing her clasping.

Kara and Jennifer stopped looking the same way and began fitting a different harness set up onto Luca's back.

"Why don't we just leave this prick down here?" Jennifer asked adjusting the rig while glaring at Cole's unconscious body.

"We can't let him take that shuttle can we," Kara said stating the simple fact. Jennifer rolled her eyes.

"I know that…why not just kill the fucker."

"What's the hold up?" Ellis called interrupting. Hayes side-stepped, looking up the open elevator shaft. Ellis was three decks up with a lighting unit attached to his belt. He had climbed the cable and opened the door on deck four. He'd extended a Strut across the shaft and was waiting to get Annabelle attached to the line he'd slung round it. The line continued through the door to a motor he'd set up in the hallway just behind him.

"Just a sec," Hayes said before crouching back to Annabelle.

Although Annabelle was awake, she was still dazed and limp. She sat slouched against the wall.

"Anna? Are you ready?" Hayes asked softly. Annabelle forced a smile, her eyes heavy.

"No. Anna. You need to stay awake," Hayes said gently tapping her hand. Annabelle nodded. Hayes gave Luca a nod and moved to her side. Luca crouched down and wrapped his arms around her just beneath the arms. Kara moved in and held her head as Luca stood. There was a thud. Kara and Hayes looked behind Luca's large frame. Jennifer was staring down at Cole. Fresh blood leaking from his nose. Jennifer glanced back at the group.

"What?…He moved," she stated. Hayes rolled her eyes.

"Okay," Hayes said crouching to the floor and lifting a motorised pulley ascender and moved round Luca. She reached into the shaft and took the line. She locked the ascender in place and Kara handed her the carabiner clip while Luca shifted closer holding Annabelle still.

"Thank you," Annabelle whispered.

"Any time," Luca whispered back, Hayes gave Ellis a thumb and he pointed a remote through the door above and clicked a button. The motor fired up and Annabelle was gently pulled from Luca's grip up the shaft.

While Annabelle approached the strut, Ellis signalled down.

"Jennifer…Hook up." He called down reaching out for Annabelle's arrival. Jennifer approach Hayes's side in the doorway. She stared up.

"Oh, fuck me."

"You'll be fine," Hayes said watching Ellis pull Annabelle toward him. He linked the carabiner clip on his belt to Annabelle's rig, bringing the ascent line close to the ladder. Hayes attached a hand ascender to the line.

"Don't let go," Hayes mocked. Jennifer gave a mocking smile in return and took hold of the grip. The motor started again, and she rose. Hayes and Kara moved away from the door as Jennifer ascended. Luca was lifting Cole from the floor, not so gently this time. Jennifer reached Annabelle's height. Ellis was kneeling in the doorway now. Jennifer reached out and Ellis took her hand.

Jennifer took a grip on the doors edge. She pulled Annabelle until she was against the threshold. Ellis took her around the waist and pulled back. Annabelle slumped on to Ellis in the corridor. He held her for a moment, and she raised her head to look down at him.

"Don't get any ideas," Annabelle whispered. He rolled gently, laying her beside him. He uncoupled softly and climbed back to his feet. He helped Jennifer into the hallway. Jennifer stood quickly, looking round at the white styling of the upper level.

"Hey," Ellis called; Jennifer turned sharply to see him struggle to get Annabelle into a sitting position against the wall. She ducked into her other side and took some weight. They sat her up. Annabelle winced with the pain in her ribs.

"Just a bit longer Bebe," Ellis said softly before moving back to the doorway. He clicked the remote again, sending the ascent equipment back down.

"Hey Anna? Why do they call you Bebe?" Jennifer whispered still crouched in front of her. Annabelle smirked and slowly gestured at her chest. Jennifer studied the bumps under her torn jacket and shirt for a moment before glaring at Ellis in disgust.

"Fucking pigs," Jennifer mumbled quietly. Annabelle lifted her head but did not respond.

Luca had turned his back to Cole while Hayes and Kara helped strap him into the rig.

"Why was this man locked up anyway?" Kara asked studying Cole's face.

"He's a suspect in a murder inquiry."

"Two murders," Luca interjected.

"Yes, two murders."

"Oh, shit," Kara responded, taking a step back. "That's why he was trying to escape?"

"Most likely, he's a bit…" Hayes froze. A screech echoed through the corridor. Luca stepped from the wall. Standing tall despite having a full-grown man on his back. The sound was joined by a smattering of clanging and shallow bangs.

Luca took a step back into the women.

"What is it Luca?" Hayes asked quietly.

"We need to go," he said calmly.

"Why?" Kara asked, knowing she wouldn't like the answer.

"That sound is not human," Luca explained, stillness in his voice. Luca stepped back again, shoving the women back.

"Lead the way Hayes," he said moving back further. Hayes looked round for a moment. "Hayes…Lead the way."

"Okay, away we go," Hayes said turning quickly. She grabbed Kara's hand surprising her and began to run away from the noise. Luca followed on their heels. The screaming and screeching began to echo around them.

Rajiv was on the floor. Knees tucked in, arm's holding them. His cheeks glistering with liquid. He bit his lower lip, tasting the salt of his tears. He had jammed himself between the wall and toilet bowl of the bathroom. The sound of screeching had gone along with the short period of something, *the creature* wailing on the door of the accommodation he'd retreated to. In fact, that brief assault on the door had been gone for some time. He stretched his mouth awkwardly and looked up at the wash basin to his left. He glared at the bathroom door.

Silence. He moved his arm from his cradling position and slowly pushed out a leg. His joint's stiff and creaking. He winced extending the other leg. He had to use the wall and toilet lid to aid his stance. Without erecting fully, he lurched over to the wash bowl. Slumped over the taps he turned on the cold and began scooping handfuls of water into his mouth. *So, thirsty*. He ducked his head and started gulping down straight from the tap. After his fill he soaked his face, removing the teary, sweaty fluid from his skin.

Continuing his cautious movements, Rajiv touched the door panel. The quick response of the slid startled him, but he kept moving toward the main door. He reached for the panel. Froze. He cancelled the move and leaned against the door. He heard something small and metallic dropping to the floor and quiet again. He waited; ear pressed. There was a squeak and a thud. Rajiv jolted from the door. *Was that a voice? Is the thing still out there?* He pressed his palms against the door. He bowed his head. His eyes shut tight. *Is everyone dead? Am I…Alone?*

Chapter 23: Deck Four

The wide oval corridors were dim. Ceiling lights skipping in and out of life. The once soft white walling seemed grey and hard with grime. Deep reds and black oils speckled the walling in odd places. The access panel to elevator four illuminated before bursting in a fountain of sparks. There was a stiff thud from inside. With the second thud, a blade of hooked steel broke through the seal of the door. A second hook lurched through above the last. Curving in the opposite direction.

"Pull damn it," Markov snapped. The grunt of two men pushing with everything they had responded, prizing the door open. Torch light from their chest mounted positions glared into the hallway beyond. The engineering team inside sloped backward in the cube. Almost everyone in the small space grimaced. "That smell is rank." Blake, an athletic blonde man with a pointed beard said.

"What the hell is that?" Carlo said looking to the stocky grey bearded man to his left. Black leathery string stretched across the opening. Markov regarded the webbing for a moment.

"Whatever it is. It is in our way. Olga," Markov said calmly. With Carlo and Blake still holding the door with the hefty breaching tools Olga stepped forward. Her hair was exceptionally long and blonde. She had plaited it behind her, and it reached past her waist. In her hands, she held a cutting tool shaped like a drill with a thin saw protruding from it. The serrated edge glistened with a diamond tip. With a stroke of her thumb the tool began to hum, and she brought the tool down over the black webbing. The blocking bands snapped away, clinging to the door edges with no resistance given to the cutting tool. Olga stepped aside proudly, looking to their leader. Markov gave a direction gesture toward the door and Carlo stepped into the hallway.

He began to cough. Markov, Olga, and Blake covered their mouths. Each one covered their faces with moulded breathing masks that they wore on their tool belts. Carlo masked up also.

"Lieutenant Markov?" Carlos called. Lazar Markov stepped out and joined his gaze. He held his torched light on a man's body resting against the wall. The body was sat in a pool of blood that had clearly came from his own chest. There were two deep gouges running down his right pectoral down to his opposite hip. Without speaking to his team, Markov took a small radio device that had been rewired in a botched way from his belt.

"Dumont? Can you hear me?" he spoke calmly. The radio crackled. Markov gently rattled the wiring.

"Dumont?" More crackling that sounded rhythmic.

"You're not clear Markov." Dumont's French accent pushing through. Markov banged the device on the side a few times.

"Dumont? Radio check. One…one…one."

"Yes, radio check good."

"We need your people down here now…We have a mutilated body near elevator four and we haven't even started." After a moment of silence, Dumont responded.

"Understood Markov. I have a team gearing up as we speak…Hold your position," Markov regarded the downed man and his team.

"Negative. We will, push on to Hydroponics and Medical. People may need our help." Another moment of silence.

"Alright. My people are moving as fast as they can. Be careful Laz."

"Copy that Andre," Markov finished, tucking the radio away.

"Okay team. We move fast. Medical first," he ordered before charging off down the corridor. The rest of the team close behind.

Ellis and Jennifer held Annabelle up as they stepped slowly through the corridor. Lights flickered everywhere. As they approached the junction, they froze. Three crewmen lay on the floor ahead of them. Blood and black slime covered their bodies. Ellis released his hold on Annabelle, Jennifer taking her weight.

"What are you doing?" Jennifer whispered, staring at the grounded people.

Ellis ran forward toward them. The body on the right jerked before being dragged away. Ellis slid to a stop and back himself to the right wall. He stared back at Jennifer and Annabelle. His eyes wide with terror. He looked down at the two remaining bodies. The bodies had been torn across the chest; one's arm was missing. He cupped his mouth as their smell grabbed his face trying not to vomit. From the right was an ear shattering scream and Ellis slid away from the junction. He squeezed his eyes tightly. There was a snarl and a squelch, like a knife being driven into a gut.

Ellis looked back at the girls again. They had both curled down to the ground. He could see Annabelle's hands shaking. He studied their faces. Jennifer was stern faced but clearly terrified. Tears began to run down Annabelle's face as she squeezed them shut. Ellis slid back toward the edge of the corner. He held his breath and quickly glanced round. He lurched back and ran to the girls.

He grabbed Annabelle by the arms and wrenched her to her feet.

"We have to go," he whispered aggressively at Jennifer before moving under Annabelle's arm, almost lifting her feet off the floor. He charged toward the junction and bolted to the left. As Jennifer came up behind him, she looked to the right. All the breath left her. A large black mass of slick tentacles lashed at the body on the ground. With each strike it shovelled flesh and blood into its centre mass like it was pulling the body inside inch by inch. Jennifer saw no eyes but knew it was looking straight at her. A section of the mass lurched outward in an arch that seemed like its head and the bellowing scream came again.

The two bodies near Jennifer's feet arched up like they were being electrocuted. Jennifer leapt away and raced after Ellis and Annabelle who had just disappeared around another junction. Jennifer slipped on the slick flooring and crashed down onto her hands and knees. The frictionless floor allowed her to slide forward onto her hip with a crack. She watched in horror as the two stumbling bodies franticly came toward her. She clambered on, slipping constantly on the floor toward the junction. There was shouting ahead of her, but she kept moving.

He left me. He fucking left me to die. She grabbed at the corner of the junction and pulled but the grip betrayed her, and she whirled onto her back. As the erratic bodies got closer. One flung its arms out and a black tentacle torn out of its flesh. Splitting from the hands right up to its shoulders. The human appendages flopped to its sides lifeless. The new tentacle arms solidified at its ends, foaming razor blade hooks.

Jennifer felt a thud at her head. She looked up at a man's groin. The first creature lunged forward, and the man flung a breaching tool across its head. The head snapped back, breaking the neck. It's newly form claw slashed down through his left shoulder, opening his body down to his stomach. Jennifer curled into a ball as the creature collided with the man over her. The first creature had landed in a mounted position and raised its weapons to continue striking down at the man. The second body grabbed her legs and jerked her back toward it. In its pull, it spread her legs and pulled her into its groin.

Jennifer screamed and hammered her fists at its face. A loud bang echoed through the corridor. The creature that was on top off the man was launched toward the side wall. It stuck in place but continued to whip its arms wildly. The body that held her bucked at her. Its stomach erupted with a flare of small stringy tentacles that latched onto her waist. Jennifer grabbed at the snakes on her body. *Get it off! Get it off!*

A second bang filled the corridor and the bodies head snapped back as a ten-inch bolt drove into its head. The capped end stopped the bolt from going all the way through. A second bolt rammed into its chest. This bolt flung the body away, the small tentacles snapping apart. Jennifer ripped at the remains on her body throwing them aside. A second man moved past her and pulled back a side handle on some type of weapon. He fired another bolt into the creature that locked it to the floor. Jennifer recoiled to the side as a woman in an orange flight suit and the longest plait she had ever seen offered her a hand.

"Come on," she said before pulling her to her feet. She cradled Jennifer with her arm and led her away. She watched another man hammering away at the first pinned creature with a breaching tool.

"Enough Carlo. Back inside," said the stocky man wielding the bolt gun. The woman led Jennifer into medical.

"What's your name girl?" The woman asked leading toward a bed.

"Uh. Jennifer."

"I'm Olga. Are you hurt?"

"I don't know."

Markov pulled Carlo away from their brutalised colleague and retreated into the medical bay.

Inside the two men of the engineering team insured the door was sealed as Olga helped Jennifer up on to the beds.

"Are you alright Jen?" Ellis asked while stood at Annabelle's side. A Doctor was applying a gel to Annabelle's lips while a younger woman wrapped bandaging around her waist. Jennifer shot Ellis a look.

"Fuck you," she snarled.

"You were supposed to be right behind me. I told these guys to get you," Ellis replied.

"He did," Olga confirmed. Jennifer watched the Doctor kiss Annabelle's forehead before approaching her.

"I'm doctor Grace Lancaster…Are you hurt?" Grace questioned studying her.

Jennifer glanced up at her and nodded.

"Tell me where it hurts?" she asked. Jennifer held her stomach and looked at the ground.

"Okay not to worry. Josephine, chair please," Grace called. Josephine brought a soft padded wheelchair from the corner of the room. They helped Jennifer into it and wheeled her to the far end of the medical bay to the last bed and Josephine closed the private curtain. Doctor Lancaster crouched in front of her.

"Okay let's take a look," she said softly, gently unbuttoning Jennifer's jacket. Grace then lifted her black shirt. Jennifer's stomach was bruised around the lower waist.

"I am sorry but, we need to take your trousers down to see how far this goes," Grace said quietly. Jennifer nodded.

Ellis placed a hand on Annabelle's shoulder. She laid her hand from that shoulder on to his.

"I'm alright Ellis. Don't worry," Ellis nodded and approached his fellow engineers.

"Thank you, guys…Sir," he said nodding at Markov. He looked round.

"Where's Blake?"

"Outside," Carlo said bluntly marching away and sitting in a chair at one of the beds.

"They killed him…Tore him up bad," Olga explained taking a seat on the bed she stood by.

"Fuck. What the fuck is happening? Where the fuck did that thing come from? Where is everyone?" Ellis said turning his attention to Markov.

Markov set the bolt gun down on the bed behind Olga.

"Security is on their way…I've told them everything I know…Which is nothing," Markov said focusing his gaze on Annabelle, who was cradling her ribs upon the near bed.

"She must know something," Markov insisted. Ellis glanced back at Annabelle and Markov stepped forward. Olga reached for his arm but was short. Ellis leapt in front of him.

"Why would she know anything?" he spoke quietly. They locked eyes.

"Nothing happens without her knowing, Ellis. She's closer to Stefan than any one of us," Markov growled.

Olga leapt from her position when Ellis was shoved aside.

"Sir. Stop," Olga said with no response. Ellis rebalanced as Markov reached Annabelle.

"Hey! Start talking." He snapped standing over her. Annabelle snapped her eyes up.

"About what?"

"Don't act dumb. What is killing my people?" his voice rising.

"I have no idea what you're talking about…I."

"Don't lie!" Markov grabbed Annabelle by the shoulders and shook her. Ellis launched into Markov, shoulder charging him to the floor. Annabelle clutched at her ribs again and grimaced.

"She hasn't seen them Laz!" Ellis yelled as Markov clambered back to his feet. Now Carlo was between the two men.

"Back off Nathan," Carlos snapped; his palms aimed at each man.

"Big mistake boy," Markov growled, standing tall. Olga was now beside Annabelle.

"How did you get hurt Bebe?" Olga asked studying the standoff.

"Cole."

"Cole is in the brig," Carlo countered.

"Big mistake," Markov said again, his eyes locked on Ellis.

"Stand down. Right now," Grace ordered sternly, now out from behind the curtain. All but Markov looked at her.

"Lieutenant Markov." He finally broke his stare.

"Yes Doctor?" Markov gritting his teeth.

"David escaped the cells. Annabelle caught him trying to leave the ship," Grace explained calmly.

"How…and why?" Olga added.

"He knows," Ellis realised.

"How would he…?" Carlo asked. Markov stepped back from the standoff.

"It's what he brought on board. This is the intelligent life Stefan mentioned," Markov explained.

"So where is Cole now?" Olga asked, moving things along.

Ellis shot a look of shock at Annabelle.

"Luca had him…They were taking him back to the cell block," Ellis told them.

"Alright, we wait for security. We get to Hydroponics and send them to find Cole," Markov said firmly.

"What is wrong with Hydroponics?" Annabelle asked softly.

"Heating systems have gone crazy on the upper decks. It's why we came down here," Markov explained. Jennifer emerged from the curtain. Her face and hands had been cleaned of blood.

"How hot are we talking?" she asked.

"About ten degrees almost…Why?" Markov said.

"Your heating system is linked with propulsion, right?"

"All ships are."

"You know that can alter our vector."

They looked at her in confusion. "The propulsion system is constantly pushing harder and faster. A ship's flight path always plans for this. If the heat system skyrockets, that's more pressure on the engine which will result in a propulsion loss."

"How do you know?" Olga asked.

"I'm a flight navigator."

"It doesn't change anything. We wait for support," Markov stated. Jennifer rolled her eyes.

"You don't have time for that. If the bridge doesn't pick up on those changes and re-calculate. This ship will be destroyed when we reach the Main belt," Jennifer explained impatiently.

"We call the bridge…Simple," Ellis said. Olga glanced at him.

"What?" he asked looking round.

"Comms are blocked. We need to reset in the Spire," Markov told them.

"So, we reset it," Ellis said shrugging.

"We still need to get into Hydroponics and fix the temperature spike. And make sure our air isn't compromised. How can we hit the spire as well?" Carlo interjected.

"I'll reset the Spire."

"Then what. You tell them we're off course…That won't help. You need to provide new instruction," Jennifer said shooting him down. Ellis studied the floor for a moment then smiled deeply.

"That's why you're coming too."

"Oh no. I'm not going back out there no way," Jennifer said stepping back.

"Yes, you are…And so am I," Annabelle said sliding slowly from the bed.

"Neither one of you are fit enough to go," Grace told them folding her arms.

"You know this has to be done Grace," Annabelle explained.

Markov moved back to the first bed taking up the bolt gun. He checked the drum on its right side before extending it to Ellis.

"There are twelve bolts left," he said as Ellis excepted it.

"One bolt doesn't stop them…Remember that," he continued tapping Ellis on the shoulder.

"Oh, fucking fuck," Jennifer mumbled rubbing her hand's through her side of hair. Grace looked at Annabelle, Her hands firmly at her hips. Grace closed her eyes and took a breath. She made for a large cabernet and yanked it open. Inside were medical instruments that were hung like a mechanic's wall rack. She took a large curved, serrated blade from its holding and offered it to Jennifer. She accepted the silver bone saw slowly.

"Thanks," she said bluntly. Grace gestured at Annabelle to approach. She chose a square headed axe of stainless steel. She held Annabelle's hand as she accepted the councilman chisel.

"You don't have to go," Grace said softly. Annabelle smiled softly.

"There's too much to lose. What happens if we fail?" She spoke softly back. Grace nodded in acceptance and the two-women joined Ellis at the door.

"It seems quiet out there," Ellis nodded.

"Oh super," Jennifer said sarcastically. Markov and Carlo unlocked the door and slid the door by hand just enough for Ellis and Jennifer to squeeze out. Annabelle stood side on with the opening and glared at Markov. He pulled his side of the door a little wider before she joined the others.

Chapter 24: Below

Luca collapsed onto his hands and knees. His skin slick, breathing heavily.

"Aaaah. Damn it, that's it I'm beached." He gasped tumbling onto his side, the weight of Cole finally off his back. Hayes swung back scanning the darkness with her torch light. Her eyes were wide, and her skin was shining. She got down low behind Luca's head.

"Luca?" She said quietly, briefly checking Cole's still unconscious face.

"I can't…I'm…I need rest," Luca managed as Kara join the floored group.

"We cannot stay here. We need a room?" Kara whispered eyeing Hayes. Wiping her brow Hayes stood and scanned with her torch.

"Shit, shit, shit," Hayes spoke to herself throwing her torch light left and right down the corridor of never-ending darkness. Kara stood quickly and took her hand making her flinch.

"We are alright. We need a break room. Come on engineer, where would you go?" Hayes focused her thoughts.

"Shower room," she replied crouching down and pulling on Luca's arm. With Kara's aid Luca slowly rose and the group moved a few more metres and into a doorway to the left. Luca tripped over the threshold but stayed on his feet.

They stepped through a second doorway. They were flooded in mist from small jets around a box room of bluish metal. The door slid shut behind before the door ahead opened. Moving through the third door they entered a locker room. It had brown wired lockers and benches that had a green tint to the seating. They unclipped the harness and let Cole slump to the cold floor. Luca dropped to a bench, rubbing his legs. The ceiling lights were dim but kept a steady glow. Kara crouched at Luca's feet and began to work his thigh muscles with her fingers. She glanced up to see Luca smiling down at her.

"That's the closest I'm gonna get, so you can stop smiling," she said and Luca sniggered. Hayes stepped slowly round a right turn to the shower units. There were very tightly set with narrow shower heads. She turned back and went left to a small kitchenette area. The cupboards where a pearl white and where also empty. Hayes let out a huff after opening them. She glanced into the sink. There was a used mug and fork inside. She held the cup to the tap and thumbed the panel.

There was a shuddering hum and a splash of black gunk vomited out, speckling the basin, cup and her flight suit. She glared down at herself for a moment before taking the mug back to the shower section. She cautiously reached into a cubical and thumbed the panel. It too spluttered but water quickly followed. She wet her hand and smelt it. She cupped more in her hands and rubbed it over the black staining on her suit. Now using both hands, she rubbed the mug as clean as she could in the jet stream.

"So, what do you think of the ship so far?" Luca chuckled.

"Oh, it's a fucking dream boat," Kara chuckled back, now rubbing his calf muscle.

"Yeah. It would be nice to actually know what the fuck is happening right now."

"I know…What was that fucking noise? What is out there in those halls?" Kara asked leaning back on her heels.

"I don't know…But anything that shrieks like that is out for blood."

"I hope Jennifer is okay…And your friends of course."

"Don't worry Ellis is smart and Bebe is strong, they will look after your friend," Luca said leaning forward.

"I don't know. That Anna took a beating."

"Her will is strong trust me," Luca confirmed. The pair looked when Hayes came back handing Luca a mug of water.

"It's not cold but at least it's clean," Hayes said sitting beside him. Luca gulped it down.

"Thanks," Luca said handing the mug back.

"I'll take it," Kara said raising to her feet and going for a fresh mug of water herself. Hayes glared at Luca as he watched her walk away.

"Hey. Now is not the time," Hayes said tapping his arm.

"I was only looking," he said softly.

"It starts with a look." The pair glanced down and across to where Cole lay.

"Are you gonna be able to get him up to the cell block?" Hayes asked quietly.

The screeching sound erupted through the walls again.

"Not if that sound has anything to do with it."

Kara froze, the mug still held under the shower head. She glanced to her right.

"Guys?"

"We're still here," Hayes replied quietly. Kara pull the mug back, now full to the brim. She drank heavily and refilled the mug. She quickly returned to the other's and offered the mug to Hayes.

"We all need to keep our strength up."

"Thanks." While Hayes drank, Kara sat beside her.

"Do you think it's close?" The three glanced at the door.

"It could be anywhere. That high pitch is really travelling," Luca said quietly, slowly stretching as he stood.

"We need a plan," Hayes added also standing and heading back to the kitchenette.

"Shall we wake him…We might need his help," Kara suggested nodding at Cole on the ground.

"I don't know…He could make things worse for us."

Hayes placed the mug in the sink but lifted it again. It's came up slowly in her grip. The mug was thick with a black stringy tar. Hayes glanced into the sink which now had a thick layer of tar inside that buried the fork she saw before. The stringy texture tightened and ripped the mug from her hand. It smashed as it connected with the sink base and the pool of tar erupted into the air. Hayes screamed as the mass latched onto her face, neck and shoulders. It quickly contracted pulling Hayes face first into the sink base with such force her feet flung from the floor. Luca launched into the room. Hayes was almost upside down; her skin and flesh being dragged from her upper torso. Hayes was silent, her face covered in the tar. Her arms instinctively pushing back of the sink unit only made the tearing quicker.

"Chelsey!" Luca yelled pulling her legs downward and hugging her waist. Now Kara was also pulling, screaming with all her strength. Hayes arms went limp, Luca kicked his boot against the unit for more leverage.

First Hayes skin tore away quickly followed by her shoulder muscles. The flesh torn clean off her bones. The unit became a wash of deep red. Luca and Kara flung backward with Hayes's mutilated body. Hayes's blood drenched them, as the three hit the floor hard. Hayes's body began rapidly convulsing with shock. Kara caught sight of Hayes's one remaining eye staring up at her. Hayes's mouth was fixed open in a scream but there was no sound.

The stringy blackness thickened and launched again. Its forming tentacles stabbing into Hayes's upper body and wrapping around the lower. It jerked Hayes away from them, throwing lashes of tentacles at the pair. As Luca lost his bloody grip on his friend, he shoved Kara hard with one hand. His strength and slipper underfoot made Kara skate back out to the bench area. She stopped, half over the bench.

"Chelsey!" Luca yelled again, clambering to his feet, slipping violently on the plasma-soaked floor. Kara saw him disappear behind the wall toward the sink unit as she struggled to her feet. She quickly whirled round to follow Luca's advance but was met with Luca's fear-stricken face launching at her.

"Run!" Luca screamed, his face cover with a thick layering of blood and tissue. Kara was shoved toward the door. She pounded frantically at the panel. For a moment, the touch pad didn't register. As Luca came up behind her the door opened to the decontamination box. Kara lost all sense of direction as the mist from the room's jets blasted her vision. Luca made for the closing door but came down hard banging his forehead on the threshold. He gripped his head in rage and saw Cole, his arm's wrapped around his ankles.

"Help me!" Cole screamed, water rushing from his eyes.

"Get off me!" Luca screamed back kicking his heels free. He heard the door close behind his head. He lurched up the door, banging on the panel to open again.

The door slid open again and Luca fell inside, the room became thick with mist and steam. He could see a mass of black writhing in the room behind. Cole's hand came through the mist, stopping the decontamination cycle from ending.

"Don't leave me!"

"Damn you, Cole!" Luca leapt to his feet and pulled Cole inside. The door he fell through closed, and the hallway door opened instantly. Luca hurled himself into the hallway almost hitting the adjacent wall. He quickly looked round for Kara but there was nothing there. He began turning frantically in the hallway like he'd missed something, but Kara was gone.

A pounding began upon the door inside. Cole stumbled toward Luca almost hugging him.

"Get away from me you freak," Luca shoved him away. The sound of metal buckling began around them, quickly followed by all familiar screeching. Luca looked hard down the corridor. A human form was moving toward them in the darkness.

"Kara?" Luca called moving toward her. He reached to his harness and turned on his torch as the arms came up in a frantic wave.

The security officer clambered toward the pair; his face guard was down yet his face was torn open from the left eye down through the cheek. His mid-section had been torn away completely yet it still moved. The torch light reflected of the same tar blackness from the creature in the other room, but it was supporting the man's upper body, not devouring it. Cole had already begun to step backward. It wasn't until Cole kicked the bottom curve of the wall before Luca snapped awake again.

He spun quickly and ran toward Cole, grabbing him by the arm and pulling him away from the advancing man. The pair reached one of the elevator doors. Luca began tapping at the panel. The touch pad slide upward revealing a second panel. The maintenance casing housed a USB port on one side with wiring on the other. Luca reached inside and pulled. Ripping the wiring free the door slid open with a gush of back draft. Luca quickly looked up and down the shaft.

"Get climbing Cole."

"What? I'll fall."

"I'll fucking throw you in if you don't climb!" Luca yelled barrelling over him.

"Alright, alright," Cole leapt for the cable and swung into the shaft. On the return swing Luca leapt inside onto the line, catching it just below him. Luca held his grip while Cole began to climb the cable. Luca looked down the shaft. He realised the elevator door at the bottom of the shaft was also open. The light from the hallway drifting into the dark tube. The light cascaded around a bundle in the middle of the floor. *Is that clothing? Is it Kara's jacket? Shit. Fuck.* Luca looked up, Cole still going strong. Luca shut his eyes and took a deep breath. He loosened his grip a little and began to climb downward toward the light below.

With a creek that echoed through the shaft, Captain Stefan Dietrich managed to shove the elevator door open. He was able to pull one side of the doors toward him. He let out a huff from his efforts before lunging into the opening. Only his top half made it. The wind being ramped out of his mid-section. With his crawling motions, he pulled himself into the hallway. He used the rear wall to stand. He glared at the red slickness of his sleeves and looked round slowly.

The Habitation deck was dim with flickering light. With each flicker, Stefan could see the blood pools and splatters all around. He grimaced sighting an arm that had been torn away from the bicep. The realisation set in throwing his form back against the wall. He fumbled wildly until his gun was up and pointing.

"Not Cole. Definitely not Cole…" Stefan locked his sight on his shaking gun in his freaking hands. He whipped his arms back to his face, taking control of his grip. He shook his head sharply. *Come on you dick*. He began to step forward. Stefan began to swing his body, aiming his handgun into the open doorways of each Hab.

The first had an overturned table with some clothing scattered on the floor. Stefan straightened in the hallway and moved to the next Hab. He stepped tactically toward the Hab sighting thick, gooey blood down the near edge of the door frame. He gave himself a moment before swinging into the doorway. The kitchenette area had clear signs of a struggle and the bathroom door was ripped open. Blood splatters decorated the white walls of the room. Something metal, fell within the halls. Stefan stepped back from the room and aimed. He began to move toward the turn to the right in the hall. He swung round, more blood and gore peppered the hall. Stefan spotted a ceiling light frame on the ground, still rocking from its fall. He continued his advance down the next hall. His footing slipped on a thick blood pile underfoot. His legs flung upward, and he landed hard on his back. He immediately curled into a side ball, wheezing to recover his oxygen.

You stupid old fuck!

After a moment, Stefan adjusted his downed form, tucking a foot under himself he began to stand. The sound of screeches began to echo all around. The erratic sound of vent shafts buckling joined the screeching calls. Stefan rose quicker and scanned his surroundings. He kept up his direction as the threatening noises got louder. A few metres ahead of Stefan a vent shaft grate fell to the floor. Stefan stopped and slowly took a knee. A slimy black bulk dropped from the shaft with a thud. Stefan raised his pistol. The tar looking blob began to open like a flower, its gooey petal crystallising into spikes. The spike petal jetted outward driving into the walls and ceiling. The bulk tightened and raised itself.

The limbs began to bend and reposition, latching onto other parts of the wall. Stefan tilted his head, checking the gun's safety lock. The bulk began to pull itself forward and Stefan fired a bullet at the centre of the bulk. Tar like droplets sprayed from the entry point, but its advance continued. Stefan tapped at the trigger three times. The muzzle flashes reflecting off the tar textures. A wiry mass stretched toward Stefan, coiling together to form a thick tentacle hand. He adjusted his aim putting a bullet through its hand palm. The hand filched and parted slightly before twisting around itself and hardening.

"Fuck you!" Stefan shouted rapidly firing another two bullets straight into the advancing reach.

Hard black chunks erupted from the hand. As if gravity ripped it down the stretching arm fell to the floor. The bulk did not stop. It seemed to peel open at its centre. Thin tentacles flicked outward as a small bulk lurched forward. Its opened. It's screeched. *A mouth*. Stefan adjusted his aim again and fired three more bullets directly into the screeching opening. As the first bullet hit, the screeching became a gargle. With the other two bullet's burring into the same point and gaping mouth flopped to the floor. The bulk stopped moving.

Stefan slumped onto his hip…He held the gun's sight over the bulk again. It did not move. Stefan slowly stood and headed back to the nearest open Hab. He stepped sheepishly over the bloody collection. Moving left he approached the bed. At the headboard wall was a small grey frame etched into the white panelling. He pressed the grey boarder at each side, and it bedded deep into the wall before sliding upward. Inside the panel was a little form bulb of black. Stefan reached into the panel and gently pulled the bulb outward. The bulb was held with six thin wires of different colours. He pulled a green and then a red wire free from the rear and twisted them together before forcing them back into the green wire slot.

"You better be listening," he said quietly into the bulb. "This is Captain Stefan…I order you to seal the bridge immediately. There are…creatures on board the Euphoria. Cole is not the concern anymore. I have engaged and killed one of them, but I hear more…" He stopped and waited for a moment. "I hear them moving around the vent shafts on the Hab deck…many of our crew have been…killed or…taken. Relay my word's to Home Base and all surrounding stations. Issuing escort order only. The Euphoria is in quarantine. When we have assessed if there is an infection…" Stefan whirled round raising his weapon. His finger squeezing the trigger but released.

Chapter 25: The Spire

Ellis rolled his face along the wall until his left eye was looking down the corridor. He gently shook his fingers to life and re-gripped the bolt gun he was aiming at the ground. At the end of the corridor was a large, reinforced door with bright red Spire access painted in large, bold white. He rolled backward to where Jennifer and Annabelle queued behind him. Both girls shining with sweat, clutching their hand weapons tightly.

"Clear," Ellis whispered before moving round into the corridor. He moved slowly forward. Jennifer and Annabelle followed closely until they reached the door.

"Hold this," Ellis held the bolt gun out at Annabelle. She glared for a moment before gently placing her surgical axe on the grated floor and took up the gun.

While she watched the corridor behind, Ellis unscrewed a panel with a one-handed power drill from his belt. He gently placed the panel on the floor and studied the wiring inside. After he had swapped a few connections round, the door jolted. Stepping back the door began to open. Black stringy tar stretched across the opening as the powerful door pull open.

"What the fuck is all that shit?" Jennifer asked studying the dropping tar strings.

"That's not the biggest worry," Ellis said pointing inside the room. Annabelle glanced back and turn to face the opening quickly.

Thick black globs of tar dripped off the walls. Stringy black lines reached over a green and brown layer of hardened pus like padding. Ellis and Jennifer covered their mouths and noses as the damp rancid smell glided over them. Annabelle grimaced just after before covering her own lower face.

"Oh fuck. That's…oh god," Annabelle said stumbling to her right. She threw up onto the side wall she stood at. Jennifer looked away, making sure she didn't do the same. Ellis coughed dryly before taken up Annabelle's weapon. He swung at the string. As each one cut it sprang to the edges like elastic. He stepped in slowly looking at a cubic section in the middle of the room. From the cube extended every wire, cable, duct and vent you could imagine. The cube began at knee height in the room but the ducting and tubing extended way down below and way up above.

Jennifer looked up and down the lines.

"Welcome to the spire," Ellis whispered.

"It's all covered in…shit," Jennifer said staring upward.

"This is just one column. There are others through those pathways," Ellis explained pointing to each side of the room. Narrow long slots at three walls of the central room. Jennifer glared at Ellis in disgust. Those same narrow opening were also thick with the mucky formations of every shit colour there was. Annabelle stepped in behind and quickly lifted a foot that almost stuck to the gooey floor.

Ellis studied the central cube of lights, switches, and levers.

"I think the system overloaded."

"Is that all?" Jennifer said watching a tar blob stretching to the floor.

"I think so. All this…whatever it is has convinced the system it's over heated."

"Simple problem. Simple fix?" Annabelle asked watching her footing.

"Well. Yeah. Just flip the breakers and reset here," Ellis said pointing two large buttons. Annabelle leaned in to see.

"Test and reset."

"Yeah. Test first obviously."

"Obviously," Jennifer mocked rolling her eyes.

Ellis turned from the panel.

"Pick one," he said pointing at one of the narrow openings.

Jennifer stepped back.

"Can't you do them all?"

"The reset needs to be quick…I won't reach all three."

"I really don't like you," Jennifer snapped shaking her head.

"Here," Annabelle said offering the bolt gun to Jennifer. Jennifer eyed the weapon and handed her bone saw to Annabelle. Ellis scowled at the lack of hesitation and stepped to the opening on the left side.

"Okay follow the piping above to the circuit breaker. Pull the lever down and come back…Simple," Ellis explained. He nodded and disappeared through the narrow slot.

"Good luck," Annabelle said moving toward her passage.

"Aww…yuck…this stuff is…fuck," Jennifer complained as she pushed into the passage. The gooey liquid dripping over her shoulders and tugging at her arms as she squeezed through. Annabelle closed her eyes before turning to her side and slipping into her own passageway. The cold of the dripping liquid made her shiver and the sticking of the goo across her chest and back made her wince.

The formation stung her body as she pushed past hardened parts of the guck in the passage. After several feet of shuffling, she reached a wider passageway. She looked down at herself and almost laughed, noticing her jacket was gooey across the bust. *Even in a life-threatening situation…I get sticky tits.* A glopping sound ahead pulled her back and she raised her blade. She released a sharp huff and ploughed forward down the passageway. As she walked, she glanced up.

Follow the pipes. There was another glop, but this ended with a thud. Annabelle swung round and saw hooked tentacles lunging at her. The hooks had her shoulders as the small slithering body followed. The lower tentacles of the creature latched round her waist as the body stopped over her face.

Annabelle thrusted her bone saw upward, slicing through the creature's rear up through its head. It fell away as Annabelle dropped to her backside. Still holding the saw with both hands, she saw that the creature was no larger than wild dog. She could make out two razor sharp hooks either side of her cut. *Those would have killed me for sure.* The inner guts of the creature looked the same as the outside except for a clearer liquid that ran out of the thing. She realised the clear liquid now covered her hands and saw.

Annabelle clambered to her feet, flicked her hands, and saw several times, the clear sticky gel stringing off to the floor. She turned quickly and moved around a bend to the breaker box. She reached the unit and paused. The breaker's lever thick with the same gooey shit. She quickly peeled of her suit jacket and cover the handle. She squatted down as she pulled the stiff lever until it locked down.

Several tiny green lights blinked to life. She heard another glopping and leapt away from the unit as another creature landed on the floor near her feet. She quickly swung her saw across the back of the creature, batting it into the wall to the left. She hurried away back the way she came. Annabelle reach the narrow passage and tore into it head on, dragging her shoulders through the muck over the walls. Bursting out the other side she saw the stunned faces of Jennifer and Ellis. Jennifer raised the bolt and aimed down the passage.

"What happened?" Annabelle had her hands on her knees recovering her breath and heart rate. After a second, she stood up straight.

"Was your boyfriend in there?" Ellis asked glancing at her. She stared back at him before he eyed her up and down. Annabelle looked down at herself and saw the clear liquid across her chest and arms.

"Fuck you Ellis," Ellis sniggered and pushed the reset button. The cube made a rumbling noise as its green lighten panel lit up.

"All done…What?" Ellis caught Jennifer's stare.

"I should use this on your junk," Jennifer growled loosely aiming the bolt gun. Annabelle pushed the weapon down.

"He doesn't realise when he's being a dick that's all," Annabelle explain moving between the pair.

"That's the fucking problem."

"Did you see any creatures, Ellis? I sure as hell did. I don't plan on seeing them again. So, let's get out of this room. Fast," Annabelle said ignoring Jennifer's response. Ellis gave a gently smile and gestured back down the main corridor. The three stepped out and Ellis resealed the large door behind them.

As the door closed with a heavy thud, screeching erupted all around them.

"Where's it coming from?" Jennifer asked.

"Don't know. Don't care. We need to move," Ellis stated, scooping up the surgical axe and marching forward. Ahead of them, two vent coverings burst into the corridor on either side. Ellis turned to the right blanking the event.

"Ellis?" Annabelle said tapping his shoulder. A creature crawled out of each vent. Ellis thumbed a panel on the wall, opening a door. Both creatures had evolved further from human. One's head was gone, black mandibles snapping right up. The second had been disembowelled, its intestines now lashing tentacles.

"Ellis?" Annabelle grabbed at his flight suit. Ellis ripped the bolt gun from Jennifer's hands and forced the axe into her palm. He turned to face the two disfigured human's lurching toward them.

"Ellis?!" Annabelle shouted at him. He pointed into the open door. "Third door on the left…There's a comm booth inside…Warn the bridge," Jennifer darted into the new corridor and headed to the left. Annabelle stopped in the doorway.

"Ellis don't be a hero."

"She need's time to send it," he explained keeping his sight on the creatures. "Go. Now."

"If they get close…You run," Annabelle pulled on his shoulder, making him look at her.

"You run."

"Yes ma'am," Annabelle turned and made off down the hall. Her eye's filled with water as she heard the door closing behind her. The bolt gun began to fire.

Annabelle reached the third room and Jennifer was already leaning over a console speaking.

"I'm the new Navigator I don't have a code yet," Jennifer snapped as Annabelle locked the door.

"The Navigator was issued a code on arrival," Annabelle recognised the voice and approached the console.

"Romiley? It's Annabelle. You need to listen to her."

"Bebe? Who is this person?"

"Jennifer Kruse boarded with Karabina Farion. Just listen to her will you."

"Understood. Send it."

"The rapid temperature change has screwed up our trajectory path. You'll need to re-calculate after adding the engines new temperature and the additional loss of power with that overheat."

"Sorry Miss Kruse. We appreciate the temperature change information, but our course has all but stopped. We are currently in wide orbit around Mars," Romiley explained. Annabelle leapt toward the console.

"We're in emergency holding pattern. You know what's going on?"

"Some idea Bebe. The Captain sent a burst transmission from the Habitation decks," Jennifer smiled at Annabelle.

"We're being rescued?"

"Uh…No. Not yet anyway."

"What the fu…" Annabelle covered Jennifer's mouth. Jennifer wide eyed and raging.

"Explain your last Romiley," Annabelle asked, her hand still fixed across Jennifer's face.

"We have no way of understanding this attack right now. The Captain has ordered lock down procedure."

"We're in quarantine," Annabelle said quietly removing her hand.

"Quarantine means no rescue," Jennifer stating the obvious with an angry scowl.

"I want to talk to the Captain," Annabelle said sternly.

"The Captain has not returned…In fact, he went looking for you. Are you alright? Something about Cole, a fight."

"I'm fine Romiley. Does the Captain know where I am?"

"Heading to medical but like I said we had a comm from the Habitation deck."

"Anything on security?"

"Security and engineering teams have been sent out but…"

"But?"

"The crew's Bio-monitors are flatlining fast," Jennifer leapt at the console into Annabelle. She threw her arms around her stopping her advance.

"We're all gonna die! Get us the fuck out of here!" Jennifer screamed swinging the axe toward the console. The handle launching the microphone from the console in a burst of static. Noticing her mistake Jennifer paused giving Annabelle the chance to shove her away.

"What is wrong with you? Are all your dog's barking?" Annabelle yelled at Jennifer's floored position. Jennifer clenched her fist around the axe handle.

"The only contact we've had in hours, and you lose your shit!" Annabelle continued pointing at the console behind her. Jennifer glared at the floor.

"I'm sorry okay…I have a temper."

"Yeah. No shit," Annabelle said with a chuckle and Jennifer smiled back and let go the axe. Annabelle offered a hand. Taking it Jennifer rose to her feet. She stumbled forward but Annabelle caught her in an embrace.

"Oh. You alright?" Annabelle let out; the pair paused together for a moment.

"Yes," Jennifer lowered her head.

"You're so…Strong…yet soft," Jennifer whispered.

"Yeah, my girls are soft sugar," Annabelle replied. Jennifer took in a lung full of Annabelle's sent. Annabelle straightened her arms and made space between them. Annabelle smiled and glanced at the console. She felt Jennifer grip her shoulders. She lurched backward as Jennifer leaned in.

"Wow," Annabelle said softly. "I'm not into girls Sugar," Jennifer gave a scowl.

"I'm not either. I didn't do anything," Jennifer snarled stepping back and looking away. Annabelle tilted her head.

"You're not the first girl to try it on sweetie. Don't worry we're cool. It's my fault. I don't know how to turn it off," Annabelle said turning her attention to the console. Jennifer studied her form for a moment before scowling again and finding a comfortable chair to sit in. She sat on one end of a three-piece sofa and folded her arm's still holding her scowl.

Annabelle move round the console and put the microphone back on its desk. She inspected the wiring.

"Well, this is fucked. There's no way to fix it," Annabelle stated shoving it back on the desk. She marched over to the couch and slouched into the sofa beside Jennifer. The pair sat in silence for a moment before Annabelle threw Jennifer a look.

"What?" Jennifer asked. Annabelle leaned toward her.

"We need to do something."

"What?"

"Oh. I don't know. Get back to medical. Or the bridge. I mean don't you want to find Karabina?"

Jennifer lowered her head.

"Of course, but…"

"But what? Won't you help your friend?"

"We don't even know where she is," Jennifer's eyes began to shimmer. Annabelle tightened her lips with a little smile.

"We can find out. Look I know you're scared. I'm scared too, but I have people here that I care about. And I'm going to find them," Annabelle stood and straightened her shirt before opening two top buttons. She took in a lung full.

"Oh, that's better. I tell ya, this body shape is a real nightmare." She glanced back at Jennifer and saw her smile. *Lighten the mood. Reset the soul.* Jennifer stood.

"How do we find them?"

"Their hard to miss," Annabelle said staring down at herself.

"I meant Kara and the others."

"Oh of course. We find a second comm. And you stay cool this time," Annabelle giggled.

Jennifer collected the surgical axe from the floor. She took several sharp breaths before heading toward the door. She looked back to find Annabelle stretching, her breasts raised high. She slowly twisted her waist. Jennifer stared at her until Annabelle dropped her arms. *Hook and line.*

"Don't like women my ass," Annabelle mocked as she joined Jennifer at the door. Jennifer smiled eyeing the floor shyly.

Chapter 26: Above and Below

Stefan lowered his gun and let out a long huff.

"You were this close to having your head blown off boy." He spat lurching forward. Gripping the boy round the neck he hustled him into the room. He scanned the hallway and came back in. The young man just stood in the middle of the room wide eyed. Stefan studied him for a moment. This guy…Really?

"Hey Ray? Do you know what's going on?" he asked gripping his shoulder again.

"I…It got into Doctor Green."

"Got into?"

"I saw her all messed up but moving like…like she was possessed…like a puppet."

"So, this is something Viral," Stefan moved passed Rajiv and searched the kitchenette cupboards.

"Uh…Viral…I don't know. I think it consumes things. Not…dependant."

"What the hell does that mean Reg?" Stefan found a bottle and held it to the tap at the sink.

"A Virus doesn't kill immediately…It need's somewhere to go first…Like it knows it will survive when the host dies." While Rajiv spoke, Stefan filled the bottle and took a mouth full before fixing it to his belt.

"And you know it's not Viral because it kills immediately yes."

"I believe so."

"I need concrete evidence Roy."

"Rajiv."

"Huh."

"I'm Rajiv."

"Oh yeah, yeah, yeah. Evidence Rajiv?"

"I'd need a sample of it."

"Can't you take a sample from the one out there," Stefan snapped waving a hand at the door. Rajiv swung to the doorway and back again.

"There isn't anything out there."

Stefan scowled and stormed past him out into the corridor and turned the corner. The Creature he'd fired on was gone. Just a slick trail of black goo from its previous position, which rounded another corner further away. Stefan stuck his head in on Rajiv.

"Muster what you can to take a sample and follow me," Rajiv fumbled into the kitchenette and gathered a mug and a steak knife, before joining Stefan.

"Where are we going Captain."

"Hunting."

Luca slipped from the cable and fell six feet. On to his heels before his backside. He growled after impact. He studied his hand's, now sticky with a yellow and green mush. He got to his feet and rubbed his palm on his thighs before bending to the clothing that caught his attention. *This is Kara's jacket.* He stared into the light mist that rose off the floor. It had the same mush trailing off in waving lines and the mist seemed to emit from it. Luca began moving forward, slowly crossing his steps as he walked. The gooey muck began to spread upward partially until it was all around him. He paused, allowing a gloop of the blacking muck to fall just in front of him before moving on.

After a few more steps he squinted hard, a rancid smell began to lead him. The feeling under foot changes and he looked down. This area was grated, and the muck was seeping through. There was an indent in the mucky slime where something had been dragged. *Kara.* He moved forward quicker for several step's and paused when he saw something making jerking movement's ahead. He saw a humanoid shape jerking upward as it moved, and it was dragging someone. He looked down, feeling round his belt. Nothing for a weapon. He gritted his teeth and charged.

As he closed the distance the humanoid paused and turned. Releasing the body, it let out a thunderous scream that stung Luca's ears. He kept running. It spread itself wide, clawed tentacles raising, fat balled up tentacles spreading to its side. Taking a broad step, he threw out his boot, landing it on the creature's half caved in skull. With a crack it flung backward, its head and back flipping down to the floor hard. The creature's legs stood firm and Luca's supporting leg gave out. As he fell backward the creature came back up swinging its right claw over his head. Without its body adjusting for the next attack its left claw drove downward. The creature's blade screeching into the grated floor. He kicked at the embedded claw splintering it where it joined the tentacle. The right tentacle swung back from the previous swing skimming his chest.

"Kara!" he yelled grabbing at her leg. The creature's head jerked to the right, fixing its sight on its package. Its balling mass of tentacles latched onto the body and yanked it away from Luca's grasp. Its right claw swung again and stopped. Luca had ripped the dismember claw from the grating and blocked the attack. He counter swung across its human legs and the creature peeled backward with a squeal. Luca lunged on top driving the claw through remains of the face. It tried to raise but its claws pinned it to the grated floor. The legs gave no aid. It's balled up tentacles released the body and slammed down to the floor to lift itself. Luca locked his arms around the right tentacle and twisted his body ripping that claw away from the creature. He slashed at the balled-up tentacle closest to him and the creature dropped flat again. He sat up and forced the second claw through the mid-section pinning it fast. The creature jerked and pulsated before becoming still.

Luca stared down at the blacken dismemberment of someone he may have known breathing heavily. Snapping awake he leapt to the…man. Under the stains of blood and black goo the man wore a white flight suit. Luca wasn't sure who the man used to be, but it wasn't Kara. Luca pushed hard on the man's face to close his still stunned eyes before standing. Luca studied the claws embedded in the creature for a moment. *Best keep it pinned.* He continued slowly along the grated floor and saw a woman's body crushed into a breach in the door ahead. Luca crouched and saw her face. *Not Kara. She must have tried to escape as it closed.* He looked to his right feeling a rush of cold air on his face. Although the green and yellow muck spread over it, Luca knew he was beside one of the huge cargo bay doors. He was on the grating that spanned the edge of bay now.

Removing a one-handed drill from his belt he opened a small panel next to the door and pull at several wires. With a spark, the door slid open dropping the broken woman on the floor. Luca gently pulled the body from the threshold, her legs barely holding. He turned the body to see her face and like before he forced her tormented eyes shut before moving through the door. The smell of death made his eyes sting now, but he pressed on into the next bay. Dim lights flickered high above him, and he could make out a large lump in the middle of the bay. As he stepped slowly forward, he began to identify shapes. Human shapes. Oh, gods protect me. Then the pile moved. A body stumbled from the mass of bodies. Luca moved closer on the walkway. Luca leaned for a better view.

"Kara?"

"Luca is that you?"

"Yes, it's me Kara. Are you hurt?" Luca asked searching the platform for a ladder.

Kara did not answer. Her shoulders began to tremble. Her eyes pooled into tears.

Luca found a vertical ladder taped in yellow and black.

"I'm here. I'm coming down to you," Luca reassured. Luca reached the bottom, his legs danced beneath him on the blood slick floor. He tightened his grip on the ladder and looked back at Kara's distort form. With the entire floor slick like oil, he crouched. With a strong push, he slid on to his knees across the room and threw his arms around Kara's hunched body. She buried her face into his chest and threw her dripping arms around him.

"Are you hurt?" Luca asked again. Kara shook her head sharply.

"Thirsty." Was the only word she could muster.

Cole climbed as high as he could go. He was right under the elevator now. It was jammed between two floors leaving him with half a floor of space. He reached and stretched for the corridor floor, but it was too far. He scrunched up his face. His arms burning furiously from the climb. He studied the underside of the elevator. He considered the wiring that ran beneath. Maybe they are thick enough. Cole studied the thickest cabling that was an inch in diameter. *Fuck it. Die from electricity or the fall.* He pulled on the cable near its connection block. His arm went limp from fatigue, and he slipped slightly on the elevator cable. He howled as the shaft cable splintered into his hand. He squeezed his weak grip back around the cable, blood began to trickle from his palm as he held.

After a second, Cole pulled himself up curling back beneath the elevator. He threw his leg around the shaft cable and hooked it with his foot. He let out three short breaths before losing his grip on the cable. He felt his knee strain and his weight settled on his leg. He scrunched up his face again feeling his ligaments stretching. He slowly stretched each arms, easing the burn in the muscles. With fresher hands he held the cable and unhooked his leg. *Ahhh. Ahhh. Fuck.* He straightened a leg slowly. He pulled hard and tensed his core. Lifting the other leg high, he kicked at the connection box loosening it. With another pull up kick, he'd freed it. *No sparks.* He wrapped the wiring cable round his wrist and swung toward the shaft opening. His hips ploughed into the edge of the floor but he was there. His upper body resting on the cold wet floor of the corridor.

In front of him was the lower half of a body. He glanced up and rolled to his side before pulling his legs in. *Don't fancy being cut in half.* He stumbled wildly as he stood and fell against the far wall. Blood soaked his hands and clothes. He stared down at the half body and tilted his head. *Is that a man or woman?* He tilted his head to the other side. *Definitely a woman's ass.*

Cole pushed off the wall and rounded the first corner. He waded into the first open Hab. Blood had been sprayed across one wall and there was a dismembered foot, still wearing a boot under the room's table. Walking to the Kitchenette he saw a piece of someone's jaw on the top. He regarded the bloody lower mouth for a moment before shoving it off the surface. He turned the sinks tap on and rubbed his hands, removing most of the blood. He crouched and pulled open the fridge door. *Yes.* He pulled out a bottle of lager and twisted off the top. *Cheers.* He gestured at the piece of jaw and gulped down the drink.

Luca held Kara tightly around the shoulders as they approached the maintenance break room. Although Kara had stopped crying, she still shivered with disgust. Kara glanced up slowly. He gently released her from his hug and showed his palms. *Stay still.* She nodded a response. Luca turned toward a brown, rust stained door. He held the rusty old handle of the door. *Basic tech this far down.* He listened for a moment before forcing the handle down and shouldering the door. With a short squeak, it opened. He studied the room quickly before leading Kara in with an inviting hand. The room was no more than a square box room. A thin steel framed table on the left side. A mouldy green bench at the opposite wall. A cyber deck had been left beside a large heating ern on the table. The table seemed to bend inward with the ern's weight. It being constantly filled to maximum. Greased up overalls scattered the room. Grimy work boots lined beneath the bench. Luca shoved some clothing to the far end of the padded bench and gestured Kara to sit.

As Kara sat, hugging herself, Luca shook the ern. A sloshing sound told him there was water still inside and he frantically searched for a container. Finding a metal pot, he slung it in one direction. Alloy washers flinging out, peppering the floor. Kara recoiled, her leg's scooping off the floor. "Wow, wow, it's alright. I'm sorry," Luca giving a concerned look. He flicked the ern's tap and swilled the pot. Shaking out the metallic water Luca added clean water to the pot. Luca crouched in front of Kara and offered the water pot with both hands. Kara drank heavily. Lowering the pot from her lips, she froze. Kara glared into the shimmering water in the pot.

"You alright?" Luca's crouching in front of her.

"Hayes. That poor girl. That's no way for anyone to die," Kara spoke quietly.

"She was tough and took no shit from anyone," Luca laid his hands upon her red stained thighs. For a split-second Luca closed his eyes. Kara took hold of Luca's hands as her shoulders began to bounce. Luca threw his arms around her as she began to cry. She pressed in tightly, her tears running down his cheek. Luca stroked her toughened hair. He pulled back slightly, catching Kara biting down hard on her bottom lip.

"Drink some more," he said raising the pot in her hands. Kara smiled with a long blink. She drank more, her eyes closed. Luca moved back a little.

Kara coughed from rushing the water down. She wiped her mouth with her fingertips.

"Chelsey. That was her name, right?"

"Yes…Ellis is going to be crushed," Luca said focusing on the floor.

"Must have been close, all of you."

"Our trio for sure…Nothing like his feelings for you though."

Kara's eyes widened.

"Huh? What do you mean?"

"Well look at you, can you blame him," Luca spreading his hands. Kara smirked.

"I'm a mess." Pulling at her matted hair.

"Nah. No way. Your Skux."

Kara gave a puzzled look. "Skux?"

"Sorry, mean's beautiful, cool, hot." Kara's eyes narrowed, her cheeks gently pulling a smile.

"Do you think I'm beautiful?" She leaned forward, her back arching, her arm's straightening at the bench. "Or hot?"

"Yeah. But Ellis, he…" Luca paused. Kara backed-up.

"He what? He what Luca?"

"He really likes you. You know," Luca stated as he stood, creating more space between them.

"Speaking of Ellis…It's time we found him don't you think?" Luca said briefly stretching his arms. Kara gave a sweet smile before slapping her thighs as she stood.

"Your right...Let's find our friends and get the hell out of here."

Luca crept from the break room; Kara close behind. Kara pulled at Luca's belt when she saw one of the humanoid creatures staring at a wall, twitching and flinching. The pair continued staying as quiet as possible until the elevator shaft came into view.

"Does this ship have any fucking stairs." She growled stopping short of the open doors.

"Sadly not...Which is a terrible design flaw," Luca smirked. Kara joined his smile before shaking her head rapidly.

"No...No not another shaft. There must be another way," Kara glanced up at Luca, her eyes filling with water yet again. Luca wrapped his arms around her, hugging her tightly to his chest.

"We get through this one and find Ellis...Agreed."

"Agreed," Kara mumbled still in his chest. He pulled back and looked into her eyes.

"Don't cry Kara. Your eyes are too beautiful for that."

Kara giggled as she wiped her eyes.

"That's a bad line Luca."

"Made you smile didn't it."

"Yes, it did," Kara said stepping into the shaft. Luca followed and glared up the shaft beside her.

"How many floors to medical?"

"Eight."

Kara shot a stare at Luca.

"Eight...I really hate this ship."

"I could go up ahead and find a toe cable like before," Luca suggested.

"No," Kara snapped grabbing him round the bicep. "No. Not on my own again. Luca."

"Understood." Several screeching voices began to echo through the area. The pair stared at each other for a moment before Kara leapt onto the cable and began shimmying up. Luca leapt on behind her and began to climb. After two floors of cable climbing, Kara began to slow.

"I'm clearly...not...built for this," Kara mumbled glancing down at Luca. He launched up the cable. His arm's linking under hers. His crotch, under hers. She gasped. Luca hooked his legs around the cable.

"Sorry...can you lock my harness around you."

"Are you sure?"

"We can't stay like this."

Kara reached back with one hand pulling one side of the harness and looping it over her shoulder. She jerked and twisted grabbing the other side and Luca let out a grunt.

"Sorry," she said looping the other side.

"Definitely not complaining," Luca whispered.

"Yeah, just keep your blood in your arms yeah," Kara warned. Luca coughed in response and the pair began to climb as one.

Chapter 27: Distraction

As the door to the main corridor slid open Annabelle stumbled back, pushing Jennifer behind her. A humanoid shape lay on the floor, its left leg bent the wrong way. Its left arm was missing and had been replaced with a tight coiling of black leathery tentacles. Annabelle pointed at three large exit holes in its upper body.

"Ellis killed it," Annabelle whispered. She glanced down the corridor, barely exposing her head to the space.

"There were two wasn't there?"

"Yeah," Annabelle crouched, her knees together. She leaned out into the corridor. She tapped Jennifer's leg and pointed again. Jennifer peeked out. A tentacle mass of human flesh lay on the floor further away. A person's boot attached to it.

"Where's the rest of it?" Jennifer whispered.

"I don't know. I hope Ellis is alright," Annabelle glanced up at Jennifer. She held a blank stare at the leg.

"Which way to the other comm room?"

Annabelle let out a gentle huff.

"Past that leg."

"Wonderful."

Annabelle stood and stepped into the corridor. She tip-toed toward the leg and slid past it along the piped wall. She waved Jennifer to her and crouched again. She pointed at a reflective streak of red and followed it with her finger.

"I think Ellis is hurt."

Jennifer glared at it and then at Annabelle.

"How the fuck would you know that?"

"My father. We used to hunt a lot. And camped a lot," Annabelle stood again and followed the fine trail of red.

"Where are you going now?"

"To find Ellis."

"And the comm room?"

Annabelle turned sharply but bit her tongue.

"In the same direction," she said softly before moving on. The pair continued slowly until they reached a second humanoid form, with its leg missing. The creature pierced with several bolts.

"Ellis has to be alive," Annabelle said continuing.

After rounding a corner, Annabelle found torn pieces of an orange flight suit, thick with blood.

"Was he attacked again?" Jennifer asked while Annabelle examined the clothing.

"Tourniquet. He might be hurt badly," Annabelle leapt up and ran to a nearby door that had jammed half open.

"Aaaaah, damn it," Annabelle snapped as she forced herself through the opening. Jennifer followed her into medical bay four. Several medical bed frames were turned over with their mattresses across the floor. Several pieces of surgical equipment scattered the floor. There was a thud.

"Fuck it."

Annabelle approached a desk across the room and peeked over. Ellis was sat on the floor attaching a surgical clamp to his leg. Annabelle rushed round the deck to his side. Ellis lurched back.

"Fuck me, Bebe. You scared the shit out of me," Annabelle held the clamp in place on his leg.

"Are you hurt anywhere else…Lock it."

Ellis pulled on the slip lock, and it snapped tight round his thigh. He growled loudly.

"No. Just the leg," he said gritting his teeth.

"Jen. Find some painkillers. The glass case with the yellow edging," Annabelle ordered peeking over the desk. Jennifer unclipped the glass case mounted on the wall and began searching the bottles. Annabelle crawled across the floor and searched the equipment on the floor.

"If that doesn't distract me from the pain, I hope the painkillers will," Ellis said was staring at Annabelle's backside while on her hands and knees. Annabelle looked back at him, holding her pose. Ellis jerked and winced in pain. Annabelle swung back to him with a fine wire and thick needle.

"That's one way we could keep the blood in your body," Annabelle said softly, hungrily grinning down at his crotch.

"I think I'm going to vomit," Jennifer added extending a bottle of painkillers from behind the desk.

"Sorry Jen…Thanks," Annabelle said taking the bottle. She popped the top and gave Ellis two pills and began stitching up the slice down his thigh.

"Are you going to be able to walk with this?" she asked finishing the stitching.

"Yeah. Sure of course." Reaching for the desk Ellis moved just a little before growling in pain.

"Yeah. You aren't going anywhere any time soon," Annabelle glanced over at a smashed glass panel where a digital display would have been.

"I'll have to get back to Grace myself. You'll be stuck here without her help."

"You took a risk just getting here. You can't."

"I thought you knew me better than that Ellis. Don't tell me I can't."

"I do know you better," Ellis admitted smiling.

Annabelle got to her feet. She found the bolt gun between two mangled bed frames and looked at the drum.

"There's two bolts left," she explained handing the weapon to Jennifer.

"Wait what the fuck."

"Stay here. You'll be safer together," she continued taking both the axe and saw. She slipped the axe handle into the back of her trousers and shifted it to a better angle.

"Fuck no. I'm not staying here."

"Yes, you are. I'll be back as soon as I can," Annabelle pressed into the gap, her bust slowing her disappearance back into the corridor.

Chapter 28: Tension

Jennifer slung the bolt gun onto the desk.

"Woah," Ellis instinctively covered his head for a second. Jennifer rolled her eyes. Giving a tut she walked across the medical bay. She began shifting boxes around on the storage shelves and opening draws.

"What are you doing?" Ellis asked impatiently, shifting to get comfortable.

"I'm starving."

"This is a medical bay. Why would there be food?"

Jennifer paused and glared back at him.

"Patients require sustenance after surgery." She bluntly stated, continuing to search. He stopped and smiled. She had found bags with clear liquid inside. Grabbing the jelly sack from its container she turned back to face Ellis, a smug grin on her face.

"Okay. I didn't think of that."

"Huh. Why would you?" She sniggered, crouching for a scalpel.

"What is your fucking problem, Jen?" Ellis barked.

"Jennifer."

"What?"

"My name is Jennifer."

"Again. Your problem is?"

Jennifer didn't answer, she just cut into the bag she held and began to sip at the contents. Ellis took a slow breath.

"Jennifer? Why do you hate me?"

"You're a sexist pig. And I have no idea what Kara sees in you."

"Fuck. You're jealous. We haven't seen each other in years and you're jealous."

Jennifer flung the empty pack across the floor.

"Kara…is…mine," Jennifer growled stepping toward him. Ellis smirked.

"What's funny?" Jennifer leaned in on Ellis baring her teeth. Ellis rose the best he could.

"If there's one thing I do know about Kara. She won't be owned...by anyone."

"You'd do well to remember that if you want to keep her."

Jennifer backed off.

"Just stay away from her."

"Kara is my friend...I'd die for her."

Jennifer turned away and walked back across the room.

"Good to know," she whispered.

Chapter 29: Fresh Sample

Stefan waved Rajiv over to his tail. Rajiv moved low and slow. Stefan looked back and shook his head in disbelief. Stefan raised his pistol and shifted across the hallway amongst the Habitats of section C. Stefan crept forward following a black Tar trail. Although random sounds of bending metal emanated through the hallways Stefan did not pause. Rajiv on the other hand slouched down and froze every single time. Stefan turned his head slowly.

"If you do that, one more time…I'll shoot you," Stefan said quietly before continuing on. Rajiv pulled a face behind him and followed. There was a clash of utensils in a nearby Hab. Stefan signalled silence with his finger and moved slowly round the doorway with gun raised. Inside the kitchenette area stood one of the crew. The man who worked as a technician had been split from the right shoulder down to his hip. The whole right side had peeled down to the floor.

Its entire arm from hand to shoulder lay on the floor. A mass of thin tentacles thrashed and lapped at the air. The creature began to turn, and Stefan began shooting. Black tar splashed at the walls as the bullets ripped through the slithering mass. The human head of the body spat out a screech and lurched forward. Just before the creature was in striking range it fell flat on its front. Stefan threw a boot into the body and there was no reaction.

"Now's your chance," Stefan said diverting his attention to the hall they stood in. The screams of other creatures began to rage all around.

"Now would be good Rajiv," Stefan said calmly, and Rajiv rushed into the room. He grimaced at the sight of the creature and bent over the body. He sliced off one of the tentacles and let it drop into the jar he'd collected. He screwed the lid back on.

Rajiv turned to Stefan and tapped his shoulder.

"Grab my belt," Stefan ordered.

"Huh?" Rajiv questioned.

"This will be fast. Grab…my…belt," Stefan confirmed. The moment he felt his belt strap tug Stefan began to move quickly in a tactical form. A vent panel burst from the left with a creature sprawling across the floor. Stefan shifted to the left and continued. An overhead light burst as a ceiling panel fell. A humanoid form slipped from the ceiling. Its legs had elongated, and it had solidified hooks sprouting from its feet. Its arms had split into wiry strings with a bulk of thick tentacles whipping around its head. Without even slowing Stefan fired at the creature's legs. It took more bullets than he thought but still he didn't slow his pace. Just as he was about to march into death the creature buckled and slump to the right.

As the pair darted passed the downed creature, more ceiling panels began to collapse like a wave. Body after body fell from the breaking supports. Almost instantly the bodies where leaping from their prone positions and gave chase. Although each one wasn't torn up or had any limbs torn away, they still moved franticly, throwing their arms around as if pulling the air.

Stefan stumbled into a stop at an elevator door and pressed the panel.

"Captain's override: Stefan Dietrich…7 8 6 4 5 8 5." The panel slide open, and Stefan fumbled at his pocket. He pulled a USB from his pocket.

"In the slot there. And jump to the cable!" Stefan shouted shoving the device into his hand. Stefan turned back at the rushing horde. Rajiv scanned the panel for a moment and found the slot.

He stuck in the USB and the elevator door's slid open. Stefan glanced back as Rajiv leapt for the Cable in the centre of the shaft. Stefan swung round the inner wall of the shaft and hung onto the access ladder. The crowd of raging bodies piled into the opening as each one stretched for Rajiv as he pulled his body tightly upward on the cable. After several bodies had spiralled to the bottom of the shaft in an eruption of blood and flesh, Rajiv stared at Stefan on the ladder.

"Can I get on the ladder now?"

"We're not heading to the upper decks Rajiv. You need to test that shit," Stefan holstered his gun and got his torchlight over his ankles. Rajiv watched the torch beam. There was only one more rung below Stefan's feet.

"Ladder up. Cable down," Rajiv concluded.

"Ladder up. Cable down," Stefan said before leaping to the cable below Rajiv. Stefan began to climb down the cable. He stopped and looked up at Rajiv.

"Hook your legs and don't slide down, you'll slice your hands to pieces."

Rajiv nodded and the pair began to climb downward.

Chapter 30: Saving Grace

Annabelle moved quickly but cautiously through the corridors. She darted her gaze at each door section she passed to work out which way she was heading in the flickering light. She saw a shadow pass an open door to Medical bay 3. When she heard a quiet crackling screech from inside, she back pedalled and took another route. *Don't fight unless you must.* Soon she came upon four bodies strung across the floor, each one had been viciously torn or dismembered. She grabbed her mouth tightly to stop herself from screaming or vomiting or both. Three were engineering and two were security. She noticed an extraordinary long ponytail on a girl. *Olga.* She squeezed her eyes closed, seeing the same girl dancing at the wake hours before. Annabelle bowed her head for a moment. Her face became determined as she stood, and she moved must faster toward Medical bay 1.

She got to the corner before the open door of the bay and hit the wall hard. She side stepped quickly to the edge. She got down low and peeked in. The bay was much darker than before with just an examination light to illuminate it. Inner lining from the bed she had sat on was everywhere. Broken glass and thrown boxes decorated the floor. She stayed in a squat position and crept inside. She moved around a shelfing unit and saw another body on the floor. There was a ceiling panel across its torso. The legs in the green medical uniform.

"Grace," Annabelle dove toward the panel and shoved the light metal away. Her rib cage pulled open, and her intestines were spilling out. Annabelle slumped back onto her heels. *Josephine. Bless your sweetheart.* Annabelle took in a long, fowl smelling breath to hold back her tears. She gagged and shifted on her legs to turn away. She looked across the room. *That display isn't smashed!* She clambered to her feet and bound across the room to the glass panel on the wall. She hung over the desk and palmed the sensor on the right side. The keyboard crackled to life.

One square of elevator floor panel popped up slightly. With a grunt and a thud, the panel sprang upward into the box.

"That's it, climb. You can do it," Luca said helping Kara inside with a palm to her backside. She turned quickly on her hands and knees and looked back down at him.

"You could have pushed my foot you know."

"I know." He replied with a wink and a smile.

Luca leapt up catching the flooring edge with one hand. Kara quickly reached in and took his free hand. Together they pull him in. Luca tumbling over her. His knees found balance on the floor, and he quickly stood.

"Sorry, you alright?"

"I'm fine. Thank you," Kara joked staring up at him, arms and legs limp at her sides. Luca bent over her and positioned her hands around his neck. He stood slowly, easily lifting her weight off the floor. His eyes locked past her.

Luca took her arm off him and gently pushed her aside. Kara almost fell from the man's strength.

"What are you…" Kara turned with the push and became silent. She stared into the hallway as Luca slowly moved to the edge of the doors. The crisp white walling of the R and D deck had been vandalised with thick blood splashes and fine blood squirts.

"Oh my god. All the people down there."

"Were up here when all this begun," Luca finished her sentence. He shot a look back; Kara had dizzied to the wall.

"Hey," Luca stood over her, his hands on her shoulders.

"You feeling alright?"

Kara shook her head sharply.

"I can feel the weight of their bodies."

Luca lowered to her eye level.

"We're almost there. The medical block is close. That's where Ellis is, and Jennifer and Anna," Luca explained, nodding.

"Ellis, Jennifer and Bebe."

Kara smiled and nodded back. Luca moved back to the opening.

Annabelle pressed the holographic symbols on the small panel on the right.

"Hello? Is anyone there? Hello?"

"Hello? Anna?" Romiley replied.

Anna closed her eyes, relief washing over her.

"Yes, Romiley it's me."

"What the hell happened? I heard shouting and you disappeared."

"It doesn't matter anymore. Listen, Josephine's dead. Grace is missing and Ellis has been injured. I need to find Grace now." Her words calm and clear.

"Can things get any worse."

"Find Grace, Romiley."

"Page, Bio-mon Grace Lancaster," Annabelle scanned her back while she waited.

"Give me the bio-mon for Annabelle Brooks," Romiley continued. Annabelle stared at the home screen of the large display. An info video played with no sound. Each section head gave an upbeat looking presentation about the Euphoria's departments.

"She's moving."

"Where?"

"Toward you…Side corridor six."

Annabelle scowled at the doorway.

"Martha Green is with her," Romiley's tone shifted "Page said their running!"

Annabelle ran from the room and bolted to the left, at the next junction she turned left again. As she turned right at the next junction, she saw Grace. Almost too late. Annabelle leapt back, to the wall at the side of the corner. Grace stumbled at the sight of Annabelle and fell to her knees before barrelling into the wall of the T-junction. As Grace landed on her side, she looked at Annabelle, her skin soaked in sweat, eyes paralysed by fear.

"Run!" Grace snapped.

Annabelle did not run. Instead, she drew the axe from her back and turned into the corridor like some warrior maiden, her arms spread with a weapon in each hand. She saw Martha Green rampaging toward her. *I've never liked you bitch.* Martha's jaw had been torn open, but it still snapped frantically. Her forearms had burst apart into a mass of tentacles. Stiffened tentacles stretched from her stomach like spider legs and were stabbing at the side walls increasing her speed.

Annabelle adjusted her form, the axe high and behind. She threw with all her strength. The axe spun toward Martha's head. The back side of the axe smashed against Martha's forehead. The weapon glancing off as her skull flung back further than it should have. Annabelle's heart sank as the thing trained toward her. She lunged forward in a roar, thrusting the saw straight into Martha's mangled mouth. The force against her was way too great. Martha's momentum, slamming them both into the wall above Grace. Marth lurched round. Slinging Annabelle round like a ragdoll. Annabelle held her grip on the saw embedded in Martha's mouth. She launched into the opposite wall side way, back first. Annabelle let out a deep groan as her lungs emptied.

As Annabelle slumped to the floor, she pulled Martha's head down with her. The mass of tentacles enveloped Annabelle's upper body and face. The spider legs drove down into the floor and pushed. The saw torn away from her face and dropped to the floor. The slithering tentacles yanked Annabelle to her feet.

Annabelle pulled her head back the best she could while the tentacles studied her face. Annabelle gritted her teeth feeling pressure around her waist. *This is it.* A mass of baby snakes spilled from Martha's mid-section. They felt their way through the buttons of her shirt and ripped it open to expose her stomach. Three snakes shifted from the rest pressing at her belly button. She tried to pull them away, but her hands were enveloped with larger tentacles and were pulled away. Martha's head slung back and screeched toward the ceiling. Annabelle turned away, mouth and eyes shut tightly.

With a squelching thud, Martha jerked backward. The tentacles at her waist went limp and slipped off Annabelle's stomach, cold liquid splashing. Annabelle heard a deep grunt and another thud. She felt pulling on her right arm. She opened her eyes as balance left her. She fell to the ground half on top of Kara. She quickly looked back at Martha. Luca was wailing furiously on Martha with the surgical axe she'd thrown.

"You, okay? You, okay?" Kara asked frantically as the two clambered to their knees and reached Grace.

Chunks of tentacle flung from the creature with spray of black tar. Luca continued to swing wildly at the creature while the three women helped each other up. Annabelle pointed passed Luca and nodded at Kara. Nodding back, she leapt toward Luca pulling on his shoulder.

"This way, come on." She called out as Annabelle and Grace ran past clutching each other.

Annabelle swung Grace round the doorway of Medical bay 1. Stopping her softly near the wall she held her hand on the door panel. Kara and Luca came in behind and Annabelle locked the door. Annabelle and Grace looked at each other and leapt together in an embrace.

"Oh, my sweet, sweet child."

"Thank the lord you're alright."

The two looked at each other again.

"I'm fine sweetheart but…So many dead. Josephine," Grace said attempting to turn. Annabelle held her tightly stopping her.

"Come and sit down," Annabelle led her to the display console and pulled a wheelied chair to her. Grace sat and softly smiled. She stroked Annabelle's cheek with her thumb. Annabelle rose and kissed her forehead before turning to the others.

"Your timing was perfect…Thank you," Annabelle said stretching up and kissing Luca's cheek and hugging him round the waist.

"Your very welcome."

Annabelle moved back and turned to Kara.

"You doing okay sugar?"

Kara grinned before scanning the room. Her face quickly shifted from a smile to a scowl to a realisation.

"Where are they? Where's Ellis? Where's Jennifer?"

Chapter 31: Break Point

Ellis began dragging himself back to a cabinet beside the x-ray scanning unit. Jennifer leaned against the storage boxes and watched his struggle. Ellis gritted his teeth with every movement he made. After a few moves, he'd eyeball Jennifer who'd simply raised her eyebrows. He'd huff with disappointment and continue to struggle. When he reached the cabinet, he slumped to the floor, breathing heavily.

"I need water." He managed. Jennifer glared at him for several seconds before shoving herself off her resting spot. She turned and took another bag of clear liquid from a draw. She made her way toward Ellis like a stroppy teenager. Halfway across the room she stopped, clutched her lower mid-section, and scrunched up her face. Ellis scowled and glanced away for a moment.

"What's wrong?" Ellis asked bluntly.

"I don't fucking know!" Jennifer snapped before doubling over.

"Jennifer?" Ellis called reaching out and hurting his leg.

She dropped to her knees and balled up on the floor. Her body began to shake.

"Jennifer?" He called again. He shifted his body grunting in pain. He began dragging himself backward toward Jennifer's curled up form. Jennifer began to jerk in a heaving motion.

"Jennifer?"

She snapped on to her back.

"Jennifer!" Ellis shouted.

Her back arched up sharply and she screamed at the top of her lungs. Ellis reached her and hunched over her.

"Jennifer? What's happening to you?"

Her back dropped back down, and she went silent. Ellis leaned over her watching her breathing heavily and fast. He touched her face.

"Jen? Are you alright?" he asked quietly. Her eyes shot open.

"Don't touch me. Pervert!" She shoved him away. Ellis fell backward and screamed in pain. She pounced on top of him. Ellis roared in agony. She straddled him and rose her fists high above her head. Ellis covered his face. Her fists ploughed down into his stomach. He instinctively dropped his hands to his stomach, and she balled up her fists again and rammed them down onto his face. His vision went blurry as one hand hit his left eye and the other hit his nose.

"Get off me!" Ellis yelled frantically trying to cover his face. Jennifer swung hammer fist blows down onto his body.

Blood began to spring from his mouth and nose. From a slice on his cheek. From his right eye. He took blows to his stomach, his chest, even his throat. He struggled to breathe as Jennifer's fists broke ribs. Ellis threw a fist at Jennifer's cheek, knocking her off him. He wheezed sharply. He glared at Jennifer who sat up quickly. She rolled away onto her knees and onto her feet. Jennifer rubbed her face, eyes burning with anger.

"How dare you strike a woman." She growled through a clenched grin. She marched down to his legs. She flicked a kick at his injured thigh. He reached for the pain.

"Aaaah. You sick…" His word cut off as she launched a kick to his groin. He let out a weak groan as the pain leapt into his stomach. He coughed. Blood lurching from his mouth. He slowly rolled to his side and held his ribs and crotch.

"Pathetic," Jennifer mocked, strolling back to the desk. All Ellis could do was watch through his teary vision as she leaned across the desk and pull back straight with the bolt gun in hand. Ellis slowly raised a hand in surrender.

"Please…Don't…Stop," Ellis said between ragged breaths. Jennifer's eyes were wide and furious. She aimed the bolt gun straight at him. She squeezed the trigger. The bolt plunged into his stomach, ramming him across the floor in a pool of blood. He screamed.

Jennifer watched Ellis as his body began to shiver. The life blood poured from his stomach and lower back. Ellis looked up at Jennifer again. He opened his mouth. Blood replaced his voice. Jennifer fired again. The bolt exploded into his face, slinging his body round in the blood pool.

Jennifer's face was blank, she tilted her head to the side staring at the body. She relaxed her hands. The bolt gun dropped to the floor.

"Jen?"

She turned slowly. Kara stood in front of her. She was shaking with rage. She held Annabelle's bone saw in her right hand. Both hands clenched tightly.

The blank stare on Jennifer's face morphed into sadness. Her eyes filled with water until tears ran down her cheeks. Kara screamed and threw the saw across Jennifer's throat. The look of sadness on Jennifer's face held as blood poured from her neck down her body to the floor. A moment later, Jennifer collapsed.

Luca grabbed hold of Kara and tore the saw from her hands. Kara's legs gave way and the two slumped to the floor. Kara began to cry hysterically. Annabelle dropped to one knee clutching her stomach. She fought to hold back the vomit. Her tears came regardless.

Grace gathered herself around Annabelle and held her tightly. Kara screamed into the air and pushed out of Luca's grasp. She was shaking wildly as she crawled across the floor to Ellis's body. She slumped over him and continued to cry.

"No. No. Nathan. Oh god no," Kara blubbered over his body.

Grace saw Luca. He hadn't moved since Kara left his grasp. She squeezed Annabelle harder before letting go. She shifted over to Luca and squeezed his shoulder before resting her head on his other shoulder.

"I am so sorry sweetheart," Grace said softly, caressing his shoulder.

"Nathan too," Luca whispered.

"What'd you say?" Annabelle asked.

"Chelsey's gone too."

Annabelle joined the two and put her arms around Luca. Grace stroked Annabelle's cheek as she moved aside. Annabelle got in close, straddling his knee. Annabelle squeezed her body against his.

"I'm so sorry sugar. Y'all were inseparable."

"We were family," Luca said with a look of shook. Annabelle kissed him softly on the cheek. She shifted closer. Luca held on tighter.

After a minute, their grip slowly loosed when they both realised, they were straddling each other. Both able to feel the other upon their knee. *Fuck it.* Annabelle rose up high and held his face against her pillows for comfort.

Grace slowly approached Kara still slumped over Ellis, water streaming down her face. Grace slowly got down onto her knees, crawled into Kara, and began to rub her shoulders. Kara looked back at her before lunging into her embrace.

"It's all my fault. I knew she was jealous. I knew she was crazy."

"You can't blame yourself for any of this. Everything has gone to hell on this ship. We must find the strength to get off it," Grace explained.

Annabelle released Luca's head. He gave her a nod.

"That was nice. Thank you."

"It's the least I could do Sugar. You saved my life. Twice."

Annabelle kissed his forehead and held him again. Luca stared at Jennifer's body, watching the blood pour from her open throat, and spreading across the floor. Annabelle looked at him staring off behind her.

She shot a look back too. Thin tentacles were slowly flicking at the air from Jennifer's open throat.

"Holy shit!" Annabelle barked, flinging herself off Luca with a spin.

"Get back. Get back!" Annabelle called louder. Kara and Grace looked at Annabelle, then saw the tentacles thickening and stretching outward. Kara and Grace kicked their legs wildly as they backed across the floor on their behinds. Annabelle leapt forward and grabbed the bone saw and quickly moved back and bumped into Luca. He was standing tall axe firm in hand.

"No more hero stuff Luca," Annabelle said calmly.

"No more hero stuff."

"Kara, Grace," Annabelle whispered waving her hand for them to join them.

Jennifer's body still hadn't moved but the tentacles continued to whip around as they continued to expand. Kara and Grace joined Annabelle and Luca who stood like a shield wall.

"Let's move somewhere else," Grace whispered.

"Good idea," Kara added. Annabelle side stepped slowly to the door and pressed the panel. The door slid open, and Annabelle glanced into the corridor. She darted out and turned back. She signalled them to follow her. First came Grace, followed by Kara and Luca reluctantly leaving the battle behind.

Chapter 32: Reunion

"Swing."

"What?"

"Swing you idiot. I'll grab the door."

Stefan and Rajiv began to shift their weight until the cable began to sway. As the momentum increased Stefan began to reach for the elevator door. Shortly Stefan grabbed a handful wiring that added the opening system of the doors. Their swing stopped. Stefan began to pull toward the door.

"Okay pull the lever, get them open," Stefan told him. Rajiv yanked the lever down and pulled at one of the sliding doors. Rajiv climbed into the corridor on the floor. Stefan reached in and gestured for help. Rajiv grabbed him with both hands and pulled him inside. Rajiv fell backward. Stefan fell on him and quickly stood brushing at his uniform.

"Okay kid. Quickest way to the labs?"

Rajiv struggled to his feet and dusted himself off.

"Ah. Yeah, this way Sir," Rajiv said walking down the main corridor. He stopped at the corner and peeked round.

"Well?" Stefan asked.

"Huh? What Sir?"

"It's Captain…Is the corridor clear?"

"Sort off."

"Uh fuck me," Stefan scowled barging passed him into the next bend. The sort of was a simple reference to the bloody mess that decorated the area.

Stefan moved fast down the corridor to the next bend and had a look.

"Which way?"

"Left."

Stefan hurried off again to the following junction.

"Straight on," Rajiv called out from behind. Stefan glanced to the right turn as he passed. He stopped and turned. He stood at the junction.

"Anna!" Stefan shouted before running down the corridor toward her. Stefan almost threw her into the air when he grabbed her.

"Oh, My god. You're okay," Stefan said backing to look at her. He saw her jacket was missing, her open shirt around the belly. The mixture of blood, black tar speckles and streaks of clear liquid down her abdomen and over her trousers.

"Jesus Christ! What happened to you?" he asked removing his suit jacket. He threw his jacket over her shoulders. He attempted to button the front.

"It's a long story," Annabelle paused.

"Seriously," Annabelle glared down at herself as Stefan tried to cover her. Stefan paused for a moment and stopped closing buttons.

"I'm glad you're alright Stef," Annabelle said changing the subject. Stefan smiled and hugged her again.

"Grace." He moved on to her.

"Thank god your safe." He shook her hand and looked at the large guy at her back.

"Luca, isn't it?"

"Yes Captain."

Stefan glanced past him.

"Where's the rest of your team?" Stefan asked fearing the answer.

"They didn't survive Captain," Luca admitted lowering his gaze.

"This is Kara," Grace said stepping to the side.

"Hello Captain. Karabina, your new navigation officer," she said professionally shaking his hand.

"I'm terribly sorry. I bet you've had one hell of a first day."

Kara just lowered her gaze.

"That's an understatement," Kara admitted. Stefan rubbed her shoulder.

"We're going to get out of this I promise you," he said before turning back to Annabelle.

Annabelle was at the junction. Her arms tight around Rajiv's shoulders. His arms tight around her waist. They did not speak. They did not kiss. They just held each other. Both with eyes held tightly shut. Both breathing softly.

Grace tapped Stefan's shoulder.

"Where were you to heading?"

Stefan kept his eyes on the pair.

"To the labs. I need to know how this thing spreads. Are we all infected already?"

"I don't believe we are. I think it's purely a physical transmission."

"I have to be sure."

"We should join you. Anna?" Grace said. Annabelle released her hold on Rajiv and turned.

"They are heading to the lab," Grace began.

"To end the quarantine?" Annabelle interrupted.

"Hopefully," Stefan answered, noting the anger in Annabelle's voice. Rajiv took her hand. He nodded at Stefan and led Annabelle off down the corridor.

The rest of them caught up with them quickly and made their way to the nearest science lab. Rajiv slowed when they reached a corridor of bodies. Some lay on the ground and others sat against the walls. Every single one cut, torn or dismembered.

"Oh, dear lord," Annabelle said softly, she felt the grip on her hand tighten and pull quicker. She regarded Rajiv. *Stern. Focused. Brave...Attractive.* Rajiv stormed passed the bodies, but still stepped carefully not to step on anyone.

They reached a science lab and Rajiv palmed the panel. The door slid open. Five science staff members had been killed inside. Stefan moved to the desk that housed the micro-scopes. He checked the body that was slumped there. A needle loose in his fingers.

"Grace?"

She joined him and inspected the body.

"He's killed himself."

"What about them?" Stefan nodded at the other four on the ground. Grace went to check them while Stefan pulled the body from the chair. Luca joined him quickly and helped him lay the body on the ground. Kara closed the door while Rajiv sat in the chair the body had been in. Annabelle stood behind his chair. He pulled the sample from his pocket and opened the container. He gestured at a tray of surgical equipment. Annabelle collected the tray and placed it beside him.

"I need a blood and urine samples from everyone," Rajiv said quietly as he began slicing into the piece of creature he'd collected.

Annabelle joined Grace while she spoke with Stefan.

"These four were the same. Suicide. Morphine injections."

Stefan regarded the bodies.

"I don't blame their choices."

"Neither do I."

"Grace? Rajiv need's a blood and urine sample from everyone," Annabelle explained.

"Okay sweetie. I'll get yours first," Grace gathered syringes and vials and sat at a triage table with two chairs built in. Annabelle sat opposite and rolled up her left arm, sleeve.

"Whoever is waiting. Take a tube from the tray," Grace said briefly pointing. "Toilet is back there. Fill 'em up." She pointed again. Stefan offered the bottle of water he'd collected to everyone, and some took a drink. Annabelle approached Rajiv with her blood sample.

"The petri dishes. Use that syringe there. One drop from each and seal the dish. Copy the initials to each dish." While he explained, Annabelle began collecting the petri dishes.

Rajiv prepared the creature sample and Annabelle began labelling the dishes. Annabelle looked at Rajiv several times with no eye contact.

"Are you okay Sugar?"

"I'm fine."

"What's wrong Rajiv?"

Rajiv glanced at her as he sliced.

"Nothing."

Annabelle stopped marking and touched his shoulder.

"Rajiv. Look at me. What is wrong?"

Rajiv glared at her. "The last time I saw you. You hit me, twice. Or did you forget that."

"I'm sorry about the punch. And especially the knee," Annabelle began leaning into his ear.

"I didn't mean to hurt you sugar. Especially there. Especially your area."

"Don't do that. You hurt me. The punch hurt. The knee even more so. But the worst part. Your willingness to strike me in the first place. That hurt me the most," Rajiv explained, focusing on his work.

"Hey," Annabelle taking his hand. He looked at her.

"I promise you. I will never hit you again. Never," Annabelle said sternly but sweetly.

"I said some horrible things, didn't I? I clearly over reacted," Rajiv admitted.

"We both did," Annabelle said before kissing his neck extremely gently, sensually. Rajiv smiled and blushed.

"Have you done the labels?" He smirked, distracting himself. Kara joined them with the rest of the samples.

Annabelle made room for her at the table.

"Thank you, Sugar. Can you place a drop of blood on the dish with the same name?" Annabelle explained.

"Sure. No problem."

"One syringe for each drop of blood."

Kara nodded as she began.

"Are you doing okay Sweetie?" Annabelle asked touching her shoulder. Kara took a breath.

"I hadn't seen Nathan for four years. All I got was that awkward reunion," Kara said as she added a dropped of blood to each dish.

"It is more than some people ever get."

Kara shot a disgusted look.

"The chance to see someone we love once more," Annabelle continued.

"Nathan was…beautiful…inside and out."

"I quickly found out he was playful but truly kind. Was he always protective?" Annabelle asked her. Kara paused, a memory playing back in her mind.

"Yes, he was," she said smiling.

"Did you know Ellis arranged your transfer," Annabelle added while sealing the dishes.

"He did? How do you know that?"

"He told me about you. I arranged his chat with the Captain," Annabelle nodded at him. "And Ellis convinced him to give you the Job."

"Really. Wow."

"Beautiful inside and out Sugar," Annabelle rubbed Kara's shoulder. Stefan came from the toilet cubicle with his tube of urine.

"Your next Anna," he said before added his urine sample to the others. Annabelle picked up her tube and made off to the cubicle.

Chapter 33: Test

Rajiv studied each sample carefully, searching for any abnormalities. Grace sat beside him examining the urine samples. Stefan sat on a chair at the digital console with Annabelle resting on her hip on the floor in front of him. As they spoke Kara nudged Luca's arm from the desk, they both sat on.

"I can't tell if that's endearing or creepy," Kara whispered looking over at the old Captain and the young beauty at crotch level.

Luca smirked.

"From what I've seen it's a father and daughter deal…Besides she's actually with him," Luca pointed loosely at Rajiv. Kara stared at Luca; her jaw floored.

"No way. That guy."

Luca nodding. Kara looked over at him again.

"No way. Really. Wow."

"Yes, I know."

"Yeah but. How? I mean, she's amazing. I would. I'm sure you and Nathan would have taken a shot," Kara suggested quietly.

Luca giggled.

"Nathan asked once."

"And she shot him down."

"More like, laid him down gently, kissed his cheek and walked away."

Kara looked puzzled.

"Oh yeah, she was so kind and respectful when he asked her. He simply couldn't bring himself to ask again. You know like: she knows I'm game, if she is, she'll let me know. They just became good friends."

Kara nodded as he explained.

"What about you?"

"Oh no, no, no. She labelled me her big brother shortly after we met."

"Is that a friend zone thing."

"Yeah, but the being there goes both ways. She'd always do her best to help me out in any situation."

"She seems too good to be real doesn't she."

"She's not extraordinary or anything. She's a friendly woman who is sexy as hell."

"Like I said doesn't seem real. That guy though," Kara returned her attention to Rajiv.

Stefan offered the water bottle again.

"I'm good," Annabelle waved a hand.

"Have another drink please."

Annabelle rolled her eyes.

"I just said I'm fine," she said snatching the bottle from his hand.

"Yes, I know. Could be worse I could be bashing your dress code." He mocked flicking a finger at her body. She glanced down; a large portion of skin was on display despite Stefan's jacket on her. She put the bottle down and forced another two clasps shut. The first was the hardest crossing the widest part.

"Happy now. I feel like I'm trapped in a bottle," Annabelle gestured her hand's upward.

"You'll be warmer."

"Hush up, Stef," Annabelle rolled her eyes. Stefan leaned back in his chair with a stunned expression. Annabelle took up the bottle and drunk. She set it aside and glared down at the floor.

Stefan watched her for a few moments.

"How much longer do you think?"

"Not sure. Rajiv needs to be one hundred percent sure right."

"I can't help myself Anna," Stefan continued.

"I know," Annabelle replied still gazing at the floor.

"I care about you."

Annabelle looked at him.

"Yes, I know you do. Trouble is, you worry about what people are thinking when they look at me…Because you're already thinking it."

Stefan's jaw dropped and he shifted uncomfortably in the chair.

"No. That's not it at all. How can you say that I." His words dropped off.

"I don't resent you for it, Stef. You can lock it in your box or your bank. Just be the dad you want to be the rest of the time."

"Please don't refer to banking anything again," Stefan said leaning in close. Annabelle rose to her knees. She kissed his hand that rested upon his knee and looked up at him.

"Yes, Daddy. Never again," Annabelle said sweetly before using his knees to get to her feet.

Kara watched the two.

"Definitely creepy," she mumbled under her breath.

"Creepy as fuuuuck," she said aloud in a playful tone while watching Annabelle approached the workstation.

"What was that?" Luca said lifting his head from a resting position.

"That's not a father and daughter thing."

"No." He replied resting his eye's again.

"No. That's a sugar daddy thing."

"People see what they want to see."

Kara shot a look at Luca who still had his eyes closed with his head against the wall.

"What?"

"Just because you think it's there doesn't always mean it is."

"Just because I think you're crazy, doesn't mean you are," Kara mocked his tone.

"Exactly."

Annabelle gently laid her arms around Rajiv and kissed his cheek. Rajiv smiled and stroked her arm.

"How we doing Baby," she spoke softly.

"Last one. Just Doctor Lancaster with the pee."

Annabelle glanced over.

"Captain?" Grace called out. Annabelle looked to him as he rose from the chair. Kara nudged Luca.

"Hey. I'm awake."

"Listen," Kara told him, pointing. Stefan approached the desk and stood between Grace and Rajiv. Annabelle shifted round to lean on the desk.

"What's the verdict team?"

"We're all clear," Grace smiled.

"You are sure," Stefan asked looking at both Grace and Rajiv.

"Without a doubt…The only way this creature can transmit is through physical contact. Fastest induction is into the blood stream," Rajiv explained, now also smiling.

Stefan nodded and walked away. Annabelle scowled and looked at Rajiv, then to Grace who in turn looked at Stefan. Annabelle sprang from the desk.

"Captain?" He sat back in the chair. As Annabelle approached, he peeked at her before slapping his face into his hands.

"Stef? What? This is good news," Annabelle said clasping his wrists and squatting in front of him. He spread his palms and looked at her.

"You know a good Captain saves lives in a disaster."

"You have saved lives."

"I condemned everyone to death."

"Oh, no. no. You didn't. This isn't your fault," Annabelle spoke as if he was her little boy.

"I had a hunch it spread like a virus. I was wrong. We should have evacuated hours ago."

"Yeah, we should have," Kara said climbing from the desk. Annabelle shot her a look, Luca attempted to grab her arm but missed.

"If we had evacuated, Nathan would still be alive, Jennifer would still be alive…"

"Back off Kara," Annabelle growled.

"…Chelsey would still be alive," Kara stopped her advance. "That was in this scenario Captain. In another it would have been a virus. You would have evacuated. And everyone out there. Ares Base. Luna Base. Earth. Would have an alien creature killing them. All of them." Everyone fell silent. Annabelle looked up at Stefan again and smiled.

Luca held Kara's shoulder. She glanced at him and he gave a solid nod.

"You made the right call Stefan," Grace confirmed.

"See. You've saved billions of lives with that call," Annabelle spoke sweetly.

"If you could save a few more that would be great," Rajiv said gesturing at them all.

Stefan looked at each of their faces until he was back at Annabelle. He brushed her doting face. Stefan returned the look.

"We need a plan."

Stefan stood with Annabelle.

"We need to get the surviving crew off without allowing a single one of those thing's near a shuttle," Stefan explained.

"Can we kill them. Could we do that?" Luca asked.

"Yeah, couldn't we vent the ship?" Kara added.

"Hum," Rajiv said half raising his hand.

"I don't think it would work. This creature survived on Pluto's moon. There's no doubt they could hibernate in the vacuum."

"Alright. No venting," Kara admitted.

"How about heat then Sugar," Annabelle asked Rajiv. "Your command code. Blow the ship," Annabelle continued turning to Stefan. He shook his head.

"Call me selfish but I don't want to spend the last of my days in prison. My override will be logged automatically."

"How much is the Euphoria worth? Several billion?" Grace added. Stefan smirked.

"More."

"Can we make it an accident? Crash the ship," Luca suggested.

"Where though? Crash on Mars? And if anything survives. I mean how many people are down there?" Rajiv said.

"At least five thousand. Men, women and children," Stefan told them.

"Oh, dear Lord," Annabelle said before covering her mouth in shock.

"So, we keep it sealed," Luca said, everyone looked at him. "I mean we still get out. Explain the situation, send a team to deal with these things."

"And sentence the response team to death," Grace added.

They stood in silence. Kara stared at the ground scowling.

"I think I have an answer."

"We're all ears Kara."

"We re-direct to Jupiter. We send the Euphoria straight in its mass. With its insane winds, extreme temperature and it's crushing force, there will be nothing left of it," Kara explained.

"What is the crush force?" Luca asked.

"It's in the millions."

"Forty-four million, estimated of course," Stefan added.

"Can you make it seem like an accident?" Annabelle asked her.

"It's frightening how easy it can be done. I'll need a minute to calculate a new course."

"We all need to agree on this. I tell the bridge crew the same. Complete accident," Stefan explained.

Stefan studied all the faces. Each person nodded in agreement.

"First thing's first. I need to return to the bridge to gather the crew and lift the lockdown. And Kara can input the change."

"The display behind you," Annabelle pointed. "Ellis…Repaired the link." She glanced at Kara. Stefan turned to the clear display behind, Rajiv approached the console and tapped at the holographic keypad.

"She's right, we have a connection," Rajiv said stepping aside from the console. "It's all yours Captain."

Stefan turned to face the console.

"Bridge come in." He glanced at Rajiv. "Bridge do you copy. This is Captain Dietrich. Respond." He looked at Rajiv again. Rajiv shrugged and studied the panel.

"The line is solid. They should hear you."

Stefan looked back at the others and gestured a hand at Annabelle then back at the display console.

"I've spoken to the bridge since the repair," Annabelle confirmed scowling.

"Bridge respond. Romiley? Page? Anyone? Why won't they answer?"

"Could they be dead?" Luca suggested grimly.

"I relayed an order through a Hab panel. The bridge should have locked down with the holding pattern."

"Did they get that order?" Grace asked.

"Yes, Romiley told me we're holding round Mars," Annabelle added.

"OK back to plan A. Kara and I will head to the bridge. The rest of you get to the shuttle…"

"Captain. I need a word," Grace interrupted. Everyone looked at her.

Chapter 34: Orders

Romiley spun in his chair, Page had done the same. Someone or something was thumping at the large doors to the bridge deck. Romiley slowly stood and approached the door.

"Captain is that you?" Leaning his ear against the door.

"Let me in. Now god damn it."

Romiley reached to his right and slapped the door release. The door began to open. The moment it was wide enough Cole lunged through tackling Romiley to the floor.

"Close it! Close it! Close it!" He screamed in a frantic panicked state on the floor. Page leapt from the chair and slapped the door panel at her side of the room. The door jolted and began to reverse its slow slide.

She hurried over to the pair on the floor.

"Are you alright Rom?" she asked helping him to his feet.

"Yeah, I'm okay." He glared down at Cole on the floor. He lay with his eyes closed, breathing fast. "Hey?" Cole opened his eyes.

"Oh, thanks man. Thank you," he said offering a hand. Romiley excepted and pulled Cole to his feet.

"Are they on this deck Cole?" Romiley asked holding his shoulders.

"Yes, they are."

"Oh, dear god," Page said clutching her mouth. Cole looked over the piloting crew who had all turned to face him in their chairs. He turned to Page.

"Don't worry about those things out there." He looked back at the piloting crew.

"Saleem. Hold this." He called out to the central pilot. Saleem nodded and with his left-hand Cole side threw a beer bottle to him. Saleem reached for the bottle.

He caught it and the bottle exploded. The blast vaporised his hand and shredded his arm to the shoulder. The glass burst in a shower of fire. Glass shards pepper all three of them at the pilot desk. Cole's right hand swung across Page's throat, a kitchen knife in hand. As she grasped at her open neck, Cole turned and began driving the knife swiftly into Romiley's stomach. Romiley's mouth was gaping as he struggled to scream. Cole driving the knife faster and faster into his abdomen. Cole pushed him back to arm's length before thrusting the blade upward, below the jaw.

In the same motion, he pulled the blade back. A jet of blood chasing the tip of the blade. Cole swung back to page who had turned toward her desk, hand's still grasping her gushing throat. Cole leapt forward and slashed at the back of her thigh and she folded to the floor. Cole paused for a moment and glanced around the room at the pilot's desk. Saleem lay dead over his console. The shock of the blast still in his eyes.

Asher and Nashi were screaming, holding their faces, glass deep in their skin and eyes. Cole approached the Asher to the right. He leaned in to look at the damage on his face and grimaced before jabbing the knife through his eye killing him. On the far-left, Nashi had fallen from her chair now and struggled to crawl on one hand, the other trying to hold her face together. Cole stood over her and aimed the knife like a spear. He quickly thrust at the base of her skull, and she dropped flat.

Cole wiped the blade on Nashi's back before concealing it. He glanced at Page as he approached the communication desk. Her hands still on her throat, her eyes open. Dead eyes. Cole studied the console.

"Where's the…oh yeah," he said spotting the head set still upon Romiley's head.

"Bridge come in," Cole leapt from Romiley's body.

"Fucking hell."

"Bridge do you copy. This is Captain Dietrich. Respond."

He moved back in and slipped the head set off Romiley.

"Still kicking I see," Cole said looking at the headset.

"Bridge respond? Romiley? Page? Anyone? Why won't they answer?" Cole flicked a switch ending the connection.

"I don't care what you have to say," Cole tapped a few buttons and began turning a large chrome dial. He turned it several times. He then pushed some more buttons before putting the headset on.

"Asgard, Agent update." He paused. "Asgard, Agent update."

"Code in Agent this is Asgard." A computerised female voice replied.

"David Arthur Cole…6 8 1 7 8 7 8 2."

"We expected to have you in person by now Cole." The voiced said sternly.

"Yes, well I didn't expect the Euphoria Captain to be so emotional."

"You are still aboard the Euphoria?"

"Correct. Long story but my samples are secure, and I've gathered additional data on the Charon organism."

"Wait one."

"Order update. Incoming."

Cole rolled his eyes.

"Send it."

"Sending coordinates. Enter into pilot console one. Re-calculate console two. Enable at console three. Bring samples and data home."

"Understood. The Euphoria is in quarantine. How do I open the shuttle bay from here?"

"Wait one."

"Captain's override: Stefan Dietrich…7 8 6 4 5 8 5. Override quarantine."

"Thank you Asgard."

"Communication scrambling in 5, 4, 3, 2, 1." A burst of white noise forced Cole to tear the headset off.

"Shit," he said shaking his ear.

Chapter 35: Evac

They watched in silence while Stefan and Grace spoke. Stefan rubbed his neck and glanced up at the ceiling. He clenched his eyes tight for a moment. Grace gestured and he nodded. She spoke again and Stefan pointed at her. It wasn't aggressive. Maybe an order. Kara wasn't sure. He looked at the floor and took a deep breath. He cleared his throat and headed for the Lab doors. Grace held her mouth for a second before revealing a grin.

They gathered at the doors with Stefan, and he regarded Annabelle for a moment.

"What is it?" she asked quietly. Stefan reached behind and drew his pistol. Holding the grip, he offered it to her slide first. Instinctively she took the USP 45 handgun and pulled the slide back a little, a bullet was chambered.

"What are you doing Stef? You know I won't take this from you," she said forcing it back into his hand.

"Two up, four down. It makes more sense for you to take it. Protect each other."

"If you fail, we all fail." She countered. "If Kara gets hurt, we all fail. If you don't make it to the bridge, we all fail," Annabelle stare was becoming aggressive.

"We'll ensure her safety, won't we gentlemen," Grace interrupted.

"No doubt," Luca added. Stefan regarded Rajiv. He reached down and took her hand firmly and looked to Stefan. He nodded in approval.

Stefan settled his grip on the pistol and got comfortable.

"Luca, the door please."

Luca turned and slapped the door release. With a gentle hiss, the door slid open. The darkness began to leak in. Stefan stepped into the corridor and checked each side. Distant lights flickered for short periods before going off.

He thumbed the torch attachment before shining the beam in both directions.

"Kara?" he whispered, she joined him.

"Good luck everyone," he continued before the pair walked slowly away to the right. Luca illuminated the harness torch and stepped out next, followed by Grace. They moved slowly to the left as Rajiv stepped out leading Annabelle. She tugged on his grip, stopping. He looked at her while she watched Stefan and Kara disappear into the darkness.

"Come on," Rajiv whispered, giving her hand a shake.

They moved slowly; Luca held the axe ready with both hands.

"Which way?" Grace asked. He glanced back before watching ahead again.

"Elevator eight jammed up on the eighth deck. So, its roof is just below deck seven. The safest way to open those doors."

"How do we get down there?"

"We have to climb down."

"No, Luca. Grace can't make that climb."

"Neither can Anna?" Grace interrupted. Annabelle scowled.

"Grace, I carry these all day. My back is extraordinarily strong trust me."

"Stop it. I still have the harness. I can help you down grace," Luca snapped as quietly as he could.

"And what if you fall. Or if Anna and Rajiv fall. It's too dangerous."

Luca stopped the train and turned.

"What else can I do Doctor…Turn the gravity off."

"You can do that?" Rajiv asked.

"I'll have to go to the Spire and…"

"No, nuh huh, no way. I'm not going back to the Spire. It's like a rotting hive of muck in there," Annabelle mind regressed to the small clambering creatures and their milky blood that was still in her clothing. She shuddered. Rajiv began rubbing her arms as if she were cold. *Isn't he adorable?* She gave a loving smile.

"Okay no Spire. We climb, now let's keep moving before they realise were here," Luca growled as he turned to watch ahead again.

They continued but paused when sighting a humanoid creature that had been cleaved right down the middle to its groin. Its arms acting like a second pair of legs with a mass of liquid like tentacles thrashing at the air and stringing hooks anchoring it together. It lumbered off around a bend. Luca signalled and moved in the opposite direction.

When they reached the doors to elevator eight, Luca jammed the axe in between the doors. He leaned on the handle wrenching the doors open. A moist stale smell attacked their noses. Luca grimaced looking into the shaft below.

"Is that like that hive thing," Luca asked nodding Annabelle over. She glanced inside. The shaft had black tar streaming down its walls. It seemed thicker in places, strangely the entire cascade of streaking tar ran up the shaft. Some of the black goo liquid strung from the walls to the cable like over weighted webbing.

"No nothing like this."

"Good to know. Take these," Luca said handing Annabelle working gloves.

"What about yours?"

"The rest of us can use our sleeves and hug the cable. You can't really do that," Luca whispered.

"I see. Thank you, Sugar."

Luca nodded at her before extending an arm to Grace. Luca began opening the harness while Grace glared into the shaft.

"You'll be fine. You're in the best hands, on board," Annabelle told as Luca crouched behind her and turned away. Rajiv turned away staring off down the corridor resenting the statement. Annabelle began to lock Grace into the Harness.

"Luca will jump for the cable. It will frighten you. But your perfectly safe," Grace closed her eyes tightly, taking a deep breath. She tried to kiss Annabelle's forehead but just lurched. Annabelle leaned forward to except the kiss, smiling.

"You ready Grace?"

"I'm ready, Let's…whoa," Graces words were torn away as Luca stood, lifting her clear of the floor.

"We'll be right behind you," Annabelle announced. Grace's stomach turned, her eyes widened, and her breath left her as Luca leapt for the cable. Slinging his arms and legs around the cable they stopped for the briefest of moments. A second rush washed over Grace as Luca began the slide down the cable.

They descended fast down the cable. Luca's engineering suit heating up against the metal cable. The moist air rushing over them like a trophic breeze. The stringy black tar that held the cable was torn away as Luca's legs rushed downward. The black liquid on walls began to shimmer. As Luca and Grace slid passed the tar gently twitched, flexed and began to reach.

Annabelle swung back to see Rajiv staring off down the corridor.

"Do you see something?" She whispered. Rajiv made no reply. She approached him slowly.

"Rajiv, sweetie? What is it?"

"Huh? Nothing."

Annabelle touched his face as he turned.

"Are you sure?" she asked sweetly.

"I'm okay, honestly." He kissed her forehead. "You, first."

They approached the door. Annabelle fitted the gloves. She readied and leapt for the cable.

"Aaaah. Shit." She growled as she slammed into the cable.

"Anna?"

"I'm okay, hurt my tits!" She growled again.

Luca tightened his grip as he neared the elevator roof near deck seven. As he reached the floor, he took the impact in the knees for a second before Grace felt the landing too. The pair fell to the right onto their side.

"Aaaah!" Luca yelled. He pulled at the harness quickly, unstrapping Grace. With gritted teeth, he rolled to face her.

"Grace?"

She glanced at him. "I hit my head," Luca got closer and looked at the wound. Her skin had split at the left side of her temple and blood was slowly ponding.

"Damn it. I'm so sorry. Can you sit?"

"Yeah," she said raising a hand. He sat her up and held his sleeve against the wound. She winced.

"How bad?"

"It'll need stitching."

Anabelle got her legs around the cable and leaned back holding tightly with her gloves. She allowed herself to slip down a few metres and looked up for Rajiv. He leapt onto the cable and growled.

"Rajiv?" Annabelle asked.

"I'm good."

Annabelle began to slide down again, this time Rajiv followed. They slid much slower than Luca and Grace with the separated weight. As the pair slid down the black tar began to shimmer and pulsate. It began to stretch and reach. Annabelle heard a thud below and stopped.

"What is it?" Rajiv whispered.

"I thought I heard Luca call out."

"We need to get down to them."

The pair continued down. Thin lines of the tar began to coil around itself forming tentacles. They began to thrash and whip toward the couple, just failing to reach them as they passed. Luca had helped Grace to her feet, she stood at the elevator's doors holding her bleeding head. He stood at the base of the cable waiting for the arrival of the other two. Annabelle appeared in his torch light.

"Luca?"

"I'm here."

"Are you alright?" Annabelle asked as Luca grabbed her at the waist. He moved her off the cable. And she saw Grace cradling her temple. She gave Luca a nod and rushed to Grace.

"What happened?" she asked inspecting her injury. Rajiv reached Luca's waiting position. Luca crouched as he aided Rajiv's landing. Annabelle tore a strip of material from her shirt and proceeded to clean the blood from Graces head.

Luca and Rajiv were at the door. Rajiv had pulled the lever to unlock the door. Luca pulled hard but the door only shifted a few inches.

"Shit," Luca said looking at Rajiv's puzzled face. The two began to pull together opening the doors several more inches. Cables of black tar stretched across the opening. Luca began throwing axe swings at the webbing wall.

The black tentacles were continuing to move and expand, twist and reach. Rajiv wrenched at one side of the elevator door while Luca continued to cut through the net of black greasy ropes. When the breach was wide enough Annabelle ushered Grace to the opening and climbed through. Staying on her knees she helped Grace through. The shuttle deck was much darker than before. Black tar liquid stretched along much of the walls and ceiling. Most of the lighting had been consumed by the mass of black goo everywhere. Rajiv crawled through next. Annabelle and Grace helped him stand. Luca laid his axe on the greasy floor before heaving himself through the gap.

Luca grabbed at Annabelle's leg. He gritted his teeth and scrunched up his face. He growled in pain. He lurched back into the opening pulling Annabelle off her feet. Luca grabbed each side of doors and screamed. Grace leapt forward grabbing at Luca's left arm. She wrapped her arms around his forearm. Luca pulled hard at the doors, trying to get back in. Rajiv was now pulling on his right arm. Luca yelled out again. Annabelle grabbed at the collar of Luca's flight suit. She glanced over his prone body and saw a swarm of tentacles lashing back and forth in the shaft. Luca coughed. Blood burst from his mouth, speckling Annabelle's face with blood.

A thick tentacle reached out, spreading at its end. It shaped like a leaf, razor sharp teeth forming at the spine. It slapped down on Luca's lower back, its teeth hooking into his flesh. Luca screamed out and the tentacle pulled. Luca was ripped off the floor, he struggled to keep his grip on the doors. Annabelle, Rajiv, and Grace were yanked off their knees to their feet. Luca's flesh tore and the four dropped back to the ground, all losing their grip on Luca. Luca hit the floor hard, cutting his face. He rolled to his side, trying to hold his wounded back. Annabelle grabbed the axe. The tentacles gathered over Luca. The oval tentacle repositioned and slapped down at Luca's face. Annabelle swung the axe upward, the blade cut through the right side of the oval. It pulled back; the half that remained came down on Luca's shoulder.

"Close them!" Annabelle shouted swinging the axe across the oval again, slicing the top off it. Clear plasma spraying upward. Rajiv and Grace pushed on the doors. The damaged tentacle whipped wildly, and they pushed the doors against it. The tentacle retreated through the opening as it became tighter until the doors closed.

Chapter 36: Together

Captain Dietrich palmed the door panel. The rustic door slid upward. He swung his pistol into the room. Steel shelves lined the door. He moved inside before waving Kara in behind. She stepped in, closing the door behind. Stefan scanned the room, peeking high and ducking low between the shelves.

"Seems clear," he said holstering his weapon.

"Okay what are we looking for?" Kara said shifting through equipment and boxing along the shelves.

"There must be climbing gear in here somewhere. Harnesses, rope and most importantly we need an ascender," Stefan explained searching the shelves himself. Kara pulled clasps open on a box and slid the lid off. Stefan crouched to a large open crate and found a para cord bundle of rope. Kara opened another box. She pulled out the strapping inside this box, it unfolded to a harness shape.

A loud clang echoed through the room. The pair stopped and looked up at the ducting system above. A quiet snarl coming through the vent at the end.

"Keep looking," Stefan whispered drawing his gun. Kara laid two harnesses beside the bundle of rope. A shriek erupted all around. Stefan shot a look behind before refocusing on the vent. Kara opening boxes methodically. She opened every box upon the shelf before starting on the larger crates on the floor. Stefan moved round getting a better sight on the vent opening. There was another clung from the ducting. From her crouched position, Kara shifted over and popped open another crate. In a form insert sat two ascenders with a double wheel system.

The duct broke at a join and slipped on its suspension cable. Two snake like arms emerged from the duct. They pushed and heaved its bulk out of the tight ducting. It dropped to the floor like a mangled corpse. Blood and black goo splattered across the floor and the creature rose slowly. Kara lurched backward onto her backside and shuffled away across the floor. Kara could make out human skin stretched throughout the fountain of black leather tentacles as it focused on her. Its many tentacles coiling around the shelves. Kara shuffled backward on her heels. One tentacle rose, the end stiffening into a point. It shifted and focused on Kara like an entranced cobra. The spike became larger and sharper. The rest lurching forward.

Stefan fired his gun. Bullets smashed and shattered through the spike. A roar erupted from somewhere inside the creature as it turned toward Stefan. The shelving bent and buckled as the creature pulled itself round. The boxes came down over Kara, she slid herself under the collapsing steel. Stefan fired at the centre mass of tentacles. It whipped and lashed at Stefan's head. He dropped to one knee and fired at the attacking limbs. Landing four shots into one limb and it tore on its own weight.

"Kara? The gear."

Kara pulled with her palms across the floor. She grabbed the Harness with her right hand and pulled back as a tentacle slammed down in front of her. Stefan fired again, chunks of tentacle and black goo spat across the room. The creature lunged for Stefan, and he backed out of its grasp. He backed up between another row of shelves. The creature crashed into the narrow space bending and buckling the structure. Kara reached and grabbed the bundle of rope. She pulled it back, but a small cluster of tentacles latched onto the rope. It pulled her back toward the large mass as Stefan came round the shelves. He crouched and lined a shot. He fired twice into the tentacles. Kara pulled the rope free and shuffled back.

A tentacle grabbed her leg, she kicked wildly before looking back to Stefan there. He aimed and pulled the trigger to a dry click.

"Fuck!" He turned his gun, noticing the gun's slide hand locked back. With a button press, he dropped the empty magazine and instinctively slapped in a second and flicked the unlock on the slide and fired at the grasping tentacle. He reached for her. They locked hands and he pulled her from under the mangled shelfing. Kara stopped on her hip. And whipped back under. The creature began to lurch around the shelving at Stefan's side.

"Kara?" Stefan yelled and she re-emerged with the Ascender. Stefan leapt at the panel and hit it with his shoulder and fired two shots at the creature sending it back stunned. The door opened and Kara ducked under Stefan's aim out of the room. Stefan ducked out behind and closed the door.

"These fucking things they…" Stefan stared down the hallway. Kara was on one knee regathering their climbing gear also staring.

The corridor was filling with humanoid creatures of tentacles, claws and hooked blades. They let out a chorus of screams and screeches as they began barrelling toward them. Stefan touched Kara's shoulder. She turned on her heel and hurried passed him. Stefan fired two bullets toward limbs near the ground and stumbled two of them before chasing after Kara. Kara dropped the gear at the doorway of an open elevator shaft. She looped the rope over her shoulder and stepped back. Stefan came round the corner and saw Kara run at the doorway and leap.

Kara leaped onto the cable in the middle of the shaft. Pushing with the inner souls of her shoes she climbed hard. She shimmied as fast as she could. Stefan reached the door and dropped to his knee. A creature appeared at the corner. Stefan began shooting. He put four bullets into its chest area, but nothing phased it. He fired low and after two more shots its leg tore off at the knee. Another creature emerged from the corner followed by more. He continued to fire at the limbs of the advancing humanoids despite some having a conveyor belt of tentacles as legs.

Kara climbed just over a deck. Her hands were bloody from the steel cable. Her skin was sweaty from the climb. She took a breath and leapt from the cable to the access ladder. She hooked her right arm over a rung and began tying the rope to the ladder. She threw the rope down letting it uncoil. Stefan continued to fire; four humanoid creatures now crawling toward him while others clambered toward him faster. Kara was shouting. Stefan turned his ear to the doorway and stopped shooting.

"Ascender!"

Stefan glanced into the shaft and saw the rope hanging to his left. He grabbed a hand full and pulled it to the floor beside the Ascender. He holstered his gun and locked the ascender to the rope. A humanoid creature swung at him as he leapt into the shaft thumbing the ascender. The device squealed as it pulled him up the rope.

He stopped with a clang at the base of the ladder.

"Holy shit." He looked up. Kara on the ladder looking down.

"Thank you, Kara."

Kara reached down and took his hand; he felt the slick cold blood on her hands, and she pulled. He climbed with his feet and secured himself on the ladder beside her.

"Are you alright?" He gestured at her hands.

"I'll survive," Kara looked up the shaft. "The ladder goes all the way?"

"All the way. You okay to keep moving?" Stefan asked gesturing at her hands again.

"Let's go," Kara said immediately beginning to climb the ladder.

Chapter 37: Departures

Annabelle and Rajiv held Luca under the arm's as they struggled toward the shuttle bay. Grace walked in front leading them. Grace palmed the door. It slid upward with a burst of air. Annabelle moved in first, Rajiv behind with Luca still between them. Grace stepped in and lifted Luca's head. Luca opened his eyes and smiled softly.

"Hold on Luca," Grace whispered.

"These god damn doors," Annabelle growled.

The four struggled through seven pressurised doors. Inside the departure area they laid Luca gently on the floor. Annabelle kept her hands on the leaking wound on Luca's back. Grace moved behind the desk and began opening lockers set in the wall.

"Where would the first aid kit be?" she asked franticly searching. Rajiv joined her in her search.

"I don't know…I've never seen it," Annabelle called out, panic rising in her voice.

"Damn it. Is he still awake?" Grace called back shifting through. Annabelle leaned over Luca's body from the back.

"Luca? Luca sweetie? Luca come on."

Luca groaned before opening his eyes. "Hey you."

Annabelle smiled at him before glancing at the searching pair.

Rajiv found a medium sized white case, he pulled it out halfway.

"This it?"

Grace turned to him and reached for the case. "That's it." The pair hurried back round to Luca. Grace knelt behind Annabelle.

"Get something for his head." She ordered opening the case. Rajiv took off his lab coat and balled it up. He tucked it under Luca's cheek as Grace rolled him on to his chest. Grace handed Annabelle some scissors.

"Cut his clothing around the wound," Grace ordered going back into the case. Grace handed a nylon strip of material with a metal pen fixed to it. She handed it to Rajiv. "Tourniquet over the shoulder, under the arm pit," Grace told him, her words calm and clear. Grace ripped open three antiseptic powder packs and poured them over Luca's exposed back. Next, she unfolded a thick padded bandage and pushed it on to the collection of puncture wounds on his lower back.

"Pressure Anna." She ordered turning for a second pad. Annabelle held the first pad down. His blood continued to leak. Rajiv strapped the tourniquet over Luca's shoulder. He pulled tight and Luca growled. Rajiv extended the metal pen and began twisting until the blood had stopped leaking from his shoulder.

Grace added another pad and Annabelle held it down again. Grace handed a small bandage and powder to Rajiv without speaking. Rajiv powdered the shoulder before binding the bandage. He looked at Annabelle, her eyes had begun to glaze, and her cheeks had reddened. She had rubbed her forehead. Luca's blood smudged across it now. Grace was mopping furiously as the blood continued to leak out from the pads. Rajiv checked the shoulder again before moving down and putting his hands over Annabelle's. Grace glanced at him as she continued to clean. He caught Annabelle's eye, tears streaming down her face.

"Talk to him."

"What?"

"Talk to him," Rajiv said firmly. Annabelle leaned over near Luca's ear.

"Luca?"

He groaned.

"Hold on sweetie. The shuttle is just through that door. We're going home. You'll see." She whispered.

Chapter 38: Bridge

Stefan rolled in through the elevator door and climbed to his feet. He checked both directions, weapon raised. He turned back and reached in. Kara took his hand, and he pulled her in to the corridor.

"Which way?" Kara asked climbing to her feet.

"Just up here," Stefan said tactically moving forward. They rounded the corner and Stefan stopped, he pushed Kara to the wall behind with his left hand.

"What's wrong?" she asked. Stefan glanced back at her. "That door shouldn't be open," he whispered before gesturing her to stay there. Stefan crept toward the large open doors, he stopped and crouched. He saw a man laying on the floor. *Romiley.* He waited for a moment. There was no movement. He kept low and approached the door. He moved to the right side of the door and peeked in.

Stefan scanned the room quickly before rushing inside. He crouched at Romiley's body and saw the stab wounds to his stomach and throat. He turned to another body to the right and realised it was Page. Her throat had been cut. He moved over to the next body which was Nashi. He inspected the burn and glass fragments on her face. Checking Saleem he saw his arm was irreparably damaged. Someone has done this. Stefan rushed over to Romiley's console. He picked up the headphones and glanced back at Romiley's body. He began tapping keys.

"Captain's override: Stefan Dietrich…7 8 6…"

"There's no point. Captain."

Stefan spun round, weapon up.

Cole held Kara by the hair with his left hand, pulling her head to the side. His knife pressed against her throat. He shifted, moving his head behind Kara's for a moment.

"I've already ended quarantine. Now. Put it down Captain," Cole snapped. Stefan held his aim.

"What did you do?"

"I can't really paint a better picture. Drop the gun."

Stefan held his aim.

"Why Cole? Why?"

Cole wrenched Kara's head back. "Drop the fucking gun!"

Stefan focused on Kara. Her face was stone, her glare directed toward Cole. Not the blade.

"I'll cut her throat! Drop the gun!"

"Drop the knife Cole," Stefan held his aim. Cole shot a look at Kara and back at Stefan.

"I said drop the gun. I'll kill her!"

Kara was slowly lifting her left hand.

Stefan held his aim. "I'm going to ask you…One…Last…" Kara pulled Cole's wrist away from her neck and lurched forward. Stefan fired. Cole flung backward as the bullet tore into his left shoulder and out at the shoulder blade. Kara fell to her knees and Stefan ran to her.

"Your tough as hell. Are you alright?" Stefan asked rubbing her shoulder.

"Nice shot."

"Thanks. Go to the console. Key in shuttle bay. Call the others," Stefan said helping Kara to her feet.

Kara approached the console. Stefan walked slowly toward Cole on his back. Kara tapped at the keys. Stefan stood over him, he watched the blood pool forming around his shoulder.

"Shuttle bay? Shuttle bay come in?" Kara called.

"They're not responding."

"The headset," Stefan said glancing at her. She looked over the desk before spotting it hanging off the console. Kara jumped as Stefan's gun fired. She spun round. Stefan fell to his side to his left. Cole and Stefan held on to the gun. Cole had thrust his knife into Stefan's ribs.

The two men lay side by side. Cole was still holding the blade with his right hand and wrestling the gun from Stefan with the other. Kara ran toward them. The gun fired again. Kara ducked as she approached. She stayed low before lunging toward the gun with both hands. Cole released the blade to grab the gun with both hands also. Kara and Cole wrestled with the gun. Kara's bloody hands made it hard for either one to grasp. Cole grit his teeth in anger. Kara grit her teeth in pain. Stefan grabbed at Cole's face. Cole shifted his body to the left and pulled Kara down between them. Kara threw her knee up at Cole's groin. Cole shifted his hips back and she missed her target. She kept her knee up and pushed against his chest. She shifted again getting her knee higher. She threw her hips catching Cole on the chin with her knee.

The gun fired again. A bullet glanced across Kara's shoulder. She screamed out wrenching the gun to her right. The gun launched from their hands from the blood drenched all over it. Cole sat up to reach for the gun. Kara grabbed his face with her bloody hands. He grabbed her hands and pulled them from his face. He brought his elbow down into Kara's stomach. She roared in pain as Cole lurched forward for the gun again.

Cole lurched onto his front and reached around the floor. From Kara's curled position, she saw Cole slapping his palms at the floor, the gun just out of reach. Kara's blood in his eyes. *He can't see it.* Kara turned onto her front and crawled for the gun. Cole slapped the floor, his little finger touching the grip. Kara pulled herself closer. Cole got his fingers over the gun. Then the gun was further away. Stefan had grabbed him by the ankle and pulled him backward. Kara reached the gun. Cole wiped his face with the back of his hand. Kara struggled to her knees. Cole kicked at Stefan to release his grip and looked for the gun.

It was pointing at his face. Cole glanced up at Kara. The back of his head exploded as Kara pulled the trigger. Cole's face slapped to the floor, a gaping hole in the back of his skull. Kara crawled over to Stefan. He was holding his stomach with both hands. His nose bleeding from Cole's kick. Stefan reached up at Kara and she took his hand. She sat next to him and covered her torn shoulder with her left hand.

"Like I said. Tough as hell," Stefan whispered.

Chapter 39: Waiting

Annabelle sat leaning against the chairs of the departure area. She held her arm around Luca, whose head was resting against her right pillow. She gently stroked his head, her hand clean of most blood. Rajiv approached quietly and she opened her eyes. She smiled softly as he crouched beside her. He held two bottles of water, one had a rag between it and his fingers. He offered the first bottle to her. Annabelle nodded and he thumbed the top, popping it open. He gave her the bottle and move round to Luca's side. While Annabelle drank, Rajiv tipped water onto the rag and wiped Luca's mouth. He opened his mouth a little and Rajiv lifted his head. He tipped water into his mouth. Luca drank a bit but spilt more. Annabelle flinched as the cold water touched her.

"Sorry," Rajiv whispered before cupping Luca's mouth with the rag and giving him more. Rajiv wiped Annabelle's breast with the other side of the rag then left it there. He gently lowered Luca's cheek down on to the rag. Annabelle stroked Rajiv's cheek. He leaned in and gave a peck on her lips.

"Thank you," Annabelle whispered. Rajiv smiled and stood. He walked quietly back to the desk where Grace was slouched. He touched her shoulder. She flinched awake. Rajiv gestured a sorry.

"How are you feeling?"

"I'm okay. Pain killer's working well now," Rajiv nodded and inspected her bandage.

"Water?"

Grace nodded and accepted the bottle. "How is he doing?"

"Just gave him some water. I'm not sure."

"I better check his dressings," Grace said stretching. Rajiv and Grace moved round the desk.

"Shuttle bay?" They froze. "Shuttle bay come in?" Rajiv rushed back round the desk.

"Was that Kara?" Annabelle asked.

"Kara? This is shuttle bay. We read you," Rajiv scanned their faces.

"Kara? Captain? Respond?"

"They made it to the bridge…Just give them a second. Help me Rajiv," Grace said crouching in front of Annabelle.

Rajiv joined them.

"The shoulder."

Rajiv and Annabelle lifted his head and turned him away slightly. Grace splashed her hands with the water bottle and lifted the dressing. Annabelle scowled. Panic in graces eyes. She turned him back to Annabelle roughly and checked the dressing at his lower back. Rajiv leapt backward and scurried around Luca's body to Annabelle's side. He grabbed her hand and pulled her, Annabelle still trying to support Luca's head.

"Get back, get back," Rajiv snapped. Annabelle directed his head to the chair they'd been leaning against.

Grace stared at the puncture wounds on Luca's back. The veins near the wound had turned black. The holes where black with tar. Grace moved away and covered her mouth.

"What is it?" Annabelle asked Rajiv who was holding her by the arms.

"It's inside him."

Annabelle covered her mouth also for a moment.

"What…What do we do?"

"We get him back out to the corridor," Rajiv said moving passed slowly. He stood behind Luca and tucked his arms under his.

"Come on. We have to do this." He glared at Annabelle. Luca opened his eyes.

"Are we leaving now?"

Rajiv jolted backward. Annabelle squatted in front of Luca. He saw her and smiled.

"Hey. How we doing?"

Annabelle tilted her head.

"Not much longer sweetie."

Rajiv moved across the floor and grabbed the scissors. Annabelle signalled with the palm of her hand to stop. She stroked Luca's cheek.

"How do you feel?"

"Tired."

"Here. Get some more rest," Annabelle suggested helping him to lay on the floor. She watched him for a moment. She then looked up at Rajiv, clearly panicked still holding the scissors.

She stood and guided him over to Grace who had tears in her eyes.

"That's clearly still Luca. How much time do you think he has?" Annabelle asked Grace. She held her own arms tightly.

"I have no idea. We still don't know how this thing works. His body might shut down first. He might go mad. He could survive for days. I don't know."

"Nothing gets off the ship remember," Rajiv whispered. Annabelle shot him a look.

"Could you be any colder," she said scornfully.

"Are you gonna suggest I'm wrong here."

"No, you're right," Grace looked at Annabelle. "He's right. But we wait. We wait for Stefan and Kara to get here."

"So, Stefan can shoot him you mean," Annabelle interrupted.

"Think logically. That might be our only option."

Chapter 40: Choices

Stefan struggled to his knees. He held his stomach as blood continued to leak from the knife wound. Kara glanced up. Stefan could barely see her face with her blood-stained hair in front. He managed to get to one knee, he winced before finishing on to his feet. He could see the torn flesh across the top of her right shoulder. She wasn't even holding it.

"Kara?"

She tilted her head, allowing her hair to move aside.

"Let's get this course set in huh?" He suggested softly, offering a hand.

Kara nodded and accepted his grasp. Both grunted and winced as Kara got to her feet. She looked at her shoulder. She grimaced and gently laid her hand over the flesh, teeth clenched. She turned to the pilot consoles and approached the console to the left.

"Can you do this?"

"I can do it; I just need a sec," Kara studied the console. As she began tapping at keys with her the hand from her good shoulder. Stefan turned and approached the monitoring console that Page had occupied. He grimaced again as he leaned over the console. He began tapping the keys with his left hand.

A. BROOKS search. A loading bar flashed four times across the screen. Departure/arrival suite. Shuttle Bay.

BIO-MON status.

Amber: Breathing abnormality, possible bruising.

"She made it." He mumbled.

Nearby BIO-MON search. Several loading screen's flashed again.

Active: 3

Inactive: 17

Stefan scowled at the screen and glanced over at Kara who was stumbling toward the far-right pilot's console. Back at the screen he selected the active option and then added status.

DR G. Lancaster: Amber: Concussion, possible head trauma.

R. Mody: Green:

L. Smith: Red: Breathing difficulty, Major blood loss, Unknown.

Unknown Clarify.

Unknown Biomaterial in blood stream.

Nearby Unknown Biomaterial. The computer searched again.

18. Stefan glanced back at Kara who was now at the centre pilot's console. He eyed the screen again.

19…20…21…22…23.

"Fucking hell, no," Stefan whispered shutting his eyes tightly for a moment. *They need to evac now. Right now.* pushing himself from the console.

Stefan headed for the door and palmed the panel before limping to the middle of the room.

"How we doing Kara?"

"Just allowing the computer to re-calculate and we get the hell out of here."

Kara felt her breath leave her as her rib cage burst open over her right lung. Blood washed the console. She stumbled, holding on to the desk before her legs buckled. She slumped to the floor brushing passed the pilots chair. She fell on her right hip, then her shoulder, then her head followed. She felt the blood from her shoulder wound cool her skin as her head hit the floor. Her body relaxed and she slipped onto her back. Stefan was standing over her. The gun back in his hand.

"I'm so sorry. If she must wait for us to reach her. She won't make it. Besides. It's better this way."

Kara wheezed heavily. She tried to speak. No air. She gritted her teeth. She pathetically kicked her leg. Stefan glanced down at her attempt.

"Like I said. Tough as hell," Stefan aimed at her forehead and fired. The back of her skull spreading out on the floor. Stefan stared down at her.

It's better this way. Kara's eyes were still open. Staring at him. He clenched his eyes and turned away.

Stefan stumbled over to the communication's console. He dragged the console chair behind him and slumped into it. He covered his ears with the headset and pushed a few keys with his left hand. His right cradling his open belly.

Chapter 41: Last Chance

Grace's head lay on her folded arms across the lounge desk. Rajiv sat on one of the chairs near Luca's ankles. Annabelle had slipped in under Rajiv's right arm, her head resting on his chest. Rajiv moved her loose hair from her face. She had fallen asleep to the sound of his breathing. He stroked her forehead. He leaned forward and kissed her on top of her head.

"Shuttle bay? It's Stefan," Grace jolted up right. Annabelle stirred. Rajiv gently nudged her.

"Stefan. It's Grace is everything alright?"

"The shuttle bay is open now. You need to get going."

Annabelle sat straight and rubbed her neck.

"That's great news Stefan. Are you okay?" Grace asked again.

"We…Ran in to Cole."

Grace leaned closer to the microphone as Annabelle stood.

"Stefan, are you alright?" Grace asked a third time. Annabelle reached the desk and leaned in.

"No," Stefan finally said before breathing heavily into the headset.

"Stefan?" Annabelle asked softly.

"Hey. How you doing?" His voice picking up.

"Stefan? What happened? Where's Cole now?" Annabelle asked firmly.

"Don't worry about him. He's dead."

"Is Kara, okay?" Grace interjected. Stefan coughed for a few seconds.

"Kara…um…Kara took the worst of Cole's attack."

Grace and Annabelle looked at each other, their skin heating up hearing the news. Rajiv joined them at the desk and put his arm around Annabelle's shoulders.

"She…Didn't make it and I…Damn."

"What's wrong Stefan?" Annabelle asked louder than she'd intended.

"I…I'm bleeding out. I don't have much time."

Annabelle lurched from the desk.

"We're coming to get you."

"No! No, you not! That's an order Anna!"

Annabelle swung back to the console.

"Fuck your order! I quit. Now I'm coming to get you." She marched toward the door, shouldering off Rajiv's attempted grasp.

"You can't!" Grace snapped leaping from the desk chair.

"She's right Anna. You can't do that."

Annabelle turned again. Red fury in her eyes.

"Why can't I?"

Grace marched round the desk toward Annabelle and held her by the arms.

"It's too dangerous sweetheart, you know that." While Grace attempted to calm her Stefan spoke again.

"Rajiv?"

"Yes Captain?"

"The bay is unlocked. Get the shuttle powered up."

"I don't know how."

Stefan coughed again.

"It has emergency auto-pilot procedures. The shuttle will take you to Mar's base. You're a scientist Rajiv. You can figure it out. Go now."

"Huh…Yes Captain," Rajiv stepped backward from the console as Annabelle glared at him. He quickly turned and palmed the door to unlock it. The door opened and Rajiv charged across the shuttle bay to the waiting transport.

"Grace?" Stefan asked after a moment of silence.

"He's gone Captain."

Annabelle scowled in confusion. She stared at the console then back at Grace. Annabelle threw her arms up, forcing Grace to release her.

"Start talking!" Annabelle spat.

"Anna?" Stefan growled, his tone killing her anger.

"Tell me what's going on?" she asked softly moving round to the chair side of the desk.

"You are going to be a mother sweet girl," Stefan said gently. Annabelle shot a looked at Grace who was now smiling softly.

"So, you see. You can't take any chances for me, or for anyone."

Annabelle clasped her hands on her mouth and began to tear up. She slumped into the chair.

"I...I can't. I can't be a mother."

"Why not? You'll be a perfect mother," Grace said proudly as she approached her and stroked her back.

"Anna. Listen to me. I know this is a lot to take in, at the worst moment. But I'm running out of time. And so are you. Those things are surrounding the area. They know you're in there. You need to leave. Now."

"I don't...I...I can't do this without you Stefan," Annabelle's eyes flooded.

"Oh, my sweet girl. You can deal with anything. Just look at what you've achieved so far," Stefan continued. Grace bent down and held her round the shoulders.

"One last step. Get on the shuttle and get off this ship before your too far out."

Annabelle held one of Grace's arms as she cried.

"Thank you, Stefan. For everything. I...Luca?"

Luca was bolt upright. His head snapped toward them. His eyes black with tar. He threw his grasping hands up and lunged across the desk. His hands found Annabelle's throat as the three barrelled over. Graced slammed against the lockers as Luca mounted Annabelle on the floor. Luca opened his mouth, and a high-pitched screech came out. Annabelle's eyes began to peel back as Luca squeezed the life out of her throat. Grace threw her foot at Luca's skull. His head snapped up at her. Grace dove at his face, fingers first. She crawled at his skin before directing her thumbs at his eyes. Grace screamed in pure rage as she forced her thumbs into the black pools. Luca released Annabelle's neck and grabbed firmly on to Graces forearms. He did not attempt to stop her gouging. The black fluid leaking from his eyes spread across her hands. Up her arms.

Grace yanked to the right. Luca altered his balance and clambered over Grace's down body. Her thumbs were still in his skull, but Luca just held her on the ground at arm's length. The black liquid becoming thicker as it moved abnormally slowly down her arms. It had reached her elbows now and Grace was not yelling in anger anymore. Her eyes were wide, and her face was twisting.

"Run. Run," Grace barely managed the words and Annabelle rolled to the side away from the pair. She rolled and pressed up onto her hands and knees. She looked at Grace.

Grace could not move. Her arms, body and head were stiff with fear and pain. If she were able to speak anymore, she would have been screaming. Annabelle could see the pain in her eyes. Annabelle rushed to her feet and screamed herself as she made for the shuttle bay door. Stepping through she slapped the door to lock and ran across the bay.

Annabelle barrelled into the shuttle making Rajiv jump.

"Go now!" She yelled.

"Where's Grace?"

"Go! Now!" Annabelle screamed, straight into his face. He spun round and palmed a large red button on the console. It blinked to green, and the warning lights erupted in the shuttle bay. Annabelle had sealed the side door but stared through its window toward the departure door. The control panel of the door sparked and caught fire. Annabelle was entranced by the small blue flame burning there.

Loud pulses of a horn began to echo throughout the shuttle bay as the departure door jolted upward a foot. Annabelle turned to Rajiv. He was hitting all sorts of buttons not knowing what to do.

"Open the door Rajiv," Annabelle growled.

"It won't open, look."

Annabelle hurled herself over the rear seating to the cockpit. A square screen the size of a cyber station read: Safety protocol breach. Ship decompression alert. In large red lettering. Annabelle leaned toward the console.

"Captain's override: Stefan Dietrich...7 8 6 4 5 8 5. Command 43 24 36," Annabelle spoke slowly and clearly. The console screen responded.

Authorisation: A. Brooks.

"Override Safety protocol. Open hanger doors."

Voice recognised: Confirm A. Brooks.

"Confirm Annabelle Brooks."

Voice recognised. With a metal grinding creek, the hanger bays massive door began to open.

Annabelle glanced to her left through the shuttle cockpit window and saw Luca standing there, elongated black fingers upon the glass. His eye sockets hollowed with black tar streaming down his scratched-up face. Annabelle recoiled toward Rajiv's chair. Air rushed from the hanger for half a second before Luca was ripped from the window and launched out into the vast blackness. His body tumbling away in silence. The air jets from the shuttle fired and guided the shuttle outside. The main thrusters fired with a thundering that shock the shuttle tremendously. The shuttle began to turn until the red planet called Mars was fully in the front window. Annabelle and Rajiv threw their arms around one another and squeezed tightly.

"Thank you. Captain Stefan Dietrich," Annabelle said quietly, her eyes clenched tight tears running down her cheeks.

Chapter 42: Captain

Stefan sat at the monitoring console. His breathing was short and ragged. Sweat danced off his skin. The display in front of him changed.

A. Brooks: Shuttle 6…Mars Trajectory.

Stefan slumped back in the chair. He slowly moved his hand from his open belly. He grimaced, looking at it. He let his hand fall to his side. He smiled and closed his eyes.

"Good luck, my sweet girl," he said quietly.

Stefan slowly rolled out of the chair, pushing off the rests he stumbled to his feet. He turned and began swaying toward the pilot's console. He barrelled over down on to his chest, his legs kicking back at the knees as he landed. He did not move. His body relaxed. His ragged breath stopped.

Milton Keynes UK
Ingram Content Group UK Ltd.
UKHW022216091024
449475UK00006B/99